Walk A
Straight Line

Walk A Straight Line

Michelle Lindo-Rice

URBAN
CHRISTIAN

www.urbanchristianonline.com

Urban Books, LLC
97 N18th Street
Wyandanch, NY 11798

Walk A Straight Line Copyright © 2014 Michelle Lindo-Rice

ISBN 13: 978-1-60162-777-3
ISBN 10: 1-60162-777-7

First Printing January 2014
Printed in the United States of America

10 9 8 7 6 5 4 3 2 1

*This is a work of fiction. Any references or similarities
to actual events, real people, living or dead, or to real
locales are intended to give the novel a sense of reality.
Any similarity in other names, characters, places, and
incidents is entirely coincidental.*

Distributed by Kensington Corp.
Submit Wholesale Orders to:
Kensington Publishing Corp.
C/O Penguin Group (USA) Inc.
Attention: Order Processing
405 Murray Hill Parkway
East Rutherford, NJ 07073-2316
Phone: 1-800-526-0275
Fax: 1-800-227-9604

Walk A Straight Line

Two friends . . . Two brothers . . .
Two weddings . . . Too many secrets . . .

Who will cross the line?

Michelle Lindo-Rice

**(The first installment of the
On the Right Path series)**

What Readers Are Saying about Sing A New Song

"Ms. Lindo-Rice writes with heart, humor, and honesty . . ." **Shana Burton,** author of *Flawless, and Flaws and All*

"Michelle Lindo-Rice has written a sweet story of the power of love despite the main character's (Tiffany) sordid past . . ." **Michelle Stimpson,** bestselling author of *Falling into Grace*

"The author's writing is crisp and her characters' emotions are authentic . . ." **Pat Simmons,** award-winning & bestselling author of the *Guilty Series*

"The author did a phenomenal job in drawing the readers' heart and spirit into the characters . . . Ms. Lindo-Rice developed an endearing, engaging, multi-layered story with realism and redemption . . ." **Norma Jarrett,** *Essence* bestselling author of *Sunday Brunch*

"I applaud the author for sharing a wonderful story of forgiveness and faith. I enjoyed the characters, plot, and anticipation . . ." **Teresa Beasley,** APOOO Book Club

". . . when you feel like things cannot get any worse or better, Lindo-Rice shows the power of God and the influence that He has in our lives . . ." Women with Words Book Club

An Invitation from God

Thank you for choosing to read my work. You did not choose this by accident, but it was by divine ordination. I grew up in the church and have been a Christian since my early teens, so I know that sometimes the road to salvation can be rocky, but rewarding. There is no greater, more fulfilling love than what I have experienced through developing a personal relationship with God. I urge you to discover, or rediscover, God's unchanging love, and hold on to this truth. God loves you.

Romans 10:9–10 says, "That if thou shalt confess with thy mouth the Lord Jesus, and shalt believe in thine heart that God hath raised him from the dead, thou shalt be saved. For with the heart man believeth unto righteousness; and with the mouth confession is made unto salvation." Yes, it really is that easy. ☺

Acknowledgments

Everyone always acknowledges God—even the potty-mouthed artists—but when I do, it's because I am thankful to Him for every single experience He has brought me through. It is because of His tender leading and nudging that I have been extended this amazing opportunity to reach some amazing people. Thank you, Lord.

I thank my two sons—the troopers who give me much-needed time and space while I write and rewrite. I love you, Eric Michael and Jordan Elijah. I'd also like to mention my three godchildren, Imani Crystal Nugent, Nehemiah Lindo, and Joseph Alexander.

I thank my parents, Pauline and Clive, who was my photographer for my author picture.

To my beautiful cousin from Montego Bay, Jamaica, Tanisa Samuels, the face of "Colleen." Thanks, Ten Ten.

To my cousin, reggae artist, Kashief Lindo, of Heavy-Beat Records, who allowed me to mention his remake of Gregory Issac's *Love is Overdue.*

To my youngest sister, Sobi-Dee Ophelia—my support, my rock, my friend. I also thank my "publicist" and younger sister, Zara Anderson, who organizes events for me. I recognize my entire family and support system.

As this novel is about friendships, I recognize my close circle of friends—Sharon Amoy Heron, Sarah Miller, Lea Philippe, Michele Millwood, Teresa Martin, Glenda Clarke, Nicole Fox, and Bridgette Murray.

A special thank you to Jane Adams whose support goes above and beyond.

Shout out to Kathy Stack, whose presence got me through my first reading as a new author. My entire work family at Charlotte County Public Schools—too extensive to name and not get in trouble, but my biggest supporters.

I am indebted to so many authors who helped me with my writing. A very special, special, special mention to Rhonda McKnight. To the Urban family, and a BIG THANKS to an amazing, supportive editor, Joylynn Jossel-Ross, who believes in me, helps me develop my craft, and tells me what the readers want to know.

Dedicated to . . .

Colette Alexander, my best friend of twenty-five years. She supports me through every discovery, heartache, and triumph. We fight, we cry, but loyalty is never questioned.

Chapter One

July 12th

"You were easily the best dancer on the dance floor."

Gina Price's body responded to the Barry White voice from behind. After an energetic bout with the Cha-Cha Slide, she'd sought respite at one of the recently abandoned guest tables. Her now crushed gold satin dress bore the after effects of her abandon, but she had no regrets. She just needed a brief power nap, and she'd be ready for round two. It took some effort, but she opened her eyes.

Starting with his shoes, her eyes swept his tall frame. The dark blue suit fit him like a second skin. A jacket hung carelessly in one hand, while uncontrolled muscles popped from under his light blue shirt. His tie had been savagely loosened and now draped over his well-defined shoulders. At the end of her journey, she saw his face.

Oh, my. He sounded like Barry White, but he looked like Shemar Moore. Um, pretty boys spelled trouble.

Her voiced oozed honey when she uttered a low, "Thank you, but tell that to my aching feet." Gina swayed her body to the up-tempo beat. "The deejay is doing his thing— 'cause this crowd is pumped. I mean, it's almost midnight, and nobody's rushing home."

Shemar Moore chuckled. "Yes, this was some reception, wasn't it? Terence and Colleen didn't spare any expense because this wedding was top-of-the-line."

"Uh-huh . . . People will talk about this wedding for years to come," Gina agreed. With the ice doves, to the still-glowing imported scented candles, orchid and lily centerpieces, and crystal one-of-a-kind chandeliers, her head spun. Such opulence and grandeur made their wedding picture-perfect from beginning to end. Even the weather had cooperated.

Gina rubbed her bare shoulders and eyed the other members of the wedding party who still held it down on the dance floor. By the looks of it, it would be awhile before the festivities died down. She snickered. There'd be some back pains and sore limbs come morning.

"Mind if I sit?" he asked.

She had propped her feet on one of the empty chairs to rest them and admire her black, gold-encrusted, three-inch heels. Yup, the shoes were worth it. Colleen, the former Miss MacGregor, had dubbed them Men-fishing shoes.

Well, she'd reeled in a live one.

Gina moved her legs and waved him into the chair next to her. "Not at all." She didn't play coy.

"I've been admiring you all evening. I couldn't leave without at least introducing myself. I'm Michael Ward—friend of the groom." He extended his hand.

Long, tapered fingers . . . Groomed nails . . . She'd give him an eight. Gina realized he waited for a response. "I'm sorry," she blushed and took his outstretched hand. "I'm Gina Price, best friend of the bride."

"Gina. Nice name," Michael replied.

"Thank you." Okay, he bored her already. Time to cut this brother loose until he got some swag or even a corny pickup line. So far, he held as much appeal as a Twinkie without the filling. Then she looked at him. Yup, he was worth a second try.

She tilted her chin toward Colleen and Terence and made small talk. "Look at them dancing like they're the only two people in the room. I mean, I had tears in my eyes when they recited their vows. And doesn't Colleen make a stunning bride?" Terence had hired a top-of-the-line makeup artist to do her face and hair, and the results were spectacular. Colleen looked like she could be on the cover of *Vogue* magazine, and Terence would fit right in with the men at *GQ*. He was handsome. Gina had to give him that. *Yeah, a handsome devil.*

"It was a beautiful ceremony," Michael intercepted her thoughts. He stood, "I'm going to get something to drink. Can I get you something?"

"Just water."

Gina watched his long, confident stride and appreciated the view from behind.

Just then, Terence and Colleen danced past her. Gina smiled and gave a small wave, though her smile didn't quite reach her eyes. She tapped her chin as she contemplated. Something about Terence didn't sit well with her. He seemed to genuinely love Colleen, and at thirty-four, he'd found success as an art designer for *Cozy Homes* magazine. He was religious and *seemed* to be for real about his love for God, not like some of those hypocrites out there.

Still, Gina felt doubtful about him. She had voiced those misgivings to Colleen, calling him Shifty Eyes. Once, she could have sworn that he had been checking her out, but she wasn't one-hundred-percent sure. So, she'd had no choice but to dismiss it. But, mark her words, Terence wasn't all he appeared. He was like . . . like a sweet, delicious piece of candy that was good to eat, but also gave you a vicious toothache.

Despite Gina's doubts, Colleen had fallen in love and after a mere four-month courtship—here they were.

Michael returned with two ice-cold glasses of water. When Gina reached for the glass, she felt an electric jolt zap through her spine as their hands connected. Did he feel that? She took a huge swig to drown her reaction.

A slow jam came on. "Would you like to dance?" he asked.

Gina hesitated. Her feet ached . . . throbbed . . . but, his body . . . his voice . . . no, her feet hurt.

Then he smiled.

Wow. That did it. She slid her feet off the chair, took his baseball-mitt-sized hand, and followed him to the dance floor.

"Well, since I don't know if you'll disappear at midnight, let me tell you about myself. I'm an architect and self-employed. I met Terence at college, and after we graduated, we went our separate ways. Then about a year ago, we bumped into each other, quite by accident, when I was commissioned to design the layout for Terence's magazine. During our conversation, he invited me to his wedding."

So, they are more acquaintances than friends, Gina thought. Good. He just went from an eight to a nine. She liked his soothing voice, and his arms made her feel secure. "Colleen and I have been best friends since we were fourteen and freshmen in high school. Since we didn't have siblings, we clung to each other. We've been joined at the hip, like Siamese twins, ever since. We went to the same colleges for our bachelor's and master's, and now we both work at August Martin H.S. I teach English Language Arts, and Colleen teaches social studies—excuse me, used to teach. I forgot she took a leave of absence. Terence doesn't want her to work."

"Oh."

His monosyllabic response made Gina wonder if she'd struck out with this one. Had she rambled too much?

Please don't let him mention the weather. People only mentioned the weather when they had nothing else to say.

"So, are you single?"

Good, she was still in the game. "Yes, I am." She caught the huge, anticipatory smile.

Michael led her through an intimate dance move that ended with a dip. "Are you seeing anybody right now?"

That voice of his mesmerized her. "No," Gina supplied, with a huge smile of her own. She held her breath, feeling the magnetic pull, when Michael slowly lifted her and curved her body to his.

His voice deepened, and he spoke right into her ear. "Good, 'cause I'm single too, and available—no kids, no ex-wives—just one brother and a mother, who's retired and living in Atlanta."

Disbelieving, Gina couldn't hold the unladylike snort. "You expect me to believe that you're available?"

But Michael quickly schooled her. He took a few steps back, licked his lips, then clarified, "Okay, I am *reformed* and officially retired from the heartbreaking business. Any games I used to play ended with my retirement."

Whatever he was selling, she wasn't buying. Well, it depends on how much, her inner self countered. When a more suggestive melody filled the room, Michael drew her closer to him. She inhaled. He smelled like ocean, outdoors, the rugged outback—and pure, unadulterated man. Her stubby legs liquefied, and her insides quivered. Engulfed in his arms, she felt like a petite china doll.

Gina snuck a glance up at Michael. His eyes held promise for some serious pleasure. Whew! *Hold it together, girl.*

Gina Ward.

Yes, she liked that. Too much. She'd known this man for what? Fifteen minutes. Ridiculous. All too soon, the song ended, and it was time to see the lovebirds off. Gina and Michael lagged behind the well-wishers and blew bubbles at each other, before he excused himself. Bereft, she looked for the other girls in her party, while shivering in the night air.

She saw a black Range Rover pull over to the curb. Curious, her eyes followed the tinted window's slow descent to reveal the driver. When she saw it was Michael, she edged closer.

"You need a ride?" he beckoned.

Did she ever! "Sure, thanks." She opened the door and put one leg in. Wait! What was she doing taking a ride from a virtual stranger—a possible stalker.

"Gina!" one of the girls called out from the limo that drove up behind Michael's car.

She waved them off, feigning bravado. "I'm good. I've got a ride." Cautiously, she held onto the door and lowered her body until she was halfway in. She chewed her lip, wondering if she should make a speedy escape. The limo hadn't pulled away yet, as the other girls were still piling in.

Perceptive, Michael surmised her dilemma. "You're safe with me."

Said the wolf to the lamb. Should she? Her heartbeat increased. Then her inner imp egged her on. Whatever—you only live once. Heeding it, Gina pushed the hesitation aside and decisively shut the door. "I'm good." She luxuriated in the feel of the leather beneath her and chattered, "You just saved me from having to crawl my way to the back of the limo with the other girls, then enduring the winding taxicab-style ride."

"It's my pleasure."

In mere minutes, Michael pulled up to her home in Rosedale. He parallel parked beside her blue Volkswagen.

"Thanks for the ride." Gina turned to look at him from under her lashes.

"Anytime," Michael returned and patted her hand. "I hope this is not the last I hear from you."

Gina rattled off her digits. He texted her so she could save his number in her phone. Michael took a curious peek at her house, but remained in his car. He waited until Gina got out of the vehicle and unlocked her front door. When she turned to give a final wave, he vocalized, "Call me. Soon." Gina nodded her assent before slipping inside.

Leaning against her door, she heaved, "Thank God." She bent, wearily undid her shoes, wiggled out of her dress, and fell into bed.

Then she thought about Michael. She appreciated that he hadn't come on to her or tried to kiss her. In fact, he'd been the perfect gentleman. She'd wait a couple of days to call him. Can't appear too eager . . . or desperate—a definite turnoff. So, Tuesday evening it is. No contact before then. Gina rolled over, looked at the clock, and moaned. Seventy-two hours.

Chapter Two

"I *love* it here." Colleen stretched her body, loving the feel of the Egyptian cotton five-hundred-count sheets courtesy of the Sandals Resort in Montego Bay, Jamaica. She turned on her side to look at the view of the ocean from their balcony and exhaled. "The ocean is breathtaking."

Terence's large hands cupped her waist and twisted her naked body toward his. He gave her an appreciative smile. "It's beautiful, but it's nothing compared to you."

"Aahhh," Colleen cooed, "I could stay like this forever." She breathed in, taking in the crisp air and sharp blue waters. Her eyes hurt from its brilliant shine. Like a siren, the sea called to her, prompting her to leave Terence's warmth, slip on a chemise, and slide open the glass door. She stepped out barefooted to get her fill.

She listened to the waves lapping against the shores and basked in its beauty for almost fifteen minutes. The cool breeze fluttered the laces lining the edge of her shimmery baby blue chemise. The scripture really was true, she thought. "How can a person see this and not believe in God? Impossible." When she didn't hear a forthcoming reply, Colleen looked behind her and saw that Terence had drifted off to sleep. "Figures." She meandered her way through sandals and clothes tossed on the floor as a result of their passion and shook Terence's shoulder.

His eyes slowly opened to focus on her.

"Let's go enjoy the water. We've been cooped up in here for almost a week," her champagne eyes pleaded.

Terence said nothing but held up the duvet covers. His arm snaked out to drag her down next to him. Giving her a light squeeze, Terence kissed her on the nose. "All right, we'll go, although I could stay right here under the AC."

"Yeah, but I don't want to spend my entire honeymoon in Jamaica in bed—as tempting as it is." Colleen slid from under the covers. Her long legs caught in the sheet, and she ended up in a huge puddle on the floor. Unabashed, she held onto her stomach as she laughed. Terence slid out of the bed alligator-style and joined her on the floor.

Disentangling herself out of the sheets, Colleen bowed with a flourish and swooped her arms. "And now, for my second act . . ."

She ambled over to the chest. Pulling the drawer open, she tossed clothes this way and that, before triumphantly saying, "Aha!" She grabbed the lime-green two-piece, hid it behind her back, and scurried into the bathroom to freshen up and change.

When she came out of the bathroom, she expected Terence to salivate at her tantalizing show. But he didn't look pleased. Perched on the bed, with one arm crooked under his head, he coolly assessed the garment she displayed. "You're going out like that?" His peculiar facial expression and disgusted tone gave her slight pause.

"Yeah." Quizzical, her smile collapsed. Now she felt uncomfortable. Did she look funny or fat or something? She appraised herself in the mirror. Nope, no difference there.

"It's revealing." Terence shrugged in a way that said more than his words. "I don't want all those men's eyes ogling my baby. Why don't you wear something else?"

Colleen bit her bottom lip. Insecurity blossomed and took root. "Okay, I'll change, although . . ." She shook her head, deciding not to voice her objection. Personally, she thought the two-piece harmless—especially compared to the skimpy thong suits that other women were wearing. But it was her nature to please. "Well, I do have the black one-piece I packed on a whim. I'll change." She wanted her new husband's approval. It meant everything to her.

With unsure, stilted steps, Colleen changed outfits. Though she felt dowdy now, she dutifully turned to face Terence.

She remained silent but stoically watched him swing his powerful legs and walk over to cradle her in his arms. "My baby looks good."

Colleen felt her spirits rise. He was happy. Her husband was pleased, and that was all that mattered. "Whoosh," she sighed. "If you keep that up, we won't make it out to the beach. I can't go back home without ever hitting the water."

She felt the rumble of his chuckle, and her body chilled when he stepped back. "Point well made, my wife. Give me a moment to put my trunks on, and then we'll head out."

Feeling cherished, Colleen nodded. She waited while Terence grabbed his trunks and took his turn in the bathroom. When he came out, her eyes popped open when she saw his barely-there trunks.

She bit her tongue to keep from seeming catty about the whole bathing-suit thing. Resolute, she pushed it from her mind.

They left their suite arm in arm. Colleen felt giddy. She swung her hips from side to side. Inside she raved . . . *I'm not alone and bitter like my mother. I am married, and I got me a good man with a job. I don't even have to go back to work when school starts 'cause my baby got money.*

Colleen and Terence frolicked in the sun. Its rays viciously pelted into their skin, leaving them well-tanned, but thirsty. They bought lots of water and punch for sale at a shanty on the beach. Soon, Colleen's bladder protested. "I'm going up to the room. I need a potty break." "I'll bring us some more," Terence slurped, greedily.

"Yes, please do," Colleen added, with a brisk nod, addicted to the flavorful punch—a swirling, colorful concoction of ice, pineapple, passion fruit, and syrup—and, a perfect cure for a parched, dry mouth.

Colleen hauled her sun-beaten body up to the hotel, dragging her towel in the sand. She dusted sand off her body. Ugh! It was everywhere. She wished she hadn't caved when Terence had insisted on burying her in the sand.

Colleen entered the suite and stripped. She left a seductive trail of clothes to entice Terence to join her for a shower and whatever else. She grinned as she headed into the oversized stall to wash the gunk off her body with vigor. Ten minutes later, wrinkled and disappointed, Colleen stepped out of the shower.

Clad only in flip-flops and an oversized towel, she sank her body in the nearest armchair. "Where is he?" He was probably chatting with the bartender or somebody about something. The man sure loved to talk.

Adrift, Colleen sauntered to the sliding door that led to their private patio that overlooked the beach. Her eyes scanned the beach trying in vain to spot her husband in those skimpy trunks. Oh, and don't think she didn't notice the other single women checking him out with their come-hither looks. Not that she'd minded, of course, but what irked her was how Terence had preened under those hot looks. Yet, he had serious problems if another man just glanced her way.

Men and their crazy, infantile, double standards. Since Terence was nowhere in sight, Colleen wandered back into the suite.

She thought about Gina back in New York. It had only been a few days, but she missed her girl. They usually spoke every day. Terrence was generous, but she didn't need to spend money on a phone call to the States from Jamaica. She'd wait until she got home.

Colleen could understand why the members of the Apostolic Church of God Seventh Day were considering making him an associate pastor. When he spoke, he was mesmerizing and dynamic. His golden tongue could swindle a dollar from a beggar. Everybody liked him and flocked to him like bears after honey. He worked a room like nobody's business wherever they went.

Gina, however, didn't buy the hype. She remained leery—dubbing him Shifty Eyes. Colleen pooh-poohed her concerns. Cynicism ran through Gina's bones.

Or maybe jealousy?

Naw. Colleen dismissed that notion. Gorgeous, petite with curves like Scarlett Johansson, Gina could aptly be described as a Man Magnet. Wherever she went, admirers flocked who hung on her every word. She pointedly ignored them, not caring for the spotlight.

Next to Gina, Colleen felt gauche and lingered in her friend's shadow—or so it seemed to her. She placed the blame on her height of five foot ten—from that vantage point, pickings were slim.

Until Terence. He was six foot four and drawn to her. Best of all, she could wear heels without worry.

She dried herself and reached for one of her scented oils.

Once she finished oiling herself down, Colleen chose a pink and white teddy with ruffles and a delicate trim. Slipping into it, she thought about Terence and sizzled. She eased onto the bed and practiced several seductive poses.

Then she heard the lock click.

Finally.

Quick, she struck her most tantalizing pose. Her chest heaved with anticipation as she waited. He stopped at the sight of her.

"Wow."

"Come and get it, big boy."

Terence hesitated for a split second before beginning to undress.

Not fast enough. Colleen flipped her long, curly hair and beckoned him to her bedside. Terence complied. She held her hands out for him to embrace her, but he paused.

Curious, Colleen asked. "What is it?"

"I feel grungy, you know, from all that sand," Terence explained.

"Oh." Embarrassed by her brazenness, she unposed her body and stretched her legs as they had fallen asleep in that awkward position.

"Let me take a shower. Wash all this grime from me." He was in the bathroom in seconds.

"Okay, what just happened here?" she said softly.

Somehow that is not how that scene always played out on the soap operas. However, she clamped her disappointment because she knew how fastidious Terence was.

Chilled, Colleen went under the covers and closed her eyes. She'd rest because when he came back, she was going to show him a thing or two. She had a creative mind, and now had the right to use it.

Suddenly, she felt something buzz against her leg and jumped. It was Terence's cell phone vibrating. She curved her leg to move it upward and grabbed it. She peeked at the number.

Why was Francine calling Terence on their honeymoon?

Colleen debated for a second before she pressed the redial button. "Hi, Francine, is everything all right?"

"Isn't this Terence's phone?"

Wasn't she Terence's wife? "I—um—he's in the shower—and I saw your number, so . . ." she rushed to explain.

"That doesn't give you the right—just have him call me."

With that, Colleen heard the dial tone. Her brow furrowed.

Terence came into the bedroom. He wore only a robe and used a hand towel to vigorously dry his hair.

"Why is your mother calling you on your honeymoon?"

Terence tensed. "My mother called?"

"Yes, just now. What's going on?"

"Why didn't you let it go to voice mail?" he asked instead. Without waiting for an answer, Terence seized the phone from her hand. "Don't answer my phone."

Colleen shivered at his harsh tone. "In my defense, I didn't think it would be a problem if I answered your phone. It could've been an emergency."

Terence repeated with emphasis, "Don't touch my phone."

Colleen didn't understand, but she nodded her head. She turned away from him and moved to the edge of the bed. She felt the bed sink under his weight. Hurt, Colleen squeezed her eyes shut to hold the tears at bay. Who was this man?

Terence knew Colleen felt rebuffed by his tone. He ached to comfort her, but he needed this moment to gather his thoughts. He knew why his mother had called—but first things first.

He heard another sniffle and knew he had to set things right. Terence reached over to touch Colleen's arm. "Are you hungry?" No answer. Just an indrawn breath followed by an even bigger sniffle. He moved closer so he could tilt his head and see her face. His heart melted, and he flicked away her tears. No one should cry on their honeymoon, unless they were tears from passion.

"Wife, do you want something to eat?"

She adjusted herself so she could look at him. Her thick lashes spiked, and dampened hair stuck to her forehead. Gently, he moved the hair away from her face. He traced a finger along the side of her arm and toyed with the frills on her teddy. "What do we have here?"

Her stomach muscles tightened, but Colleen remained silent. The ruffles in front provided a thin covering. He pushed them aside and splayed his hand across her abdomen. He could rip the flimsy material with just a shake of his wrist. Terence wanted his wife, but knew he needed to return his mother's call.

He gave her a perfunctory pat, leaned in, and kissed her ear. Then he ordered, "Call room service. Get me the salmon dinner. I'll be right back."

Expecting her compliance, he slid from under the covers and picked up his cell phone that had fallen to the floor. He took two steps before—*Wham* in the back. Terence spun around. What the—

She'd thrown a pillow at him!

Wham—another hit him in the chest.

With a low growl, he warned, "Colleen, cut that out. That is just childish and frankly—"

Wham. This time the pillow smacked him across the face.

With two huge steps, he took her flailing hands into his. She stopped resisting as she realized her puny strength wouldn't prevail. In a controlled, firm voice, he declared, "I'm going to talk to my mother; and then we will eat. We are not going to fight on our honeymoon. I insist."

Colleen huffed and stared him down for several seconds. Then, her shoulders relaxed and she apologized.

That's better, Terence thought. He crooked his head toward the menu by the phone and went to call his mother, whom he knew would be peeved. Five minutes was her maxim for a return call. He'd kept her waiting long enough.

Chapter Three

With a whistle and a spring in his step, Michael left his Fifth Avenue Upper East Co-op located across from Central Park. He enjoyed his daily jogs in the park, loving the smell and bustle of the city.

He swiped his private access card to activate the elevator that would take him from the penthouse to the lobby. Once inside, he returned to his whimsy. Where was he? Yes, Gina. Her curves and that body made her dangerous. Her intelligence and quick wit kept him on his toes, but her eyes struck him like a tidal wave—dark chocolate pools that sparkled with mischief and devilish humor.

After Karen, Michael vowed to stop using women as playthings. He gave up the marionette strings, choosing, instead, to treat them with respect. At thirty-two, he was ready to settle down. No more games. No more drama. That's why he was moving slow with Gina—real slow. This time he was in to win it—to borrow the mantra from Randy Jackson.

When he exited the elevator, he greeted the front-desk clerk and doorman by name. "The Porsche please." The clerk—Maureen—made the call.

Boy, he was a smiling fool. His good mood could only be attributed to one person. *Gina Price.*

They'd been all over New York City—on picnics, to the theater, on excursions through Washington Square and the Village—and, as the weeks flew by, his determination grew. In his business life, he pursued his goals using tenacity and perspicacity. And within one minute of meeting Gina, he'd spotted a keeper—a must-have.

Gina had grit. She had spunk.

Michael grinned. He just loved a challenge. He pressed the voice activation on his car phone and dictated, "Call Keith," to secure a dinner invitation to his brother's house. Two months was long enough. It was time for Gina to meet his brother.

Michael watched Gina tug at her dress for the third time. The black spaghetti strap dress fit her like a glove and featured a dip in the back that went on for days. She carried a light jacket in her hand as the September air could get crisp at night.

"You look fabulous," he felt the need to say again. He took her hands in his as they entered Café Baci's—an Italian restaurant in Westbury, Long Island. He'd chosen here, because with its brick-faced floors, wraparound bar and wooden chairs, the restaurant boasted ambience, superb service and impeccable cuisine.

"Now, leave your dress alone before you rip it and cause a Third World War in here," he teased.

She smiled sheepishly. Her hands were back in her hair ensuring that it was still tight. "I've no idea why I'm so nervous—well, I do know. Michael, you speak so highly of your big brother, and you adore him. I just want him to like me."

"I understand, Gina. But, please don't be nervous," Michael replied. He bent over to look her in the eyes. Tucking his finger under her chin, he said, "My brother is cool, and you're going to love Eve. Trust me when I tell you that you have nothing to worry about."

"I know, but I just want to make a good impression."

"Keith will love you," Michael predicted confidently. "You're stunning! You've got it going on, girl!"

Gina took several deep breaths. Even that simple natural act fascinated him. This woman was special and worth waiting for. He sounded whipped, even to his own ears.

The hostess ushered them to Keith's table, but his brother wasn't hard to miss. Keith did to women what gasoline did to fire. Keith was exceptionally fit and well dressed. To top it off, the man was ridiculously handsome, and that was no exaggeration. He had piercing dark brown eyes, dark chocolate skin, and a smile that could melt ice. Michael always teased that Keith should have been a model for one of those romance novels that women seemed to enjoy reading, but his brother scoffed at the idea, stating he'd prefer to use his brain over his body any day.

Michael hadn't been forthright with Gina. Keith wasn't so easy to please—probably a result of his uncanny penchant for picking up undercover psychopaths. Ever the big brother, Keith deftly identified several reasons why they weren't suitable—er, stable. Michael hated Keith's prying. But, to his chagrin, Keith was usually right.

Well, not this time. Gina Price *was* the one. He was sure of it.

Michael introduced Gina to Keith, and they took a seat. Within minutes, a waiter came to take their appetizers and drink orders. Michael ordered zucchini fritti and calzone bambini for them to share.

"Where's Eve?" Michael asked, once their food had arrived.

"She couldn't make it. She had a new client. Eve's in the real estate business," Keith directed the last part of his statement to Gina, before taking a huge gulp of his iced tea.

"Oh, that sounds interesting," Gina said, still nervous. She gripped Michael's hand under the table. He squeezed her hand to encourage her.

"She's also very pregnant with his child," Michael declared.

"Yes," Keith confirmed. "She is . . . very pregnant."

"Well, that was a pregnant pause," Michael noted. He laughed at the obvious pun, and waited for Keith to provide an acerbic response. But, their waiter, Peter returned to clear their appetizer plates, then took their dinner orders, so the moment passed.

Michael chose the salmone rosato; Keith the chicken parmigiana; and Gina decided on the penne ricche. Michael kept the dinner conversation lighthearted and humorous. Keith could get real deep and philosophical as he went on, but he also made an extra effort to put Gina at ease. Pretty soon, the three of them were talking and laughing like old friends.

Gina excused herself to freshen up; Michael eyed Keith watching her go. He was glad for the brief respite so that he could get his brother's opinion. He waited until Keith turned to face him. Keith did not utter a word. He just looked at him, and then gave him a big, thumbs-up sign.

Michael felt a smile lift from his heart and extend to his face. His grin became a full-fledged laugh. Keith joined in and lifted his right hand for a high five.

Gina entered her home that night, smiling. Standing against the door, she reveled in the fact that for the last three hours, she had been entertained by two of the most charming men that she had ever met! Michael was so attentive, and Keith, well, he was something else. She placed her hand over her chest. Michael hadn't prepared her adequately to meet him.

Keith was *hotness to the tenth power*.

On the drive to her house, Michael had told her that Keith had given her a thumbs-up sign while she'd been in the bathroom. Gina moved her head from side to side, with attitude, and snapped her fingers. "You know it."

She slipped out of her stilettos and headed for her living room. It was her favorite spot in the house. She had decorated it with light yellows and browns, giving the room a real airy and soothing effect. She chose to hang paintings that were relaxing to give the room more impact. After dealing with the rough kids of NYC, Gina needed somewhere that would calm her nerves.

She snapped her fingers. She'd almost forgotten the paperwork. She reached over to pick up the large brown envelope hanging over the edge of her nightstand. Carefully, she undid the clasp and took out the contents. There was a request for a character reference from the law firm of Bohlander & Associates on behalf of one of her former coworkers, Payton Marshall.

Gina would gladly comply with the request. Payton had been her mentor, and an excellent teacher. Picturing her blond curls and soft blue eyes, she couldn't imagine Payton as the murderer the press made her out to be. Payton had been convicted of brutally slaughtering her husband due to the continuous abuse he inflicted upon her. Gina shook her head. Payton had covered her plight well, because the entire school had been shocked.

Goes to show that one just never knows what a battered wife looked like, because Payton had been the epitome of poise and gentleness. She seemed like she had it together, but she'd never said a word. Gathering her notepad and paper, Gina composed a rough draft that she would edit and type to send to the law firm. She hoped they would be able to help her friend.

Chapter Four

"Super Sabbath? What's that?"

"It's a big to-do, where we invite family and friends to come out to church. It's the first weekend in October, and we're having a catered luncheon," Colleen explained. Clad in her silk camisole, she propped her feet on the bed to paint her toes. Her neck cricked from holding the cordless phone between her shoulder and ear, but she wanted to be ready when Terence came in. She'd found a bright red shade that she wanted to test out.

"I'll try to make it, if I'm not going to see Payton," Gina added.

Colleen rolled her eyes. "Gina, Payton did the crime. She needs to do the time. Why can't you accept that?" This was a sore topic between them. At first, Colleen supported Gina's dogged efforts, but it was time to let that go.

"I just know there's more to it than that, Collie. Her husband beat her, and no woman should endure that. She was battered, and kudos to her for taking a stand," Gina interjected.

Colleen huffed. "Yes, but she killed him—she didn't tell anyone, she didn't fight back. She killed him."

Gina sideswiped the issue. "I'll try to make it. I promise."

"I know you're trying to change the subject, Gina, but I'm your friend. I just don't want you getting disappointed if things don't work out."

"Why don't you pray for her, Colleen? Isn't that the Christian thing to do?"

Gina's mocking statement rankled her. She knew Gina wasn't preaching at her—the same Gina who refused week-by-week to come to church. The Holy Spirit held her tongue. "I'll pray for her. But, there is such a thing as praying amiss."

"Take that off your toes this instant!"

Startled, Colleen almost dropped the tiny bottle of glitter red nail polish on the carpet. Her quick reflexes kicked in, and she saved the beige plush carpet from a nasty stain. She did, however, drop the phone.

"Is that Terence?" Gina's voice pealed through the line.

Ignoring Terence, Colleen grabbed the phone. Terence had shoved his hands in his grey sweat-suit pockets. He eyed her toes and demanded, "I said take that devilish color off your toes."

Embarrassed, Colleen whispered into the handset, "Gina, let me call you back."

"Colleen, what's going on? Colleen—"

She disconnected the line. Of course, Gina redialed. Colleen ignored the shrill ring to scuttle after Terence. He had some major explaining to do.

"Who were you talking to?" Terence inquired.

"Just Gina. I was inviting her to our Super Sabbath when you so rudely demanded I change my toes."

Terence looked down at her toes with curled lips. He snarled, "That's right. I don't want you wearing that." Just as abruptly, he changed the subject and shrugged out of his sweatpants. "I ran five miles today. You need to get on that treadmill as well."

Was he calling her fat now? She was a size six and the five pounds she'd gained on her honeymoon hadn't done any damage. But, no, she wouldn't take the bait. She would be the better person. "Forgive me if I'm more concerned about Gina's soul than some measly pounds."

Terence winced at the barb. "Just be patient, Colleen. God has a path mapped out, and Gina has to find God on her own and in her own time."

Colleen steered into a safer topic. "Well, He used you to bring me into the light, or should I say, return to Him."

Terence smiled. He looked really handsome, so handsome that she was eager to help him out of his shirt. She kissed his cheek and massaged his temples. The sandalwood scent of the cologne he'd applied earlier in the day still held the warm, masculine fragrance she'd come to appreciate on him. Her agile fingers worked their magic, and she felt his body tense. She lifted her eyes to his and read his unspoken request. Colleen pressed on his shoulders until he sat in the chair by her vanity and proceeded to give him a light massage.

"You know just what I need," Terence moaned in between words.

Colleen smiled at the sheer pleasure on his face. She pressed harder, knowing that his muscles were taut with stress. Soon, she felt them loosen under her ministrations and stilled her hands. She stepped away, intending to undress and take it to another level.

"No, wait, I have to talk to you." Terence grasped her hand and gave her a light tug. Pliant, she fell into his arms and sat on his lap. Terence hugged her from behind. Colleen's body heated. Whirls of desire built within her. She wanted her husband and pressed her body closer to him. She reached behind her to rub his head.

"Remember what we tried the other day? I want to do that again," she purred. She trailed her fingers down his body and in one brash move, flipped around to straddle him. Colleen bent and blew tender kisses on his ear and neck. Her hands developed a life of their own.

Terence, however, had another idea. He stilled her hands. "I have a great suggestion for Super Sabbath. I think that would be a good time for you to get rebaptized."

"*Re*baptized?" Of all the things she'd thought he would say, that was the furthest from her mind. Her ardor cooled. Colleen pulled out of his arms and crisscrossed her arms in defiance. Terence ignored her and brought up an inconsequential matter. "I'm out of body wash."

"There's a spare bottle under the bathroom sink." Colleen flailed her arms. Terence tore his T-shirt over his head and went to get the wash. She intended to follow him but noticed the red nail polish on the bed and picked it up. She placed it on her night stand, then confronted him though he'd entered the shower.

"What do you mean, rebaptized? I already rededicated my life to the Lord, isn't that enough?"

Five minutes. She fumed in silence for five minutes while she waited for him to get out of the shower and walk into the closet.

"Yes, but your rebaptism would leave no doubt about your renewed commitment to God. Plus, it would put a stamp on my ministry, as I led you back to Christ, so to speak," Terence addressed her, still inside the closet.

"Isn't it about my relationship with God? Isn't it about God getting the glory?"

Terence walked out, dressed in a crisp white undershirt and plaid pajama bottoms. He made Colleen feel naked in her silk camisole and underwear, so she reached for her robe and slid it on.

"I am not trying to steal God's thunder," Terence replied. "I am trying to be seriously considered for ministry. I think you *should* do it."

Something about his tone sent off a warning bell. Was he saying she *had* to do it? "Terence, I can't believe you feel I should do this. Well, I am not going to do it. I did the whole repentance thing already—you know, you were there."

"Yes, but the others do not know. The single women need to see you do it openly as an example to them."

Quizzical, Colleen held up her hands. "You are not making sense."

Terrence's voice took on a different quality. "Are you calling me stupid?"

"No, but I think—"

"Seems to me you've done enough thinking." Terence rested his hands on his waist. "I'm the head of this family and you will get rebaptized two weeks from now. I don't want to discuss it again."

Colleen knew that for him the subject matter was closed. Her heart raced, and the hair on her neck raised. She couldn't believe he had just used the whole "head of the family" line. God made man the head, but she was not the tail. She squeezed her eyes shut and willed herself to keep from making a fuss.

"It'll solve two problems." Terrence approached her and pulled her body toward him. "I'll get what I need for the ministry, and Gina will surely come for an event like that."

His last statement gave Colleen pause, but she said, "That's true. I just don't think—"

"Don't think, baby. Just do. Do it for me." Terence kissed her.

Colleen melted under his touch. She should be doing it for God, not for him. But her heart complied, because she loved her husband and wanted to please him. "Okay." That one word fell off her lips like a thousand-pound boulder.

"You don't know how happy that makes me." Relief peppered his words. "I can't wait to tell my mother." He released her, climbed into bed, and pulled back the blankets.

Her hands flew to her hips. Had she just heard him right? "Your *mother*?"

"Yes, she suggested it."

Colleen should have known. His mother was like a thorn in her side. When Terence purchased their home in Valley Stream, she'd been overjoyed . . . until she realized Francine lived seven minutes away. Francine was always showing up when she felt like it, to point out something she wasn't doing right.

Yup. Colleen punched her pillows to release some tension. She had no doubt that the entire rebaptism idea wasn't altruistic, but it was a jab at her. She knew it, but she couldn't prove it. She got into her bed with a heavy heart.

"What's the matter?" Terence asked.

You're a mama's boy, that's what's the matter, she thought, but said, "Nothing." *God, give me strength.*

"Well, I am pleading for the pillows," Terence joked.

Colleen didn't laugh. From her side of the bed, a tear fell. She discreetly wiped it. She wasn't even sure why she felt the need to cry, but she knew a voice inside her was asking, "Who's going to plead for me?"

Chapter Five

Had he heard right?

Gina Price? Keith straightened. He sat around the burgundy oblong table with the other partners in the firm, where they gathered to discuss pressing cases. He raised his finger and piped up, "I'll take it."

"Huh?"

Keith knew he'd taken Carolyn Usher by surprise. "The Marshall case—I said I'll take it."

"But, there is nothing substantial here. All we have is a recalcitrant witness and the character recommendation of a schoolteacher. In fact, I was going to suggest that we drop this pro-bono case and research another that we have a newsworthy chance of winning."

He was a senior partner and didn't have to explain himself. "I said I'll take it." Keith extended his hand, arched an eyebrow, and pierced her with an imperial stare.

Displeased, she handed him the manila folder. Keith perused the contents and held back a grimace. He didn't stand a chance of winning this one. Maybe he'd spoken up too soon. Keith flipped through the paltry contents and read Gina's letter.

Her earnestness tugged at him. Without making his excuses, Keith abruptly left the semiannual pro-bono case meeting. He had a phone call to make.

He called Gina and asked her to meet him. Of course, she wanted to know why. "I'd rather discuss it with you in person. I'll be there at one. Don't be late." He covered his demand with a light chuckle.

From inside his BMW, Keith watched her approach. Gina looked like a little doll with dangerous curves in her floral dress and wedges. A slight wind ruffled the ends of her dress, and he caught a glimpse of her legs. He released an involuntary, guttural groan. The wind swayed the dress, giving him a brief outline of her body. *Michael has found himself a diamond,* Keith thought. No doubt about it.

Gina bent over through the window, unknowingly giving him a generous view of her chest had she leaned over. Just a little more to the left, he thought. Keith crooked his finger and directed, with a friendly and neutral tone, "Get in."

When Gina opened the door and slid into the seat, her dress pulled up and gave him another view of her legs. He watched as she adjusted herself. It was a good thing that he was taller than she was, or she would have thought he was a creep for ogling his brother's woman. *This is not going to be easy.* He'd better watch himself, or he'd be in big trouble.

Keith pulled his mind back from precarious waters and pulled the vehicle away from the curb. He kept her engaged in small talk for the short ride while he navigated the busy Queens Boulevard. He honked his horn to another driver and slid into a parking space.

He touched the small of her back as he led her into the Mesa Grille. Within minutes, they were seated for lunch.

The waitress commented on how well he and Gina looked together and what a beautiful couple they made. Keith waved her off, realizing that she was fishing for a confirmation while shamelessly flirting. He thought that was tacky, but he was used to it.

Gina opened her mouth, but before she could correct the misperception, Keith piped up, "Thank you so much for the compliment."

Gina said nothing, but once she left, he saw the question in her eyes.

"I didn't want her to think I was available. Women are always flirting with me," Keith stated.

She laughed, revealing beautiful teeth. "So you used me to fool an innocent woman and possibly broke her heart."

"Yeah," he said, without any remorse. *Yeah, right. Admit it to yourself, at least. You like that people think you two are an item.*

The waitress arrived quickly with their order, and the two settled down to eat.

"So," Gina began while taking a bite of her salad, "what's up?"

"I saw your letter."

Gina wrinkled her nose and tilted her head. "What letter?"

"I'm a senior partner at Bohlander & Associates." Keith waited.

Gina's eyes widened and a broad smile stretched across her face. "You're the attorney on Payton's case?" Her face brightened the room like the sun after a rainstorm.

Keith looked at her sparkling eyes and felt a stirring within him. Her joy washed over him, chipping at the shell around his heart. His heart flip-flopped. "I just took over the case today." Gina moved to bombard him with questions. He raised his hand and chuckled at her enthusiasm. "I'll need to review her case so I'll know how to proceed." Keith's voice dropped. "So, you and I may need to confer in case you have to testify on the stand. But I'm hoping it won't come to that. This case is difficult, but that's my specialty."

Gina nodded and bounced in her chair. "Oh, gladly, whenever you're ready. I'm just happy to help in any way I can."

Ready—apt word. Keith cleared his throat and maintained his cool. "I'll let you know."

Gina shook her head. "Wow. What are the odds that you would be the one on Payton's case? Small world." She bent her head to take another bite of her meal. Her hair swept across her face, and Keith yearned to reach over and touch it. Her skin looked smooth and soft. What would it feel like against his hand?

Keith dropped his fork on the table. "Gina." He said her name lightly, like a whisper.

Gina's fork stilled in midair, and she leaned forward at the mention of her name. Slowly, she put the utensil down on the table and gave him her full attention.

Awareness built and the atmosphere tightened. Keith savored the way her name rolled off his tongue, so he said it again.

"Whatever it is, Keith, just go ahead and say it. Because you're making me nervous." She waved a hand. "All sorts of things are running through my mind right now."

Keith hesitated. This was difficult for him to say, but he knew it was now or never. He took a deep breath. "When I finally met you the other night, I must confess, I was ready to meet yet another floozy that Michael had found somewhere. I wasn't prepared to encounter such a beautiful and poised woman. I was especially *not* prepared to react the way I did once I saw you."

Gina crooked her head, but said nothing. Keith took a sip of water before he elaborated. "In other words, I didn't know that once I saw you, the only thought that would enter my head was that I wished that I had met you first." *There, he'd said it.*

Gina blinked several times and her mouth opened and closed like a fish. Then her eyes widened. "But . . ."

Keith strove to put her mind at ease after his bold admission. "Don't worry," he injected to lighten the air between them. "I have no intentions of following up on this emotion—"

Gina interrupted, having finally found her voice. "So that's why you brought me here? I mean, how am I supposed to respond to this?"

"I just wanted you to know so that you won't get the wrong impression when we see each other again, because I intend to keep my distance. I know that these feelings will sort themselves out in time."

Speechless, Gina couldn't provide a more coherent, articulate reply than, "I see." But, he deduced that she really didn't get it. She didn't understand that she'd literally taken his breath away. "Relax," Keith advised. He laughed and gave Gina a small pat on the shoulder to reassure her. "Everything will be all right. You'll see." His grin depicted a confidence he didn't feel.

She nodded. "I hope so, because I don't want, or need, any drama," Gina declared.

"I am drama free."

"Somehow, I doubt that."

"Somehow, I don't," he countered.

Gina looked at him.

Keith looked at her.

Neither spoke.

Both recognized drama, with a capital "D."

"If that man is drama free, then I'm Hillary Clinton!"

After her "meeting" with Keith, Gina had entered her house, closed the door, and now leaned against it to compose herself. Keith's declaration had taken her completely by surprise. At lunch, she'd had to grip the chair or she'd have fallen flat on the floor. She wasn't even sure how she'd remained composed the whole time. She'd had to force herself to remember the rudimentary steps to eating.

Brothers.

Honestly, a part of her felt flattered that she had attracted the attention of two gorgeous, dynamic men, but they were brothers, and she was a one-man-kind-of-a-woman.

Gina breathed in deeply several times to settle her nerves. She kicked off her sandals and walked to the sofa. Caught up in her thoughts, she slanted her body in the comfy couch and slung her legs on the end table. Keith had created an awkward position with his confession. She was dating his brother, and Keith was about to be a father. But still he dropped this bombshell. What did that say about his character?

Gina dragged her hands through her hair while she contemplated. His declaration had seemed out of character. Keith hadn't struck her as the kind of man to make a move on his brother's girl—at least, not the Keith that Michael boasted about.

To Gina, it felt like a soap opera—but his confession flattered her ego.

Gina heard a vibration. She went to peek at her cell phone. Michael had texted. Thinking about you.

Guilt surfaced, and her stomach knotted. Michael had been thinking about her while she had been out with his brother. She shouldn't have gone anywhere with Keith, but her curiosity had prevailed against her good sense. Besides, she had no way of knowing that Keith would've made such a startling confession. Gina pondered. Should she tell Michael where she'd been?

That would be a *no!* If there was one thing she had learned in her relatively short existence, it was that you never volunteered any information. What Michael didn't know wouldn't hurt him.

The next evening, Michael requested Gina accompany him for dinner at Keith's. Keith had invited them both. Michael informed her that Eve would be there as well. Gina looked forward to it. She was curious to finally meet Eve and to see Keith's house.

They entered a private driveway that led up to a huge house. It looked more like a minimansion than a regular house. Keith was obviously doing well financially. Michael led her up a flight of stairs until they were at Keith's front door.

The door was unlocked.

She saw Michael turn the lock, enter, then sniffed in delight. "Something smells good," he bellowed.

"I'm back here." Keith hollered from somewhere in the back. Michael headed toward the voice, so she followed.

Gina felt her insides flutter. She wondered if her nervousness showed on her face. She felt guilty, like she had betrayed Michael. Again, she debated whether she should have told him about having lunch with Keith. She tried hard to act normal, but her paranoia increased.

"So, what're you cooking?" Michael asked, peering into the pots. He was completely unaware of the turmoil rumbling through her system.

Keith took the spatula and slapped Michael's hands away. "Get out of my pots. You know better," he warned, but his tender smile belied the reprimand. It was obvious to Gina how much the brothers loved and respected each other.

"I'm making pot roast with carrots and potatoes," Keith replied. "It will be ready in about five minutes."

Michael wandered off with something that suspiciously looked like a piece of meat. He carried his stolen goods on a paper towel in his hands, leaving Keith alone with Gina for a moment.

Gina smiled with Keith at Michael's ploy.

"Welcome to my home, Gina," Keith greeted.

I guess he's not having any problems. Gina felt disappointed. Keith's face and mannerisms had not given anything away. He appeared cool, calm, and collected.

"Hi." That was her eloquent comeback. She averted her eyes and looked around the room. Gina tapped her feet nervously. Awkwardly, she tried to think of something—anything—to say. "I love your home," she stuttered in an attempt to ease the tension in the air.

"Thanks," Keith replied, then gave her a smile. She saw him raise his eyebrows as if to demand that she lighten up.

Play it cool. Gina expelled a breath. Suddenly feeling warm, she removed her light blazer showing off her backless cocktail dress. She needed to find Michael. That's who she was here with. She saw that he'd gone to stand by the patio windows to devour his steal. She was much safer over there with him. That *other* one rattled her nerves.

Gina's breath caught at the view. Her eyes roamed the meticulous lawn and artfully placed rainbow assortment of flowers. The sweet fragrances permeated the air and teased her senses.

She felt Michael reach for her hand before drawing her to him. *Please don't kiss me. Not here, not now.*

Michael kissed her with passion. Figures, now he decides to be more aggressive. Gina felt funny kissing him with Keith in view, but she still enjoyed it. Michael felt her acquiescence because he quickly deepened the kiss.

However, Gina pulled away. She rested her hand on his chest and crooked her head in Keith's direction. "Your brother is in the next room," she whispered.

Michael only laughed. "Trust me, if it was him, he'd be doing the same thing."

Do not look. Do not look.
He looked.

Look away. Look away.

He didn't. He watched the whole thing.

Finally, they broke apart. That was some kiss Michael and Gina had shared.

Keith was angry with himself. He could not believe that he had actually stood there spying on his brother and his girlfriend's tender moment. He was a pervert, an ogre, for ogling his brother's woman.

Keith had seen Gina's hands move down Michael's back before she broke the kiss. He had seen Michael's hands on her bare back, and he could imagine how soft her skin must feel. *It should be me.* He felt an inexplicable churn in the pit of his stomach. It was grinding him on the inside. What was wrong with him? This had never ever happened to him before. He and his brother had never shared the same taste in women.

A pair of hands encircled his waist. Startled, he jumped.

"Miss me?" Eve purred in his ear.

Keith turned around to greet her. He untangled himself from her grip.

"I didn't hear you come in. How was your doctor's appointment?"

She pouted. "Everything is fine, and you would've known that if you had been there with me."

"I'm sorry. I had a case. You know that. I explained it to you earlier," Keith answered patiently and reached out to pat her protruding stomach.

"I know," Eve said, before she relented. He saw the exact moment she spotted Michael and Gina.

Eve tilted her head. She moved her eyes up and down Gina's silhouette. Keith could see the oh-so-familiar female dissection process that began whenever another woman was in his space. Eve considered every woman competition. Even his brother's girlfriend. "That's her?"

"Yes. That's Gina."

"She's pretty," Eve remarked.

"Yes, she is," Keith replied in a careful, noncommittal tone; then he decided it was best to not give Eve a chance to render her final verdict on Gina's appearance, because she'd surely find something wrong with the dress or the hair or the makeup. "Michael, Gina, come here for a moment." He made the necessary introductions between Eve and Gina, but his mind registered that the couple had entered the room holding hands like . . . lovers. He couldn't help but wonder, were they?

He directed everyone into the dining area. Keith had lit the entire room with candles in lieu of regular lighting. He wouldn't admit that he had painstakingly done it all with Gina in mind. He glanced at Gina. Her lips looked red and swollen. Those same lips were now curved in appreciation at his handiwork, as her hands grazed the tablecloth.

"Nice," Eve murmured and pulled Keith closer to her, marking her territory. He allowed her the pleasure and motioned for everyone to be seated.

As they ate, everyone complimented him on the food. Keith accepted their praises but every opportunity he could steal, his eyes fell on Gina. It was easy to do too since she was seated directly across from him. He watched her with deep intensity. He saw Gina bite into the meat. He saw her stick her tongue out to lick gravy from her upper lip. He watched her scoop the potato off the fork and into her mouth. *It was killing him.* This had never happened to him before. Attraction had punched him in the guts.

"Michael, I almost forgot to mention that Keith and I will be working together," Gina said.

"Really? He didn't tell me that," Michael returned.

"Yes . . ." As Gina filled Michael in, Keith ducked his head and concentrated on his meal. Eve's eyes were burning holes in his skin, but he refused to look her way.

Michael cupped Gina's hand and assured her. "I'm sure you're in good hands, Gina. With Keith on the case, it's in the bag."

Keith barely acknowledged his brother's bragging, because Eve poked him in his side. He gave her a look. *What?*

She scowled. He would catch heat later.

However, Keith wasn't concerned. As Michael's thumb stroked Gina's palm, searing heat rose within him. Jealousy. It was green, and it was ugly. Keith strove for temperance. He loved his brother, and Gina was his brother's woman.

He wanted her.

He couldn't have her.

That had to be the end of it.

Chapter Six

What was *she* doing here? That was his first thought. His second reflected gratitude that Gina wasn't with him.

"Hi, Mikey," the woman said, using the pet name she always called him.

Michael's good mood evaporated. He dropped his briefcase and gasped. Immobile, he swung his head from left to right, taking in the plethora of open albums and scattered pictures. From her position on the floor, the woman looked at ease, as if she belonged there. Michael placed both hands on his hips and asked the sixty-four-thousand-dollar question. "Karen, what are you doing here?"

"I, uh . . ." Karen Newton searched for words. She shuffled and gathered the pictures to stack them into piles. "I came by, and since I still had my access card, decided to let myself in. I got bored, so . . ." Karen splayed her hands at the display.

"So, you decided to break in?"

Karen shrugged.

Michael exhaled. He resisted the urge to toss her out. He ambled over to where she sat and squatted to examine her. She'd put on some much-needed weight, because her usually gaunt face looked rounder. He took in her half-inch long nails and the huge hoops hanging from her ears. Karen had abandoned her natural look and had returned to relaxing her hair. She also had it cut and colored various shades of auburn, or chestnut. He wasn't sure which. Whatever, he was pleased by what he saw.

When they had started dating, Karen had stopped working and had hibernated in his penthouse, doing nothing. She had let herself go to the point where Michael had had to pay someone to come in and do her hair and nails. But now, she looked like her old self.

"You look good—" Michael acknowledged and rose to his feet. He moved to sit on the couch, right before he added to his compliment, "and your hair. It suits you."

"Thank you," Karen replied, before addressing the big question. "I guess you must be wondering what I'm doing here." She gathered his albums and other memorabilia, then placed them back under the coffee table that they had picked out together. When she was done, she joined him on the couch.

"Yes. I never expected to see you again after, you know . . ."

"Well . . ." Karen explained, "time has passed, and I started thinking that, well, perhaps I had been too hasty to just let us go."

"Well, that was totally understandable after the way I hurt you," Michael reasoned. His body showed nonchalance, but on the inside, he screamed, "I can't believe this is happening. Why is this happening?"

"Are you seeing anybody?" Her expectant face showed she hoped for a negative response.

"Kind of . . ." Michael trailed off. *Kind of? It was either yes or no.*

Karen raised her eyebrows at him.

"Yes," Michael clarified, "I am seeing someone."

"Oh . . ." Karen's shoulders drooped, and she sighed. She hung her head.

Her shaking tipped him off that she was actually crying. Michael's heart went out to her, and he reached out to hug his old love.

"I just . . . I just realized that I still love you . . . and . . . I just . . ." Karen sobbed and sniffed. She wiped her nose with her hands, and that simple act touched him. Michael turned toward the end table, plucked out a couple tissues from the box, and handed them to her. Karen blew into a tissue to get some semblance of control. He took another and gently wiped her face.

"I never intended to break down like this. After all, it's been almost a year. I shouldn't have expected you to be waiting, especially when I made it perfectly clear that I wasn't coming back," Karen admitted.

Worried, Michael's eyes wildly scanned the room. He couldn't meet her eyes. After her big suicide attempt, the last thing he wanted to do was reject her completely.

"I just feel as if I'm going to die without you," Karen groaned.

"Please don't talk like that." Michael held his head as the weight of her words hit his shoulders. What should he do? "You're not going to die, Karen," Michael expressed. "I mean, just look at you. You got it going on." Their eyes met. He felt a familiar stirring. No, this could not happen. Karen shifted closer and rubbed her face across his neck. He couldn't believe she'd resorted to the oldest trick in the book. Well, he wasn't falling for it. Michael jumped to his feet. "Karen. This cannot happen."

Karen stalked him. This must be how the bug feels when it realizes it's been caught in the spider's web. She pinned him with an intent, predatory gaze. Panicked, Michael used his hand to impede her from getting closer. "Look, it's over between us, and I'm with a good woman, and I'm not trying to hurt her. So leave my spare keycard here on your way out. I'll give you ten minutes and if you're still here, I will call the cops."

He retreated into his bedroom after his ultimatum. He hated being so cold with her, but he wasn't taking any chances, for his traitorous body might betray him. True to his word, he was out in ten minutes. He wasn't prepared for the sight before him.

The next day, Michael called Keith. Foregoing the perfunctory greeting, he stated, "I slept with Karen."

"You did *what?*" Keith bellowed over the line. "Did you say, *Karen?*"

Michael raged. "Yes! Karen! She was here when I got home. I demanded she leave. I gave her ten minutes before I vowed I'd call the cops. She was naked. You know no man could resist that."

"That's a poor excuse. When will you stop thinking with your—ah—well, fill in the blank!" Keith roared. "Gina is a class act. Karen is the closest thing to trash that I know."

Resentment burned inside him at his brother's disgust. "Karen is not trash. I wish you'd stop calling her that." She possessed redeemable qualities, despite her erratic behavior. But, Keith refused to give Karen a chance once he had her pegged.

Keith was silent for a second. Then he conceded, "Well, maybe trash is a harsh description. But she is psychotic and, dare I remind you, suicidal."

Michael couldn't disagree. Karen had cut up all his clothes down to his socks in a fit of rage; she had slashed his tires and had broken all his favorite music discs. Still, Michael had not ended things because he had given her good reason to be angry. He had dogged her out.

There was also the fact that she wasn't lacking skills in the bedroom. Maybe it was because she wasn't too far from certifiable, but there was nothing that Karen hadn't been willing to do or try.

However, Gina made him a better man. Yet, better man or not, he hadn't called her all day, which was unusual for him. Every time Michael picked up the phone to dial her digits, guilt engulfed him. He felt as if he were about to choke on it. Call him paranoid, but he just felt as if Gina would be able to tell by osmosis what he had done. She seemed as if she could see through his very soul whenever they spoke. No, he couldn't chance it. He had to avoid her for a few days until his equilibrium returned.

He also had to figure out what to do about Karen. She had still been at the penthouse when he'd left. Michael vowed to get rid of her, pronto. Now that his head had cleared, he admitted that Karen was a parasite, and he knew that she was about to latch on with all four claws. He could not afford for that to happen, but how could he slither out of this one?

Michael felt like a coward, but he was going to have to get out of Dodge for a few days.

Atlanta?

Hmmm . . . Michael thought. Atlanta sounded good. He had a legitimate reason to go there because he had some work he needed to get done there. He had been contracted to design the layout for a new chain, Simmonds Synthetics. He had delayed his start date, because he knew it would take a few weeks and he hadn't wanted to be away from Gina. But now was the opportune time to go. He figured if he left now, he would kill two birds with one stone. He could get some space to think and get paid for it.

Without another moment's hesitation, Michael called and booked his first-class flight. His fingers shook when he dialed Gina's number. He sighed with relief when he got her voice mail. He left a brief message explaining his "sudden" trip, and hung up before he made any foolish confessions.

Chapter Seven

Colleen scurried over to where Gina waited. She'd missed the 1:08 p.m. Long Island Railroad train to Manhattan, and had had to wait fifteen minutes for another. Then, the ten-minute trek from West 4th across the park made her even later and colder. It was a good thing she'd worn her cashmere sweater. She and Gina met up by their favorite gyro and pizza shop. They'd been coming here since their college days at New York University—always crowded with limited seats but so worth it.

Gina was being her usual impatient self, tapping her feet and looking around in every direction. Colleen chuckled. She knew what was coming next.

"Late. As usual," Gina said, as soon as she spotted Colleen. "I ordered a large pizza for us to share."

"Sorry I'm late and thanks for ordering because I'm starved." Colleen bent down and hugged her friend. They broke apart, looked at each other, and hugged again.

"I missed you. You look good. Seeing you is so much better than just talking on the phone," Gina said.

"I agree. And so do you, look good, I mean," Colleen answered, while she situated herself at the table. "I can't believe all this time has gone by, and we're now just getting together."

"I know," Gina concurred. "But, you're a busy married woman now, and you know how crazy back to school can be. August just flew by, and now, here we are in the third week of school. Plus, didn't you and Terence go out of town for Labor Day?"

"Yes, there was a church trip to Pennsylvania and a cookout, and . . . Girl, who knows! Church life is hectic and busy. There is always some function going on or some crisis. It never ends." While she spoke, Colleen rummaged through her purse and retrieved a beaded necklace that she'd brought back from Jamaica for Gina.

"It's beautiful!" Gina exclaimed, while examining the beads. She clasped it around her neck. "Turquoise is such a beautiful stone. Looks expensive."

Colleen lowered her chin and arched her eyebrows. Gina laughed as understanding dawned. Terence had given her a hard time when she decided to purchase it, but Colleen had stood her ground. She had let him know that she was going to get it whether he liked it or not. Seeing her determination, Terence had backed off. He had even magnanimously paid for it with his credit card, and Colleen let him, without any remorse or guilt.

"So, how is Terence?" Gina toyed with her necklace. "How was the honeymoon?"

This was the first time Gina mentioned Terence's name without a snide rejoinder. Colleen pretended to swoon with dramatic disbelief. "What? No biting comment?"

"Maybe I'm reforming my ways." Gina raised her hands in mock surrender. "If you're happy, then so am I. I'm not going to interfere, especially since I do not even know the man, and he is your husband at this point, so . . ."

Colleen appreciated that. "Thank you. And, to answer your question, he's doing fine." She looked at her watch. Terence had probably called her at the house already. He usually rang at one o'clock to say hello. Colleen was always at home, waiting to hear from him. However, even though she would never admit it out loud, she felt a little uneasy about his daily phone calls, which came like clockwork. She couldn't shake the feeling that he was really checking up on her.

He was jealous, controlling, and possessive, but kept that side to him veiled under politely worded requests. The requests, however, were more like demands.

Their pizza came, and both women bit in. Colleen loved the homemade sauce filled with the right amount of tomato and basil. Gina loved the thick mounds of stringy cheese when she took a bite.

"So Bohlander & Associates accepted Payton's case!" Gina said, between bites.

"Good for you, Gina. They're a top law firm."

"All I did was write a letter on Payton's behalf," Gina demurred. Then she added. "Michael's brother, Keith, works for them . . ."

Her pizza finished, Colleen nodded at the appropriate times while Gina elaborated, but her thoughts drifted to Terence. She refused to entertain the notion that she might have made a mistake and jumped the broom a teeny bit too soon. Her pride prevented her from telling Gina.

Besides, in her heart of hearts, Colleen believed that somehow, things would work themselves out for good. That's what the Bible said, and God's Word was gold. She and Terence were just undergoing an adjustment period, she reasoned. Things would get better between them.

"Are you even listening to me?" Gina cut into Colleen's thoughts.

She jumped out of her reverie. Gina had been saying something about . . . Stumped, Colleen could only shake her head. She gave Gina a sheepish grin.

"See what married life does to you! It affects your brain." Gina cracked up good-heartedly.

Thoughtful, Colleen rested one hand on her chin. Gina glowed. Her eyes sparkled. Her sunny persona appeared for two reasons—Money or Men. Colleen would stake her vote was on the latter.

"So, you and Michael hit it off, huh?" Colleen pried.

"Yeah, we sure did. He's away now in Atlanta for a few weeks, but that is just a slice of the pie . . ." Gina filled her in on her lunch date with Keith, and her fantasizing about him.

"Brothers!" Colleen shook her head with a slight grin, not the least bit surprised to hear that her friend was mixed up in such a love triangle. This was not the first time Gina had attracted the attention of brothers.

"This sounds like Jason and Justin Browben all over again," Colleen said, reminiscing.

Gina hissed through her teeth. Colleen wiggled her eyes and ears. She would never let Gina live that down.

"That was ages ago," Gina smirked and rolled her eyes. Her cheeks were rosy from embarrassment, though. "This is nothing like that. *Believe* me."

Colleen delighted at her friend's discomfort. Jason and Justin Browben were identical twins who both had taken a strong liking to Gina in college and who had become her shadow. Gina called them Double Dragons and Twin Trolls, but that didn't make a difference to either of them.

"I wonder where they are now," Colleen said.

Gina shuddered. "I don't care. As long as it's nowhere near here! I'll never forget their invitation to a three-some."

Colleen slapped her thigh. "I had forgotten about that."

"Well, Michael and Keith are nothing like Jason and Justin. They're like mincemeat compared to these guys." Gina bragged. "And just wait until you meet Keith. The man is beautiful. I'm sure he'd cringe if he heard me say that, but it's the truth."

Colleen raised her eyebrows at the airy inflection in her friend's voice and became a little concerned. "Girl?"

"What?"

Gina refused to meet her eyes.

"You know what!" Colleen persisted. She leaned over to look Gina in the eyes. "You're attracted to him!"

"Him, who?" Gina hedged.

"Cut out the games, Gigi," Colleen warned. "You're too smart to play dumb. Gina, you can't be messing with two men, especially in this day and age. Plus the fact that they're brothers . . . Ugh!"

Gina hung her head. But Colleen didn't care about the censure in her voice. She knew her friend needed a tough talking to.

"I *do* like Michael," Gina insisted, "But there's just some sort of magnetism about Keith that draws me to him." She whispered the words to Colleen, as if she were in a confessional.

"Well, Keith is engaged, so you know that nothing can ever come of that," Colleen warned, using her schoolteacher voice.

"You do not have to reprimand me like I'm one of your students," Gina answered, a little testily. "I would never try to play two brothers like that. Haven't I always walked a straight line?"

Colleen exhaled and relaxed. "You're right, girl. I'm sorry if it seemed as if I was judging you. But I guess I'm just being overprotective. I know you always do the right thing. Speaking of doing the right thing, are you coming to our Friends and Family Super Sabbath? I'm going to be getting rebaptized and I need someone there who's in my—"

Colleen's cell phone rang, interrupting the conversation. She saw relief wash over Gina's face. Gina welcomed the reprieve. "Hi . . . Yeah . . . I ah . . . I have no idea . . . All right . . . Give me a couple of hours." Colleen hung up the phone. She looked over at her friend, who was giving her *that* look. A look that Colleen knew all too well, for it was usually followed with a snippy comment. "Don't give me that look," she scowled at Gina with irritation.

"What look? I guess you just got your summons to return home, huh?" Gina balked. "I'm not surprised. Even when you both were just dating, he'd always find a reason to call you away whenever we hung out."

"That's not true," Colleen denied, but Gina's accusation pierced her heart, because it resonated with truth. She had made the same observations herself, but was not as willing to admit it out loud.

Defensive, Colleen sought to wipe off that smug expression on her friend's face. "Well, at least I don't have to worry about mixing up names and keeping track of my lies."

Gina's mouth popped open with shock and appall from Colleen's crass statement. In all their years of friendship, she had never come at her friend like that. Gina's face contorted with hurt. Colleen squirmed. Pride prevented her from apologizing.

"Well, *Sister* Hayworth," Gina began, with tears stemming her eyelids, "I guess there is no need for us to continue this discussion, is there?" With that, she snatched her handbag, tossed a twenty-dollar bill onto the table, and walked out without even a good-bye.

Once Gina had left, Colleen felt miserable. She couldn't believe that she had taken a cheap shot like that at the very best friend she ever had in the whole world. Especially since what Gina said about Terence was true. She knew she could have apologized or said something to ratify her nasty comment, but she hadn't. Gina's spine had been ramrod straight, and Colleen knew that she had hurt her friend with that crude remark. She all but called her friend loose and trifling, when that was the farthest thing from the truth. Colleen didn't have any idea what the matter was with her lately.

Lie. She knew. Her new attitude could be summed up in one word. *Terence.*

She looked at her cell phone and pressed Gina's speed dial code but stopped just before it could ring. She'd call her, later.

Later, turned into days . . . days turned into weeks, but Colleen couldn't bring herself to make the call. Gina had texted her a couple times, but she refused to answer. So, it was no surprise that Gina didn't come for Super Sabbath, which Colleen was glad about, because it was surprisingly uneventful. She had seen the whole day as an ordeal, and maybe Gina would've picked up on her discomfort with the fanfare of her rebaptism celebration. A part of her wondered if that wasn't a subconscious stimulant for her fight with Gina.

Then one day, Colleen entered her house, having just returned from a shopping spree. She had enjoyed herself, but had to admit that it was just not the same. Colleen missed Gina. Shopping was something that they almost always did together. Though Gina was usually kicking and screaming, it was always still fun.

She hunched down in the couch, dead tired.

"How was your day?"

She'd had her eyes closed but cracked them open at Terence's question. He had come out of the kitchen to greet her. She could tell because he held the remnants of the turkey sandwich she'd left for him before going out.

"Okay," Colleen said, and boosted her tired body high enough to give him a kiss on the cheek. "But it feels weird, not working. This is the time of year I'd usually be dress hunting with Gina for the high school's Homecoming Dance. So I decided to go shopping. I've rarely gone shopping without Gina," she bemoaned.

Terence merely shrugged. Secretly, Colleen believed that he rejoiced that she and Gina were not on speaking terms. Why would he? That meant that Colleen was paying him even more attention, and he was basking in every moment of it.

She hoisted herself upright when Terence went over to where she had placed the bags. He peeked into them, looking for something. "I'm sorry, honey, I didn't buy you anything this time," she yawned. Still he persisted. Why was he so interested in her purchases?

Terence hauled out a pair of pants and looked over at her. Askance, he raised one eyebrow. Colleen's heart thundered in her chest. She leapt off the couch, eyeing him like a cornered prey. The air between them intensified under his silent question. "They were on sale." Colleen's voice quivered. She rubbed at her arms to kill the goose bumps, hating her transparency.

Terence did not reply. Instead, he dove through the other bags. She stammered, "What are you doing?" He ignored her. Colleen shivered as her husband maniacally divided the clothes she had purchased into two piles. "What are you doing?" she repeated, with more emphasis.

"Get rid of those," Terence ordered and abruptly departed.

Colleen watched him go before expelling a small sigh of relief. She held up her hands. They were actually shaking. Colleen picked up the pants—the culprit. Terence was angry that she had not taken his subtle advice to only wear skirts since he was about to become the church's associate minister. He had stated that as a pastor's wife, she should wear more demure dresses instead of what she was used to wearing. But Colleen was not having it. She was her own woman, and being married was not about to change that.

If he thought for one second that just because she was now spending his money, she had to answer to him, he had another think coming. If that was what he expected, Colleen would just go back to her job at the school. It was at his insistence that she'd resigned and devoted herself to his ministry—well, she hadn't resigned, just put in for a year's leave of absence. She could have her old job back any time she wanted.

You know what, she wasn't having this. Colleen threw the pants on the floor and strode into the kitchen. She confronted him. "I am not taking them back!"

Terence's eyes narrowed. His body stance said, *Who is she talking to like that?* But he didn't say that. "Yes, you are," he said quietly.

He always spoke in a low voice. Yelling was just not his style. But Colleen was not fooled for an instant. She could hear the underlying steel, and it did not sit well with her. She ran her fingers through her hair before she caught on that it was a dead giveaway of her uncertainty. She clasped her hands together to keep them out of her hair.

Though unsure what her next move should be, she knew that she wasn't happy with the way that things were going. Colleen liked pleasing people, but at this moment, she wanted to please herself. Gina's comments from weeks ago still rattled. She didn't want to be taken advantage of by anybody, and that included her husband.

"It shouldn't matter what I wear," Colleen changed tactics. "You never had a problem when we were dating. And you may not want me wearing pants, but don't think I don't see you checking other women out."

Terence scoffed at her sentiment. "All the other wives wear dresses, and I feel that you should, too. Baby, I'm not trying to change who you are. I just want you to fit in with the ministers' wives. Even my mother agrees that you need to dress a little more conservatively. "

Colleen bit her lip to keep from screaming. It was all beginning to make sense to her. Francine was behind this. She'd probably made some comment that put this idea into Terence's head. Colleen knew that Francine didn't really like her. Francine wanted to keep her son to herself and at her beck and call. Colleen recognized this and made up her mind to ignore Francine's antics, but it was difficult.

Terence leaned toward her and kissed her full on the lips. Colleen knew that this was his way of persuading her to change her mind. She vowed not to be manipulated by his charm. Then, she sighed as she felt Terence's passion increase. He continued his tender manipulations. Colleen's passion rose. "I'll try," she promised as she leaned into her husband's embrace, seeking more.

The better she felt, the more she capitulated. It wasn't such a big deal, Colleen convinced herself. She could wear dresses every day. There were so many cute styles, and she had long boots for the winter. She supposed she could compromise on this, because, after all, it was not going to hurt her.

Terence smiled with barely concealed pleasure at her acquiescence.

Colleen noticed the slight air of superiority on Terence's face and hated that she'd become putty in his hands. It was almost like he was reveling in the control he had over her, and a part of her resented it, but a stronger part of her wanted to agree to anything he told her to do. She felt powerless, like all he had to do was touch her and she would do whatever he asked.

Chapter Eight

Michael entered his hotel suite and dumped the luggage he held to the floor.

"Well, aren't you going to even *talk* to me?" Karen whined. "I know I caught you off guard and how much you hate surprises. But I was desperate."

She addressed Michael for the third time that evening, but he barely glanced her way. He was too ticked off to even respond, and her voice grated on his nerves. Michael couldn't for the life of him figure out how Karen had finagled her way to Atlanta. He'd been in bliss for the past three weeks—before she'd just shown up, uninvited.

After he'd spoken to Gina the night before, he'd place a courtesy call to Karen. Just to check on her. Mistake number one. In their brief conversation, he'd told her his location. Mistake number two. He'd left his AmEx card in his house. Mistake number three. Boy, did he regret his big mouth.

Karen must have hopped on the next thing smoking the minute that he'd gotten off the phone with her. When the concierge told him that there was a woman waiting for him in the lobby, he'd practically sprinted, expecting to see Gina. He hadn't bothered to conceal his annoyance when he'd spotted *the leech* instead. Yes, Michael had seen *all* of her, now; however, the very sight of Karen revolted him. He was tired of her. What had he ever seen in her?

"Mikey, come on. Please. Talk to me," she wailed.

Michael continued to disregard her.

"I can't stand it when you get into one of your pouting sessions just because something didn't go your way. I didn't force you to sleep with me."

Karen was right. She hadn't forced him, but now he was paying for it. Michael knew that it was childish to ignore her, but she had complicated his escape plan. He was here to get some breathing room, to think and strategize. He had no intention of being entangled in a love triangle, so, he had to figure this out. *Why didn't I just stay away? That was all I had to do. Walk away!*

Frustrated, Michael would have kicked his own butt, if he could have, for his stupidity. He sighed. He couldn't avoid her forever. So, he proposed, "Tell you what, why don't you go get something to wear; and then we'll talk."

Karen jumped at the chance of going shopping and spending his money. She grabbed the card he offered and left the suite before he changed his mind. Michael shook his head at her predictability. He'd never noticed how shallow and selfish Karen really was. Meeting Gina had enlightened him about how good women behaved. Now he was potentially ruining his chance to have everything he had ever wanted.

No, he would not allow that. He would figure out how to fix this, and Gina would never find out.

Since he knew he could talk freely as Karen wouldn't be back any time soon, Michael used his speed dial and waited for his brother to pick up the line. "Come on, come on, Bro, pick up."

Keith answered on the second ring. Michael knew his brother was still upset with him, but he needed to confess to someone. "Um, Karen is here with me."

"*What?*" Keith's shout made his ear ring.

"I didn't bring her, Keith. I simply called her last night to check on my place. She surprised me. I didn't invite her. When I came in this evening, the front desk informed me that a woman was waiting for me in the lobby. I thought it was Gina. I don't even know how she found out I was staying at the Georgian Terrace. She must have used my credit card to pay for her flight. It's a good thing I had reserved a two-bedroom suite." He heard Keith's loud sigh, but continued, "It's as if she is digging her claws into me all over again, and I have no idea how to shake her off without her going ballistic again."

"Well, that's what happens when you sleep with a psychopath. As far as I'm concerned, you brought this on yourself."

Michael winced at his dispassionate tone. Keith didn't empathize with his plight. "I know." Michael sighed deeply and rubbed his chin. How had his life gotten so complicated already?

For several seconds, the line remained quiet. Then Keith spoke, "Okay, I'm going to attempt to put my personal feelings aside. I know you feel guilty, but the milk's already spilt, so to speak. Put Karen on the next flight, or wrap things up down there, and get home," Keith offered. "You had your closure with Karen, now end it, for good. Unless . . . you still have residual feelings for her?"

"No . . . I don't know. I'd be lying if I said that I didn't care about her." Michael felt confused and perplexed. He rubbed his temples, knowing a migraine was coming on.

"Well, you'd better figure things out fast."

Michael hung up shortly after that. He gathered his wits and called Gina. She must have been waiting for his call because he didn't remember hearing it ring.

"Hello?"

Michael gulped. Act normal. He lightly returned, "Hi, yourself."

"I've been looking out for your call," Gina greeted him, blissfully unaware of the rocks that lined Michael's stomach.

He crossed his fingers, though he knew she couldn't see. Here goes. "Yeah, I had a small conflict with the layout plans for the new Simmonds Synthetics building, which took up most of my time yesterday and today."

Gina switched topics. "So, you miss me?"

"Of course," Michael responded to the sultry tone in her question. "Actually, all I've been doing is thinking about you."

"Good, because the longer you're gone, the more I'm missing you."

Michael smiled and pressed the phone closer to his ear, subconsciously attempting to be nearer to her. Gina's voice soothed him. He vowed that he was going to do right by her. As soon as Karen returned, he would send her on her merry way.

"Well, I guess I'll be going to the Homecoming Dance this Friday night by myself."

Michael heard her overstated sigh and slapped his head with his hand. "Oh no. Gina, I completely forgot!" She had told him about the Homecoming Dance held the third Friday of every October, but it had completely slipped his mind. There was no way he'd make it. "I didn't write it down on my calendar."

"Don't worry about it. It's only a silly dance. Take care of your business, that's more important. My friends will just have to meet you another time."

Gina was so agreeable that Michael felt even worse. She should not have let him off the hook that easy. His insides churned at his deception. But then he heard the lock click. Michael knew Karen would act the fool and do something stupid if she knew he was on the phone with another female.

"Well, Gina, I've got to run."

Gina impulsively blew him a kiss. "Okay, get your rest and we'll talk tomorrow." Her seductive promise brought all kinds of images to his mind. He didn't care if Karen heard now. He'd told her that he was dating someone. "I will," he said, softly. Michael ended the call just as Karen entered the room.

She showed off her purchases from the boutique in the lobby. He listened and bit his lip to keep from yelling, "Shut up."

The evening dragged on and Michael felt antsy. Karen entertained herself by watching television while eating strawberries and chocolate. She was too caught up in whatever she was watching to pay him any attention, which was good for him.

He had to think of a way to detach this parasite from under him, without her leaving any marks from sucking his blood dry.

Despite all the upheaval in his personal life, Michael had a productive day at work the next day. He had also finally met Tyler Simmonds, owner of Simmonds Synthetics, to discuss his expansion plans. Tyler was considering opening yet another branch in Atlanta and wanted to get some preliminary designs and suggestions. He had been impressed with Michael's work and wanted to consult with Michael to get some innovative ideas.

Michael had been awed by the other man's drive and determination. He had even met Tyler's wife, Camille. The two seemed so close and in love that Michael found himself thinking about Gina. He and Gina could have something like that all the way. All he needed to do was get his act together.

In his bed that night, Michael promised himself that he'd have a serious talk with Karen and make sure she understood that they were through. As soon as they were back in New York, she would be out of his home and out of his life. For good.

The next morning, Michael strode into Karen's bedroom. Rough and not caring, he jerked her awake from her sound sleep. "Get dressed," he commanded. "You're going back to New York today. And I expect you packed and gone when I return." He'd had his secretary purchase Karen a ticket.

Karen wiped her eyes to clear them, and when she lifted the covers, he registered that she was naked. Probably hoped he would've joined her the night before. But Michael was past all that. She had played her last card. With a made-up mind, he folded his arms and turned around.

"Mikey."

He did not respond.

"Mikey," she called to him again.

He didn't turn around to look at her. He knew who he wanted, but he wasn't foolhardy to push fate.

Michael ignored her and walked toward the bathroom. He sensed when she walked behind him. He wasn't sure if she'd put clothes on, but he wasn't about to find out. A visual of her delectable physique flashed across his mind. He steeled himself. Clenching his fists, he told himself, *You're better than this.*

When she touched him, he flinched, but didn't turn around. "I meant what I said, Karen. I am not falling for the same old ploy again." She grabbed onto the back of his arms, but still he didn't comply.

Her hands felt wet. Tears? Sure enough, he heard the telltale sniffle. *Oh boy.* A woman's tears had always been his undoing. He felt himself caving. No, he told himself, do not give in.

Seconds passed. Sweat beaded his chin. Just as he reached his threshold, Karen removed her hands and left. Michael jumped at the sound of the door slamming. He took both his hands and clasped them like he was about to pray.

Then he looked upward and whispered a heartfelt, *"Thank you, Lord."* Just one second more and he would have folded. He and Karen would be tangling in the sheets this very instant. Michael gave Gina a call and squelched his disappointment when the call went to voice mail. "If there aren't any delays, I'll be back Monday night," he informed her. "I'm coming straight from the airport to your house. Baby, your face is the first I want to see."

Chapter Nine

Pick up the phone, please.

Colleen tapped the heel of her shoe on the tile floor while she listened to the phone ring. It would serve her right to get voice mail, but she was hoping she didn't.

"Well, it's about time," Gina said, without preamble. "I didn't think it would take you this long to call. When you ignored my texts, I decided to give you some space."

"I don't know why it took me this long," Colleen admitted.

"I know why. It's Terence," Gina complained through the line. "I feel like you're allowing him to come between us. I know you're married, and you're all into church now and all that, but I've been your friend forever, Collie. Forever."

A tense silence followed, and the sound of static filled the line. This was the first time in over a decade that the two friends had been at odds like this with each other. It was as if they were strangers.

Colleen couldn't abide it. "Gigi," she began, with the endearment, "Terence isn't . . ." She paused, because denial would be a blatant lie. "I mean, I'm just going through an adjustment and being newly married is major work, but there's no crack in the bond of our friendship—it's too strong to break. I'm sorry for my behavior, Gina. It was cruel and mean and . . ." Colleen stopped and began to cry.

"I didn't intend for you to cry, Colleen. Listen, friend. It would take more than a thoughtless statement or a few weeks to destroy what we have. We're sisters."

Colleen breathed a huge sigh of relief, glad that her friend was so forgiving and had let her off the hook. "I love you, girl, you know that," she said with emotion.

"I love you, too," Gina replied. "I'm glad you called, and truthfully, I was going to call you, if you didn't call me by this weekend. And if you hadn't answered, I would've been at your door. But that's a moot point now, I guess."

"Let's get together tomorrow. Ring the weekend together, like old times," Colleen offered.

"Oh, I can't. It's the Homecoming Dance this Friday night, remember? I have a hair and nail appointment after work tomorrow."

"Oh yeah." Disappointment filled her. She asked, "What about Saturday, after I get out of church? Or, better yet, why don't you finally take me up on my offer to come to church instead?"

"That sounds good."

Colleen wasn't sure which one Gina was committing to, but she didn't push. She'd just ended one fight and wasn't about to start another. "Well, listen, I am on my way to Wednesday night prayer service," Colleen said. "We'll catch up."

"Sure thing. Love you."

Colleen hung up the phone, feeling glad that she had made a move at restoration. A huge load had been taken off her chest, and she could breathe freely. She really hated what she'd said to her friend, and the friction in their friendship had bothered her tremendously.

Thankfully, Gina didn't know the meaning of holding a grudge. It was her willingness to forgive that made their friendship invaluable. Colleen looked at her watch. Yikes. She had to get moving before Terence came looking for her. They should've left ten minutes ago and Terence was scheduled to preach.

In stocking-clad feet, Colleen rushed to her vanity to find a natural shade of lipstick to wear. She picked up a pink gloss and glided it over her lips. Then she dabbed perfume on her legs and behind her ears. Satisfied, Colleen stepped back to observe herself. Her eyes widened—amazed at her transformation. Was Gina right? *Who is this person staring back at me?*

She wore a mustard skirt that was a respectable knee-length. Her beige blouse was a little larger than what she was used to wearing, and it was tucked neatly into her skirt. A nice set of pearls and matching studs in her ears completed her look. The only thing left to put on were her expensive—and ugly—black pumps. They'd been a gift from Francine and Colleen hated them. Francine's own shoes rivaled runway models, so Colleen knew she'd bought these out of sheer spite.

She turned her head to make sure her long mane pinned in a neat bun at the base of her neck still held.

With a loud sigh, Colleen looked down at her nails designed in a French manicure. She moaned. She resembled nothing like the woman that she was a few months ago. Gone were her brash and bold colors. Now, she looked like a schoolmarm from the frontier days. Teachers did not dress like this today. At least not any her age. She was one so she should know.

Colleen stepped away from the mirror just as Terence entered the room. He strolled over to her. She stood motionless as he gave her a quick kiss, and then appraised her. Colleen was happy to see the pleased glint in his eyes. He quickly headed into the shower to get dressed.

I guess I passed inspection, she thought. Although she didn't like the idea of fighting with him, she also didn't like making all the concessions either. Terence had bought these clothes for her. She would be ungrateful not to wear them. She touched her neck . . . And these were his mother's pearls.

"Babe, will you sing for us, tonight?" Terence called from the shower.

Colleen's mind screamed. *No!* "Yes, hon, if that's what you want," Colleen answered, but on the inside, she burned with resentment. He knew she hated singing in front of people. She'd told him countless times. She stuffed her feet into her shoes and grabbed her coat. Why'd he even bother asking? It's not like she really had a choice. He'd only make her feel guilty if she didn't.

Later that night, as they stood by the door and greeted the parishioners leaving the church, Colleen welcomed the fact that she and Terence made a striking couple. Everyone praised her on her solo and Terence on his inspiring message. Colleen plastered a grin on her face, shook hands, and greeted people—most of whose names she had not yet memorized. Faces blurred before her, but she put up a good front, trying to project the image of a good pastor's wife.

An older woman came up to Terence to speak to him in private. From the corner of her eye, Colleen saw Terence step over to the side to listen to her. Not knowing what else to do, Colleen just stood there, waiting, with a stupid smile planted firmly on her lips. She felt a pang of loneliness hit her at the sight of a group of women, about her age, talking and laughing. She hoped to make friends but didn't join them. She wished Gina were here. Gina never had a problem making friends.

"Hello, again," a deep voice resonated right in front of her.

Colleen jerked in surprise. She had been so caught up in her reverie that she had not realized that someone had approached. "Oh my goodness!" She clutched her throat and heat seared her cheeks. Colleen sought to retrieve his name. She'd met him before. She knew it. God rescued her. *Aha!* "I didn't see you standing there, Brother *Felix.* I'm sorry."

"That's all right," Brother Felix replied with a laugh. "I enjoyed your song earlier."

"Why, thank you," Colleen said, basking in his praise. He was a handsome man, and it felt good to be on the receiving end of his compliment.

"Hello, *Brother* Felix," Terence addressed the man, though he was a little distance away. Colleen heard his stilted voice as he asked, "Haven't seen you in a while. How are you?"

"Fine, fine, and yeah, I do need to come more often," Brother Felix answered, but his eyes were still on Colleen.

Colleen didn't know what to do, so she looked away to focus on her hands. Terence walked over and took her hands and gripped them hard. *Ow!* Colleen naturally bit her lip to keep from uttering a sharp cry. She glanced at Terence, trying to figure out what was going on. Terence had a stoic look on his face and did not glance her way.

Does he realize that he's hurting me? Colleen twisted her fingers in his to give him a subtle hint to loosen his hold. But Terence squeezed even harder than before. Pain shot through her crunched fingers. Colleen looked at Felix and saw his eyes pinned on her. His concerned frown and burrowed brows made her act fast. Colleen forced a smile onto her face until Felix's facial expression relaxed.

"See you around," he said and quickly departed.

As soon as they got home that night, Colleen challenged Terence. "Why were you squeezing my hand so hard?" she yelled.

"Because." That was Terence's quiet reply.

"Because? You *hurt* me!" Colleen accused angrily.

"Well, I was trying to squash your flirtation with Felix James," Terence stated, matter-of-factly. His eerily calm tone gave Colleen chills up her spine. But she was dealing with an alpha male and wouldn't back down. "Flirting?"

Colleen huffed. "Are you serious right now? I wasn't flirting! He just said hello to me, Terence. That's all." Colleen grabbed his hand to get his attention, but he shrugged her off. To her chagrin, he was still frighteningly unruffled and leisurely undressed as if he had done nothing wrong. His unconcerned attitude irked her to no end. At that very moment, Colleen felt like splitting his head wide-open. "I want an apology," she demanded.

Terence ignored her and went to relieve himself. Vexed, Colleen didn't bother undressing; instead, she grabbed her pillow and blanket, then trounced to the living room. "I'll sleep on the couch," she said. Colleen fluffed the pillows and shifted her body, but she just couldn't settle. Tears pricked her eyes. Suddenly, she felt scared and alone.

Terence was not who she thought he was. *He is wicked and heartless*. What had she gotten herself into?

She heard Terence flick on the television from inside the bedroom and opened her mouth in amazement. He seriously intended to leave things like that between them and had no intention to apologize. What about not going to bed angry and all that other stuff he yammered on about in church? Her temper kicked in. That's it! She wasn't going to stay here a minute longer. In one fluid motion, fueled by rage, Colleen sprang off the couch, kicked the blanket, and tossed the pillow on the floor. "Take that, Mr. Fastidious!" She quickly grabbed her keys and left.

Terence heard the front door slam. He went out to investigate and saw the headlights of Colleen's Lexus tearing out of the driveway. He wasn't worried. An hour passed . . . Then two. Then it was the next morning, and she still hadn't returned.

Terence rested his hand on his chin in thought. He hadn't done anything wrong, but evidently, he must have done something for Colleen to leave in such an uproar. She'd been distressed at the way he held onto her hand outside the church, but that was nothing. It wasn't enough for her to just up and leave.

Well, she'd had her time-out. It was time for her to come home now. He needed to settle matters between them and fast. The head pastor, Bishop Greenfield, was scheduled to pay a home visitation soon under the guise of dinner and conversation. However, Terence knew the deal. He needed his wife front and center, willing and co-operative. Terence knew that Bishop Greenfield wouldn't ordain him as an associate minister if it appeared that his home was in chaos. After all, if he couldn't control his own home, then how could he effectively run a church?

Terence thought about Colleen. He knew she had to be happy because he'd given her free rein to shop and do as she pleased. She didn't have to work, because he made more than enough to support her. A lot of women would kill to be in her position. And what did he ask of her in return? Nothing much in comparison, Terence reasoned. He only admonished her to do what he thought was apt as a pastor's wife. Nothing more.

He reached on his nightstand where he'd left his cell charging. He'd call Gina. He bet that's where Colleen had spent the night.

"Hey, Gina, I needed to speak to Colleen. Is she there, by chance?"

"No—no. I haven't seen her. Is everything all right?"

They spoke for several seconds before he ended the call. Terence pressed the END button. He wasn't sure if Gina had been lying about not knowing his wife's whereabouts. Friends lied to cover for each other all the time. Yet, he couldn't come out and accuse Gina outright of dishonesty, but where else would Colleen be?

Terence expelled a huge breath. His heart pounded . . . Unless, she'd found out about . . . No, she couldn't have. Could she? Scenarios raced through his mind.

Terence tasted palpable fear. He was too close to where he wanted to be and couldn't lose everything because of one heedless act. Panicked, he got on his knees and fervently prayed. "Lord, please, I've asked for your forgiveness in that matter. It was just a moment of weakness. Don't punish me this way, please, Lord. I sincerely love Colleen, and, Lord, if you send her home, I will be different. I promise."

Terence got off his knees, feeling a lot better. While praying, God had given him a divine inspiration. Without a moment's hesitation, he picked up the phone to make some calls. He knew what he had to do.

Chapter Ten

"She's not your problem or your concern. Whatever you do, don't call her," Keith lectured himself. He paced the kitchen, waiting for his coffee to brew, while engaged in this mental tug-of-war. He hankered to call Gina—just to hear her voice—but he needed to be honorable. Keith attributed that his strong desire to call stemmed from the fact that Michael had dogged her out, then assuaged his guilt by hightailing it to a whole other state. But, he still would not betray his brother in any shape or form. He couldn't cross that line. However, he was sorely tempted to try to warn Gina to back off.

She needed to run far . . . far away from Michael.

And into my arms?

No. Keith protested. He just didn't want to see Gina hurt. That was all. Keith closed his eyes and willed her face into his mind. He remembered watching her eat and felt his insides begin to respond. There was just something about her that made him feel alive. Gina had brought a little savor to his mundane existence. Somehow, she had managed to cut through the red tape he called life, and had gotten through to him. It was as if their minds had been engaged in their own conversation, with everyone revolving around them none the wiser. She stimulated him mentally.

This is crazy!

Keith was very surprised at his behavior. He could not believe that he was standing here fantasizing over his

brother's woman, especially since he had a baby on the
way. That was not only immoral, but it was also downright sordid! Keith berated himself repeatedly for this
futile attraction. He counted on one hand the number
of times he'd seen Gina. Yet, here he was, behaving like
some infantile . . .

Keith stopped suddenly and dragged his hands across
his face and over his head. He absolutely refused to give
Gina another thought.

Eve . . . Eve . . . Eve . . . Keith said her name over and
over, like it was a mantra, to shift his mind away from
Gina. He mentally conjured a visual image of Eve in his
mind. He saw her smiling at him as she protectively held
on to her growing stomach. *Yes, that's it.*

The telephone ringing so early jarred his concentration.

"Keith, I need a favor . . . Take Gina to the Homecoming Dance for me. It's tomorrow night."

Michael statement was not a request. He rushed on
without waiting for a reply. "Thanks, Bro," and disconnected the call before Keith could utter a single word.

He looked at the cordless, and then put it back on
its cradle. From his brother's quick, rushed tones, he
wondered if Karen was in listening distance. Or, Michael
could've been on his way to a meeting, Keith supposed.

Well, whatever the reason, Michael had some nerve.
Because of his own stupid and irresponsible actions,
Keith now had to help him clean up his mess. His brother
had not changed with time. From the time that they were
young, Michael had always expected Keith to bail him
out.

Asking me to take out his woman. Keith reached into
his pocket for his cell phone. *How preposterous . . . How
presumptuous . . . How promising . . .*

The following night, Keith dressed in a dark-gray suit,
with a black shirt and gray tie, and made sure his shoes

were parade shine. He was just about to leave when Eve popped in. Keith quickly brought her up to speed. He made sure to sound unaffected to give her the feeling that he was just doing a favor—blah-blah-blah—no big deal.

Eve wasn't buying it. "I don't like it. I don't care if you're doing Michael a favor. In my book, two people going out somewhere, all dressed up, constitutes a date."

"Well, it's not," Keith refuted. "And, I'm already committed to go, so . . ."

Eve dug inside her purse to search for a stick of gum. She popped it into her mouth, chewed, and scrutinized him under hooded eyes. "Michael is obviously an imbecile to send Gina out with you."

Keith took umbrage. "What's that supposed to mean?" It was pure reverse psychology, of course, because he knew Eve was no fool.

She sucked her teeth and mimicked his words, "What's that supposed to mean?"

Keith looked heavenward. "Don't start."

Eve's head swung back and forth like a bobble head. "Michael must be clueless when it comes to women, Keith. You know that. He's a genius at work, but when it comes to women and his love life, he's a complete idiot. Even a blind man could see the tension emanating between the two of you. I think you like her."

He wasn't taking that bait. Keith plucked at the lint on his pants and prepared to leave. Eve's gum chewing escalated. She sounded like a cow chewing its cud, but now wasn't the time to point that out. Besides, she wasn't done.

"You jumped at the chance to take her out. Admit it," Eve accused. "Gina's no supermodel, but she's refreshing, and that can be real enticing . . ."

Keith shrugged, but didn't argue. He wasn't about to add any fuel to the fire. Let Eve think whatever she wanted to think. He knew the truth.

That she was right.

"She's one of those women who would be appealing, even if she wore a potato sack," Eve continued, gauging his reaction.

Outwardly, he remained aloof. But on the inside, he fervently agreed. He searched for his keys.

Eve wouldn't let it go. "Keith, I'm worried. I mean, things are finally good again between us, and you seemed like you've come around with the baby . . ."

Keith noted the worry etched on Eve's beautiful face, and he empathized. He could have given her the reassurance that she desperately sought, but he wasn't about to say something he didn't mean. He awkwardly reached out to pat her on the stomach, but that was all he could do.

"How stupid could Michael be?" Eve whispered. She had probably meant that for her ears only, but Keith had heard her.

He dwelled on that sentiment as he drove to Gina's house. Why was Michael so trusting?

At exactly five o'clock, Keith rang Gina's doorbell, wondering for the hundredth time why he had let Michael manipulate him into coming.

Please. Nobody can twist your arm, and you know it.

"Okay," Keith muttered under his breath, "so, maybe I wanted to come."

Gina opened the door, and Keith raised his eyebrows as he saw her. "You look gorgeous," he declared. Scanning her, Keith tried to figure out what was different. He kept looking until he figured it out. She was wearing makeup, and it transformed her into a hot, luscious diva. Her lipstick made her full lips look even more kissable and inviting.

"Come in. I'm almost ready," Gina invited. "So, is Eve all right with you being my date?" She held both hands up to form quotation marks as she said the word.

No. "She understood." What an understatement, he mused, thinking about their run-in. Keith focused his attention on what she was wearing. Gina was dressed in a black cocktail dress, appropriate for chaperoning a school event, but it sported a split in the front that he could truly appreciate.

"Ah, can you help me with my zipper? For the past five minutes, I've been trying to get the zipper and hook done before you arrived, but to no avail. I feel like I have two left hands when it comes to performing any fine-motor task. I'm such a klutz. Did you know it took me a good ten minutes to get my earrings, necklace, and bracelet on?"

She was rambling, a true indication of nervousness, so Keith just nodded. He didn't mention the interesting view he had been given.

"Okay, turn around." Keith motioned with his fingers, and Gina complied. It took effort for Keith to concentrate, but being the gentleman that he was, he performed the small, but necessary task. His hand brushed against her skin, and he stifled a gasp. Her skin felt baby soft. If it were anyone else, he would think this request on Gina's part was a subtle invitation.

She has beautiful, soft skin.

Gina took a deep breath—a sign she'd not been un-moved. He noted her jitters and whispered, "You look stunning."

"Thank you. You don't look too bad yourself. Thanks for coming with me to the dance in Michael's place. You didn't have to."

His heart jumped at her bright smile. "Nonsense, it's my pleasure, believe me."

They looked at each other and smiled. Their smiles said even more than they did. They said how much they were going to enjoy the night without feeling guilty. They said how glad they were to be given this night alone, with just the two of them to see if the attraction was real.

Gina's cell phone rang, ending the intimate moment.

Her eyebrows creased in concern, and his heart constricted. He hoped everything was all right.

"No . . . No, I still haven't seen her or heard from her. Is she okay? . . . Okay, bye."

Gina clicked the END button, and stared at her phone.

"Is everything all right?" Keith asked.

"I hope so. That was Colleen's husband, Terence. He was calling to see if I had seen or heard from her." Gina fidgeted with her necklace and bit her lip. "Something's up because he called me yesterday morning as well."

"Well, I'm sure she'll call when she's ready." Keith comforted her with a light squeeze. "They probably had a spat, and she went somewhere to cool off."

"Yeah, but . . ." But she sounded skeptical.

"You look worried," Keith stated. "Do you want to skip the Homecoming Dance?"

"No, I can't. A few of the teachers bowed out because there's this stomach bug going around. So, my principal would have convulsions if I didn't show up. Plus, I was actually looking forward to going. Let me call her." She pressed the speed-dial button, but the call went directly to voice mail. Frowning, she tried again. Voice mail. Gina left a terse message urging Colleen to call. Then she sent a text.

She rocked her heels back and forth as she vacillated over what to do.

There she goes, biting that delicious bottom lip of hers. Keith cleared his throat. "Tell you what, let's go, and if, when we return, you still have not heard from her, I promise to help you find her."

"All right," Gina agreed, and she took out a fall coat from the hallway closet. Before going through the door, she said, "I still feel uneasy about Colleen not calling me or anything. That is so unlike her. Whenever either one of us has a problem, we always call each other. But, then again, if she and Terence did have an argument, chances are that she wouldn't want to tell me about it."

"Why is that?" Keith queried.

"Well, she knows I have misgivings about Terence. I've been very vocal about that," Gina said. "So, in this case, I may be the last person she calls."

Keith wanted to ask more about it, but he didn't want to dampen the mood. It was selfish, considering Gina was worried about her friend, but he'd been looking forward to the dance. They entered the gymnasium, and Keith felt as if he'd been thrown back in time to high school.

He looked over at Gina. At that moment, this night was no longer about her duty as a chaperone. It was about them. Keith led her to the dance floor. After a feeble protest, Gina started dancing. He saw her look around at the other kids that were dancing. "Forget them. Let's have some fun." That was all the encouragement she needed, and she moved closer to him. As they danced, Keith repeated in his head, *She's Michael's woman . . . She's Michael's woman*. It wasn't working.

Gina would've kept up with the teenagers, but Keith pleaded for a break. When he came back with some punch, he saw Gina on the phone.

"I just checked my voice mail. Colleen left me a message that she's okay. She promised to call me. She canceled our plans for tomorrow night. So, I guess I'll just have to wait for her call. I feel better hearing from her, though."

Keith was all smiles hearing that. Gina was now at ease. Once the dance ended, at ten p.m., they drove around, chatted, stopped to eat, and took the time to enjoy each other.

Keith's digital clock said 1:00 a.m. when he pulled into Gina's driveway and parked, with swift ease, behind her VW. He turned the ignition off, and they both sat there, in limbo. "I'm not ready to leave you, yet," Keith admitted.

"Me, too." Gina turned to him. "Thank you so much, Keith, for a wonderful evening and a wonderful night."

Keith smiled into her beautiful face. All he could think about was how much he wanted to kiss her. Gina read his thoughts and moved the door handle to open the door.

Keith followed suit and walked Gina to her front door. Gina dropped her house keys. He bent over to pick them up. "Allow me?" he lifted an eyebrow. She bobbed her head. He unlocked her door and stood aside for her to enter ahead of him.

Gina faced him and said, "Well, I had a great time . . ."

"Me, too," Keith heard his wistful tone—not at all manly. What was this woman doing to him?

"It was fun . . ."

"Yeah, it was . . ." Keith agreed, but words were not his preferred mode of communication at the moment.

"Yeah," Gina twisted her fingers, before she looked up at him with those dark eyes of hers.

He ached to discover what shimmered behind their depths. Gina tilted her face upward. Keith interpreted her thoughts. He knew what she wanted. He wanted the same. With a groan, he bent and rested his head against her forehead. "You know why we can't, don't you?"

"Yeah," Gina nodded. She reached up and touched his face.

Keith stilled. He was determined not to react. Then she hugged his arms. He wasn't that strong. Keith enfolded her and inhaled her scent. He could get used to this, he thought. He tightened his embrace, relishing how she felt.

Oh, this was not smart—and he knew it.

Gina exhaled against his ear, and he shivered.

Whoa.

"*Gina.*" Keith emphasized her name to signal his genuine agony.

"Keith," Gina whispered back. "Do you want to . . . ?" She trailed off, not completing the question.

He released her and stepped back. Her question hung between them. Keith wrestled with himself. Gina was ready. He saw it. He reached his hand up and moved his head lower. *I just want to feel what her lips feel like pressed against mine . . . That's all. Then I'll go,* Keith thought.

At the precise moment that their lips were about to make contact, Keith's cell rang. They both jumped apart, feeling like two schoolchildren caught in the act.

Gina shook her head to clear it, and she regained control of her faculties. Keith saw the rejection before she voiced it aloud. "Keith, I can't do this to Michael. He's good to me, and he deserves better."

Keith's phone rang again, and he let it ring. "I'd better go . . ." He said, albeit reluctantly.

"Yeah," Gina agreed. "It's for the best." Her tone belied her words.

Chapter Eleven

Saturday evening, Colleen opened the door to her home with as much dread as an inmate returning to her cell, which was exactly how she felt. She had seen Terence's car in the driveway. She thought he'd still be in church. But he was probably waiting for her. He couldn't very well show up to church without his lap dog on his arm, could he?

"Welcome home, Colleen. I've missed you," Terence said, as she stepped through the door.

Colleen hung her head, not saying a word, but she hated him.

"I knew you would come back," he said amicably. "The Lord showed me that you would come to your senses, and when better than today? His day."

Colleen merely bit back a retort. She was not going to say anything to him at all. She felt Terence's arms encircle her waist and literally bit her lips to keep from telling him not to touch her. She felt his lips on the back of her neck, and soon, he started nibbling all over. Colleen stood still and let him.

She could hear his breathing escalate as his desire grew. He quickly undressed her and turned her around to face him. Colleen almost said something when she saw the look of satisfaction on his face. She desperately wanted to wipe that look off his face.

"You're mine," Terence told her. "I'm glad you're home." Then he crushed her to him and started to kiss her. When she remained unresponsive a minute later, Terence stopped and looked at her.

"Why aren't you responding?" he asked, but to Colleen, it was a subtle command.

She looked at her husband. *You know why!* She wanted to scream those words at him. But she didn't. Instead, she lifted her arms and brought them around his neck. Then she moved her hips against his before reaching up to kiss him. She felt Terence relax and allow her to do her thing. Colleen kissed him until she heard Terence groan. She took the rest of her clothes off and then said, "Take it; it's yours."

Colleen's statement made him feel strong and invincible, but she was appalled that he became turned on at her declaration. He gripped her arms, and his breathing labored as his passion rose. With another guttural groan, he deepened the kiss and his hands roamed her body. Colleen responded, but she didn't return the sentiment. Not after what he'd just put her through.

As he kissed her, he whispered, "As much as I hate to admit this, I think your time away has definitely been good for you. I like this woman before me. You're willing and compliant, and everything I could ever want." He looked up at the ceiling with appreciation. "Thank you, Lord." Terence bent his head to kiss her again. Feeling his sweat on her forehead, it was all Colleen could do to keep from screaming.

She rolled her eyes and stifled a sound of utter disgust. *Was he seriously thanking God, right now?* She squeezed her eyes tight to keep from crying. Then she felt Terence pull away to look at her. Colleen quickly transformed her face to look like sheer bliss. He must have bought it too, for Terence continued his ministrations. Colleen felt used, but she did not stop him. She purposely let out a moan, and another for good measure. Terence had no clue that she was faking it, and she would, until she figured out what to do.

Lord, if you're listening, help me through this. Please, help me, Colleen prayed. Immediately, she felt doubt attack her. Was God hearing her? Would He answer her prayer?

Colleen.

That was Gina's first thought when she woke up that Sunday morning. Colleen was at the forefront of her mind. She called her without delay. Terence answered the telephone. He was as sweet as sugar before handing the phone over to his wife.

Gina rolled her eyes heavenward and pretended to gag on the phone. She knew her gestures were childish and that they were futile, since Terence could not actually see what she was doing. But Gina felt better just doing it. The man just made her grit her teeth.

Colleen got on the phone. The two women chitchatted for a minute before deciding to meet up later for lunch. Gina rang off without asking her friend the question plaguing her mind, which was, "What's going on, Colleen?"

Michael called her five minutes after her conversation with Colleen. Gina felt a little remorseful. She hadn't thought about him even once since she'd last spoken to him. Her head had been filled with Keith. She'd gone to sleep with Keith on her mind, thinking about what almost happened, what would have happened if his cell phone hadn't rung. Gina knew, without a doubt, that she would have slept with him. Her body felt alive and sizzled around him.

Gina knew from Michael's message what he wanted. The problem was that she did not know if she could give it to him.

At about 8:30 that night, Michael swerved into her driveway. She opened the door to let him in. He was out of the car and up the steps in a flash. She didn't get a hello in before he kissed her like there was no tomorrow for all the neighbors to see.

Gina couldn't help her reaction to Michael's passionate embrace. She groaned. His body weight involuntarily forced her to take a step back. That was all the invitation he needed. Michael entered her home and without breaking the kiss, shut the front door behind him.

Gina did nothing to stop him either. She doubted she could have anyway. He was a man on a mission. She pushed at his shoulders to come up for air, but Michael wouldn't let her.

Before Gina was cognizant of his actions, all her clothes were at her feet. "Michael!" She pushed against his chest and stepped back. With a vigorous shake of her head, she sought to regain some semblance of control.

"Gina, you think way too much." Michael's sultry look ignited her insides. Her inner woman awakened, and her resolve vanished.

Why should she fight this? Besides, what reason could she give Michael, apart from the truth, for not sleeping with him? They'd been dating for almost three months. She couldn't hold out forever.

"You're right."

Taking that as capitulation, Michael enfolded her in his powerful arms. Gina liked this new bold, aggressive side. It was scintillating. Without breaking the kiss, Michael led her to the couch. He whispered, "I love you and it's time I showed you."

Her knees weakened, but she couldn't repeat the words. Michael was too caught up in the moment to care.

While she responded, she thought, *Are you using Michael to forget about Keith?*

Those words made Gina pause, but Michael was now sealing the deal, so to speak. He withdrew protection from his pocket and said, "Don't want any surprises for either of us."

Gina looked up at the ceiling and wondered why she was allowing this to happen when she was not ready. Not by a long shot.

Michael panted above her, and Gina squeezed her eyes shut. Concentrate. *Get into it!*

Before she knew it, he was done. Within minutes, he fell asleep.

Gina felt a tiny whimper of disappointment. She couldn't fault his skills, but . . . call her picky . . . this wasn't earth-shattering.

That sounded shallow. She yawned and felt sleep loom. She snuggled under his large body. Next time, Gina consoled herself, the earth would move.

Chapter Twelve

Colleen waited for Gina at their usual booth at the Applebee's in Five Towns, at around four thirty in the afternoon. Gina was coming straight after work. Punctual, her Volkswagen came into view. Colleen waved her long arms to get Gina's attention.

Gina spotted her and gave a light wave. Then she headed her way. Colleen knew that Gina was shocked that she was already there, considering her penchant for tardiness.

"Hey, I can't believe you beat me here." Gina hugged her before sliding into the far corner of the booth.

"I knew you'd say that." Colleen chuckled and gave her a light kiss on the cheek.

The women ordered deluxe burgers, well done, with fries. They both ordered a mudslide. Once the waiter walked out of earshot, Gina confronted her.

"So, what's going on with you and Terence? Trouble in paradise with Shifty Eyes?" Before she could answer, Colleen saw Gina hold up her hand. "Sorry about that, I promised myself—no barbs—no shots below the belt. Colleen, I'm sorry. Please tell me, what happened?"

Colleen looked at Gina, who was being a good friend at the moment. "No need to apologize. It's okay. I need to talk to you." She saw Gina sit up straighter, but still Colleen hesitated. She honestly didn't even know how to put into words the way she felt. Colleen did not know exactly how to voice her fears aloud. "Things between me and Terence are not going the way that I'd like," she stated, simply.

"What do you mean?"

Colleen sensed that Gina was determined to keep her tone neutral and friendly. She battled with what to say, but Colleen needed to talk to someone. "Well, it's like . . . It's as if he wants to take complete control over my life."

"What exactly do you mean?" Gina's tone became harsh, and Colleen read her body language. She knew where her friend's mind was going.

"Is he hitting you, Colleen?" Gina crooked her head, her anger displayed through her elevated voice and furrowed brows.

"No." Colleen waved off the thought. "It's not like that. It's more like he gives me these requests that are more like demands, you know . . ."

"And, what happens if you don't follow them?" Gina queried. Then, she switched gears. "Honestly, it bothers me hearing you talk like this. Colleen, this is so not like you that I don't even know what to think right now."

"I don't know . . ." Colleen bent her head as uncertainty gnawed at her insides. She bit her lips trying to pull out the magic words to dissipate Gina's anger and her fear.

"Well . . ." Gina summoned a patience she didn't possess, "can you tell me why he called my house looking for you twice? I called you so many times that I lost count, and I left several messages. I was really worried. And especially now since you're being vague."

"I left. I went to a hotel to cool off. I didn't feel like being around anyone, you know. I just wanted to think . . . But . . . Terence called and canceled all my credit cards." Tears filled her eyes. "I was so embarrassed when the concierge told me that my cards were all rejected. It was a good thing I still had my Visa bank card from my personal account. But for his spitefulness, I stayed away for three nights. I didn't go home till that Saturday evening—which is why I canceled our plans—but, of course, he was there."

"I hope you told him off." Gina's fury was transparent. Her teeth bared, and she growled. "What right does he have to do that to you? The man is unbelievable. I wish you'd come to my house."

Colleen beseeched her. "I know I could've come to you, but I just wanted time to talk to God."

Gina exhaled a huge sigh. "This is why you should have kept your job. I'm glad you took my advice and didn't close your credit union account. You need to leave that man right now and go back to work," Gina demanded. "I wish he were here now, because I would certainly give him a piece of my mind. Imagine his gall to do something like that. He's a control freak, Colleen. This is a wake-up call, and you need to get out of there."

"No," Colleen said, "I'm not going to do that."

The waiter came over with their orders.

Gina tapped her feet, anxious for him to be on his way so they could finish their conversation. As soon as the waiter was out of earshot, Gina jumped back to their conversation. "Did you just say what I thought you said?" she fumed.

"Yes, I did. I've been thinking about it, and I've decided to keep trying." Colleen put her hands up to keep her friend from saying another word. "We've only been married for three months. I need to give it more time. I'm not trying to have a celebrity marriage. This is real life and marriage is work. I have to try."

"What about him?" Gina pressed. "What's he doing to try? It seems to me that the only person who's trying is you. How come you're the only one changing? I mean, look at you, Colleen. You're different. Your hair . . . your clothes . . . *everything* is different."

Colleen's spine stiffened. She resented her friend for pointing that out, even if those very concerns plagued her mind. Who did Gina think she was—her mother? And it was easy for Gina to talk that way, because she just had to breathe to get a man, while Colleen hovered in her shadow. Well, that was before Terence. Terence loved her, not Gina.

"I'm sorry that I'm not like you, Gina. I don't have men at my beck and call. But Terence loves me. *Me,* Gina. He wanted me, not you."

Gina's eyes widened, and her jaw slackened. "What're you talking about?"

"You know. It's hard for me to find a man. Nobody ever liked me." Colleen took a deep breath and sighed.

Gina swished her head from side to side. "Come on, Colleen. Quit the nonsense. You know that's just not true."

"Don't shake your head at me. I know what I'm saying. And, yes, it is true. It was that way all through high school. You had all these boys going crazy over you. You always have. Who do I have now? Terence. That's who. So, excuse me if I want to keep him."

"Colleen, you should not be desperate, trust me." Gina moved closer to emphasis her point. "You don't have to settle for just anybody who's going to change you and make you into something that you're not."

When she remained silent, Gina continued, "Colleen, you're an incredibly attractive woman. Everybody sees that but you. The only reason why you, quote, unquote, *couldn't get a man,* was because of your own low self-esteem."

Gina's revelation floored Colleen. "Me? Low self-esteem?"

"Yes—you." Her neck swung back and forth like a pendulum as she sought to get her point across. "You lack self-confidence, Colleen. All these boys in high school would ask me about you, but you were too busy feeling sorry for yourself to do anything about it."

Colleen sucked her teeth and rolled her eyes. "You can say whatever you want to say, Gina Price. But I know better."

"You know what, Colleen? I realize that nothing I say will sway you. You're going to think whatever you want to think—you're just plain stubborn. You're amazing, and I don't know what else to say or do to get you to see that. I guess you have to come to that realization on your own. I give up." Gina's hands flailed in the air.

However, Colleen remained adamant. She refused to listen to anything Gina had to say. "You're only saying those things to make me feel better."

Gina scooted her chair closer and touched her on the cheek. With tear-streaked lashes, she said, "I'm saying them because they are true, Colleen."

Colleen shook her head. She just didn't see what Gina claimed she saw. She didn't note how her thick eyelashes and high cheekbones attracted a second glance from many men. She wasn't aware of how those same men had been entranced by her legs when she wore her high heels. Colleen didn't know how many men ached to touch her radiant hair and run it through their fingers.

No, Colleen saw a woman who was destined to become a lonely, miserable, dried-up spinster, just like her mother if she didn't make this relationship work.

Whenever she thought about her mother, Colleen became even more determined to make her marriage work. She was going to try harder to make Terence happy and to keep him. Nothing Gina could say would make her change her mind.

Determinedly, Colleen changed the topic of conversation. "So, enough about me. What's going on with you and Michael?"

"You mean Michael *and* Keith."

Michael stopped. Someone was in his place. His eyes adjusted to the dark as he beheld the intruder.

Karen was asleep on his couch. He strode over, shook her awake, and demanded, "Karen, what are you still doing here? I thought I told you I wanted you gone."

Karen sat up, wiped her eyes, and burst into tears. "Please, Michael . . . I have nowhere to go. Please . . . I'll do anything." In desperation, she got on her knees and begged.

With quick reflexes, Michael pulled her to her feet. "Karen! Don't belittle yourself like this. Just leave with some dignity, please."

Karen cried so hard that her shoulders shook. "I just don't want you to kick me out, Mikey . . . Please."

Torn, Michael twiddled his thumbs as he contemplated. He took at her tear-stained cheeks and read the humiliation written on her face. He hated to see her cry and felt heartless. Unwillingly, her tears brought to mind a previous time when Karen had cried like this. It had been when he'd hurt her. Right before she tried to commit suicide.

Michael's heart leapt with fear. Karen had scared him senseless with what she'd done before. He wouldn't be able to live with himself if something happened to her. He couldn't take the chance for *that* to happen again. Michael reached over to Karen and comforted her. "Okay, Okay. Listen, I am going to help you. You can stay here for a little while longer. I'll help you find a job and get you on your feet. But then you have to leave, okay?"

Karen nodded and hugged him in a tight embrace. "I'm so glad you're going to let me stay, Mikey. Honestly, I have nowhere to go. I was desperate enough to . . ." She bent her head as shame engulfed her. Her cheeks were a bright red.

"Don't worry about it," Michael urged gently. "Consider it forgotten." He prayed that he had made the right decision. Gina could never find out.

How was he going to keep her away from his apartment until Karen was gone? That was going to be tricky. Gina had hinted about wanting to spend a night of luxury at his place, and he was anxious to accommodate her. He'd have to stall Gina for a little longer until he could get Karen out of his hair.

Michael thought. He could just put Karen up in a hotel or get her her own apartment. But, then he'd never get rid of her and he'd be stuck paying her way for life. What a nightmarish thought! He touched his chin as he debated. It's best if he kept Karen here in case she had some manic episode and decided to trash the place. Better his place than a hotel. He'd just let her stay here for now.

Maybe Keith would help him. He made a mental note to give his brother a call. He needed to get some help. Like yesterday.

Chapter Thirteen

Deep in thought, Keith entered his home and headed straight to his study. Today had been a tough day. He'd brought the paperwork home on the Marshall case to finish working on his closing arguments, which would take him all night. He sighed. The evidence was stacked against Payton Marshall, but Keith knew she was innocent. She had been a battered wife, but there was no way that she had murdered her husband. He just had to help her prove it. This was the part of the job that he found stressful, defending a client that everybody, including the judge, believes is guilty. Keith was doing the best he could. Losing was not an option to him.

Eve opened the door to the study and entered. Keith barely acknowledged her.

"I guess that snort is your way of saying hello?"

Keith busied himself with his papers, hoping she'd get the hint and leave.

"Busy, huh? But I bet if *Gina* were to call, you would suddenly have something to say."

He blinked his eyes and gave her a disapproving stare. Don't even dignify that with a rebuttal, he told himself. "Eve, I don't have the time to deal with your theatrics tonight," he told her firmly.

"Just admit it," Eve whined, coming into the office and plopping into one of his chairs. "I saw the way you were looking at her when she was here for dinner."

Keith put his papers down, extremely annoyed with her for breaking his concentration. He was in no mood to deal with her. Eve required a special patience that he didn't always possess. But Keith knew from experience that she would go on and on until she solicited a response from him. He did not know why Eve persisted, especially when he refused to let her get to him.

"You were looking at her like a dog in heat," Eve continued, still goading Keith into giving her some form of a reply.

He couldn't let that go. "Okay," Keith said switching gears and looked directly at Eve. "I take it this means that you want some attention. Did you sell any houses today?"

He saw Eve perk up, and she wisely dropped her other argument. "Yes! The Elliots finally found something! My bonus is going to be a big one!"

Keith smiled at her. With her wide smile and bright eyes, Eve was as happy as a child who had been given a piece of candy. He supposed that he could try to make more effort to actually talk to her, since she was having a baby. Keith knew that he should be more sensitive toward her. It was just that she didn't make him sizzle the way . . . *Don't go there.*

Truthfully, if it weren't for Eve's delicate condition, he doubted that they would've been together this long. She did have the brains and the beauty. Her perceptiveness was also right on cue. But Eve was shallow. She had to be the center of his world all the time. Keith found it very irritating. But, he supposed, he could still exercise some patience with her. He looked at her and smiled at her. She smiled back.

Keith went over to her and placed a kiss on her forehead. Then he hugged her, trying to be charming, and not the ogre he acted.

Eve warmed to his touch. "I love you," she closed her eyes and declared in an airy voice.

As soon as she uttered those words, Keith froze. He stepped away from her as if she had slapped him. Eve jumped to her feet with her chin lifted in defiance. He knew that his blatant rejection had hurt her.

"You can't change that, Keith. I'm entitled to love whomever I want. It's my prerogative. And, I do love you," she reiterated. "I refuse to feel guilty about my emotions, and you need to understand that."

No, I don't understand that. "Please, just leave," Keith said quietly. "We agreed never to talk about love, and I am going to hold you to it."

"But—" Eve began.

"No, Eve," Keith said, calmly cutting her off. "Love is not an option for us, and you know that. Do you need me to remind you why?" He hunched his body in a stance challenging her to go there. Because tonight, he was in the mood to go there and lay everything bare.

"No, Keith, I don't," Eve caved, tearfully. "You're right. I had just hoped that with time . . ." She trailed off.

Keith saw her shrug her shoulders in defeat and tears filled her eyes. She whispered, "I don't know why I even mentioned love to you. I know that's something you don't want to hear. I'm fooling myself for thinking you will change your mind."

Eve hiccupped through her tears, but Keith didn't respond. He couldn't lie to her. He couldn't just tell her what she wanted to hear, just for the sake of saying it.

"Sometimes I wonder if you have steel where your heart is supposed to be." He saw her hang her head; then she left the room without another word.

Keith waited until she was gone; then he put his head into his hands. He groaned aloud. *That didn't go well at all.* He berated himself over his lack of tact and for hurting Eve, but he knew that she didn't love him. She'd just managed to convince herself that she did. Keith refused to feed into that lie, especially about something as serious as love.

He'd only been in love once before, when he was in law school. Vanessa Arnold had been in medical school, and it had been love at first sight. In her arms, Keith's mind had been at peace and at rest. He'd slept like a baby. That was unusual for him, because his mind was constantly active.

But, sadly, months before their wedding, Keith had lost Vanessa as a result of a drunk driver—a low-life scumbag who'd fled the scene. Crushed, Keith pursued criminal law to help other helpless victims.

Keith remembered Vanessa's lifeless body and shuddered. Then, he mentally forced those evil thoughts away from his mind. Overcome, Keith reached into the box of tissues on his desk to wipe his eyes. That's how he knew he didn't love Eve. And Keith knew that she did not feel that way about him. Truth be known, the only woman who even came remotely close to stir him like that again was Gina. A woman he couldn't have. A woman who had everything he wanted.

Chapter Fourteen

Had he done this to her on purpose? The question had racked her mind for days. Colleen carefully removed her blouse and tried not to cringe. She slowly took her arms out of the sleeve and then, just as gingerly, removed her undershirt. Involuntarily, she stifled a cry as pain racked her body.

She got up off her bed and went to her vanity to take a look. Her back and shoulders were badly bruised. Colleen sighed. She didn't know how she'd managed to keep from wincing when Gina had hugged her in the restaurant the other day. Now, here it was, days later, and she was still in pain. But Colleen was too scared of the consequences she'd face at home if she had made her friend aware of what had happened to her.

Even though she had seen them before, Colleen could not restrain the gasp from escaping her mouth. The purple marks were painful to the touch. She wondered what Bishop Greenfield would say if he saw these. He was coming over to dinner that very night, presumably to give Terence the good news of the pastoral position. For a minute, Colleen thought about not making an appearance, or purposely waiting until the bishop had arrived to wear something that would reveal her bruises. But Colleen quickly pushed those thoughts of subterfuge aside. She was sure that Terence would find a way to make her pay for them.

Colleen recalled exactly what had happened when she returned home the night of her brief escape. She remembered Terence hugging her and how she had allowed him to make love to her.

But, somehow or other, in a moment of passion, Terence had knocked her over on her back, and Colleen ended up with bruises on her arms and back. She had cried out in pain when she hit the glass table. Colleen remembered looking at Terence in amazement as he had grabbed her to apologize. He kept telling her over and over that it was an accident.

Colleen wasn't sure if she believed him because Terence was not a clumsy person by nature. So, even though Colleen had accepted his apology, a part of her strongly suspected that her injuries were no accident. Terence was both cunning and deceiving. He had orchestrated the events so Colleen could not say for sure that he had purposely pushed her.

Colleen didn't know why she had not had the guts to tell Gina about her bruises. Normally, she wouldn't have hesitated. But Colleen realized that there was still that naïve little girl inside of her who just could not accept the fact that her husband was not only controlling, but also abusive. She could be wrong. Terence could be telling the truth, after all. What if it really was an accident? What if she wrongfully accused Terence of something heinous that he actually had not done?

What if you are just being obtuse about something that you know to be true in your guts?

Terence entered the room to see what was keeping her so long. He stopped short when he saw the purple bruises on her back. To Colleen, he appeared genuinely startled at the telltale marks on her body. She saw guilt reflected on his face before he backed out of the room in silence.

She pretended to be unaware of his presence, as he didn't think she'd seen him.

She played along, having become adept at pretending.

Terence entered the kitchen and went to talk to his mother about what he had just seen. Lady Francine Hayworth had offered to come over and cook a nice meal to honor the bishop's presence and her son's impending appointment for associate pastor.

"Mom," Terence tapped her on the shoulder. He shared, with a guilty whisper, "I think I hurt Colleen real bad the other day. I went upstairs and she still has bruises."

Francine merely dismissed his concerns with a wave of her hands. "Nonsense, boy, she had it coming. Listen to me; don't get all prissy on me now. Quit acting like a wimp. Didn't I teach you better than that? Have I ever steered you wrong? Who was the one who told you how to get Colleen to do your bidding? Hmmm? Me, that's who. And didn't it work?"

Terence nodded. Francine's sly remark about using his lovemaking as an artful means of manipulation worked like a charm. When he wanted Colleen to agree with his wishes, he kissed her senseless.

"And I bet you she's not complaining," Francine smirked. "I'm a woman. Trust me, I know what I'm saying. Now, listen to me. Did you make it look like an accident like I told you?"

"Yes, but . . ." Terence stopped unsure. His heart had constricted at the sight of the damage that he had "accidentally" inflicted upon his wife. "I'm not sure I should have done that. I think I took it too far."

Francine puckered her lips and rolled her eyes. "Terence, I thought I raised you better than that. Would I tell you to do something if I didn't know that it was the best thing to do? You called me for advice, remember? You asked me for guidance. Colleen has to learn real fast about being a preacher's wife. She needs a lot of training. Now, go prepare yourself. The bishop will be here soon."

Francine shooed away his concerns, and Terence walked off like an obedient child. He did not say anything more. A good son never argued with his mother. He'd learned that the hard way as a child.

But still, Terence felt disquieted. No matter what his mother said, he just didn't feel right about what he had done. He should never have called his mother to tell her about Colleen's disappearance. He probably shouldn't have invited her two cents into his intimate life either.

Even though his mother vehemently denied it, Terence suspected that she did not like Colleen at all. Come to think of it, she didn't like anybody he'd ever dated. Terence shrugged. He didn't know. He turned his right hand over to look at a faded scar on his arm. He trailed his fingers across it—remembering.

He bunched his fists as memories threatened to surface. His mother was always right. To defy her was to pay.

Francine watched her son leave and pursed her lips in disapproval. She took her aggression out on the pots by banging them hard. She hoped Terence had heard how much he had upset her. That woman upstairs was doing something to her son. Maybe she was putting some roots on him. She had to be, Francine was convinced. Terence had never second-guessed anything that she'd ever told him to do before, and Francine resented Colleen for it.

If Colleen, for one second, thinks that she can take my place, then she has another think coming!

That was why Francine made sure that she was here tonight. She was proud of her son's accomplishment, and she wanted to be sure that the bishop was well entertained and treated right. Francine wasn't too sure about Colleen's social or cooking skills, so she decided to handle the matters herself. She also did not want Colleen getting any praises on her son's behalf. Colleen had better be prepared to share the limelight. Francine intended to be right there to hear and to take credit for all the good things the bishop had to say about *her* son.

Francine only prayed that the girl did not disgrace herself by wearing something revealing or inappropriate. She was seriously glad Terence had taken her advice and had made Colleen change her look and her wardrobe. Honestly, she didn't know what Terence saw in Colleen. Francine wouldn't have chosen Colleen for her son. Colleen had been the only thing Terence ever stood up to her about.

He had refused to listen to his mother and had married that light-skinned, bony girl, against her wishes. And, come to think of it, why couldn't Terence have married someone a little darker? *Is he ashamed of my dark skin?* Francine cut the vegetables with a vengeance then. "She looks nothing like me, and she's an ostrich. I have to crane my neck to look at her." Never mind that Terence's father had been light-skinned, tall, and had wavy hair.

Maybe that's what bothers you.

Tsk . . . I don't care anything about that fool. Francine scraped the carrot so thin that she had to throw it out and start over.

Terence hadn't budged, not even when Francine threatened to not show up at his wedding. He had told her that he was going to marry Colleen whether she came or not. Francine nearly had a heart attack when he'd said that. So, of course, she'd attended the wedding, but she wasn't pleased about it one bit. Her only child had been prepared to take that momentous step without her presence, and to Francine, that was almost unforgivable.

But, like a good Christian mother, she had forgiven him. How could she not, when her son could do no wrong? *Colleen definitely has roots on him, though. Nothing anybody says can convince me otherwise.*

Colleen entered her bedroom on the verge of tears. *That woman is going to make me hurt her!* Every chance that Francine got during dinner, she used it to put Colleen down. Oh, she'd been polite about it, but Colleen was not fooled for an instant. The woman was plain batty! She seemed to thrive on making Colleen feel uncomfortable. No matter what Terence said, Colleen knew better. Francine had it in for her.

All I've ever tried to do is to be nice to her, but I don't think she even knows the meaning of the word!

Colleen dabbed her eyes with some baby oil to remove the makeup. The woman had nitpicked at every single thing Colleen did or said that evening. She'd made cutting remarks about her skin, her hair, and her height. Her sly comments about the way that Colleen dressed and did her hair had made her feel as if she were a common tramp. Anything that Colleen said, Francine found something to say to negate it.

But worst of all, Terence had seemed ignorant about what his mother was doing. He never once defended her, and that infuriated Colleen more than anything else. In fact, Terence seemed to transform into a ten-year-old boy whenever his mother was present. He referred all his conversations back to his mother, as if he were begging for her approval.

Colleen wondered why she was even needed when his mother went out of her way to assume all the responsibility of being the woman of the house. Francine made sure that Colleen was left out of the conversation as much as possible.

The bishop hadn't appeared to notice anything, including Francine's rude behavior. Colleen supposed it was because he was too enamored with Francine's assets to pay attention to anything else. Terence's mother was incredibly beautiful and looked years younger than her age. In fact, she looked half her age. As a matter of fact, when Colleen first met Terence's mother, she had mistakenly believed that she was his sister. Colleen just wished the woman would get a man and stay out of her son's business.

Terence entered the room. He started undressing and was humming one of the hymns from church. He was so happy that he was actually whistling.

Colleen silently seethed.

"Tonight was a success, sweetheart," Terence praised, as he came over to Colleen to place a light peck on her cheek. "Bishop Greenfield told me he would be giving his recommendation to the church board."

Colleen's spine stiffened, and she retorted. "Shouldn't you be thanking your mother? After all, she did everything."

Terence correctly interpreted her underlying message and defended. "Mom was just trying to help, Colleen. I would think that you would be grateful that she was here to cook and entertain. You didn't have to do much."

"That's just it!" Colleen emphatically stated. She splayed her hands and explained. "Francine didn't *allow* me to do anything, Terence. She did everything. Then she insulted my hair and my clothes—"

Terence interrupted her before she could go on. "I don't think my mother meant anything by it at all. You just took it wrong. That's just the way she talks sometimes. She didn't mean any harm."

"You're defending her. I can't believe it! I'm your wife, Terence, not your mother—Me!" Colleen shot back at him. It rankled her that Terence acted as if his mother was some innocent Southern girl. His mother was cold and selfish. She wanted her son all to herself.

"Quit!" Terence warned. He raised his hand in a gesture meant to silence her. "Enough about my mother already!"

Colleen instinctively stepped back and clutched her chest. She didn't know if Terence intended to hit her. Just for a second, Colleen felt scared. Then her temper kicked in. "You lifting your hands to me? Are you going to hit me now, Terence? Is this going to be another *accident?*" she asked sarcastically. "Didn't your mother teach you how to treat women?"

Colleen stopped when she saw anger flare in her husband's eyes. Perhaps she had gone too far. Terence took a menacing step toward her; then he paused. Colleen saw him regain control of himself.

"I don't want to talk about it anymore," Terence informed her calmly; then he walked away.

Colleen stood there for a few moments after Terence left. His placid tone of voice had caused chills to run up her spine. To her, it would have been better if he had screamed or snarled instead of giving her such a stoic response. It was downright spooky, and it needed to stop.

Gina's warning flashed through her mind. Maybe she should just cut her losses and leave before things got too out of hand. Then Colleen rejected that thought. Despite it all, she loved Terence. Even though Colleen was discovering this new, seemingly heartless side to him, a part of her still loved her husband. She knew she sounded like a simpering *Lifetime* movie, but this was her life. Now that she was walking in these shoes, Colleen knew she'd never make fun of another woman again.

She looked at herself in the mirror, remembering a time when she used to brag about never taking any mess from any man. "If it were me, I would be out the door!"

Colleen used to say with a snap of her fingers. Well, that was before she fell in love. That was before she got married. That was before she became dependent on a man. That was before she knew herself.

She thought about the saying that a person learned something new every day. How true that was. Colleen was quickly learning something about herself. She was realizing that when it came to matters of the heart, she could get just like any other woman in love.

Stupid.

Chapter Fifteen

He just might lose this one.

The prosecution was kicking his butt, and this might be the end of his impeccable track record. Keith was putting in some serious hours to attempt to counteract every single shred of evidence they were presenting. He may have to put Gina on the stand, and the thought of her going through cross-examination gave him a stress headache. They'd met several times to go over what she'd say, but you just never know. He massaged the bridge of his nose and eyes.

His phone rang.

"Keith Ward," he said, distracted, still immersed in the Marshall case.

"Hello. It's Gina."

Keith immediately smiled. All thoughts of his case flew out of his head at her unexpected, yet much-welcomed call. His headache vanished. "Hi, Gina." Keith had a wide grin on his face that he did nothing to temper.

"I was just calling to see how you were doing," Gina hedged.

Just like that, Keith knew why she'd called. She and Michael had . . . He took a gulp while a piece of his heart cracked. But he would handle his feelings later. Right now, he was going to convince Gina that she had done nothing wrong.

"Gina, it was only a matter of time," Keith assured her. Though inside, he was dying.

"Listen, nothing happened between us . . . I'm okay. Are you?" Keith's heart pounded as he awaited her response.

"Yeah," Gina said hesitantly. "I guess so."

Keith gripped his pen, fighting raging emotions, but he sought to put her mind at ease. "Gina," he reiterated, "nothing happened, so you have absolutely nothing to feel guilty about. We're friends, remember? We even shook on it."

"Yeah, but . . . He's your brother."

Keith yearned to console her. He wished he didn't understand her so well, but he knew how her mind worked. *That's why you're perfect for her.*

"Would you like me to come by later so we can talk about it?" Keith gently inquired. He wanted to see her to make sure she was all right. But he also had ulterior motives. He needed to see if Michael had managed to put a satisfied glow in her eyes. Maybe then he would be able to put daydreams of them being together out of his head.

Gina hemmed and hawed on the other end of the line. "I . . . No!" she panicked. "I mean . . . Yes! I want to see you."

Keith knew that she wanted to see him. But she didn't want to see him. He could relate to her uncertainty. Her dilemma made him feel consoled because he didn't know how to handle the feelings that he was having.

Gina rushed off the phone after her admission.

Keith brought his mind back to work, trying to cool his excitement at the thought of seeing Gina. He missed her, and Keith welcomed that emotion. It made him feel alive, and he hadn't felt that way in years. Since he was alone, Keith allowed himself to think about Gina and reminisce about the moment they had almost kissed.

For an instant, Keith felt like kicking himself for not making love to her when he had the chance. But then he pushed that bad feeling aside. Now that Gina had been with Michael, he knew that his opportunity was gone. She was now irrevocably his brother's woman.

A couple of hours later, Keith pulled his car into Gina's driveway. He saw her look through the window before coming to open the door for him. She greeted him with a soft smile and led him into her kitchen. Keith looked around, satisfying his curiosity about her place. The last time he hadn't entered far from the front door.

He heard her house phone ring, and Gina went to take the call. She waved her consent for him to look around.

She didn't have to tell him twice. Keith took her up on the offer. This might be his only chance, and he intended to take advantage of it.

From her tone, Keith figured that she had to be talking to his brother, so he was only too glad to make himself scarce. He was not too keen on hearing her sweet-talk Michael. Keith wandered back into the living room.

He liked the whole setup of the place. He walked into the dining area. Gina's home was nice, but Keith did not see any hint of the woman he was getting to know. He came to the stairs. He listened keenly and heard Gina still talking on the phone.

Boldly, Keith went upstairs. He peered into the first two bedrooms and a bathroom. Then he went to a door that led to what was obviously the master bedroom—her bedroom. Without thinking about it, Keith opened the door and went in.

With a whistle, he stopped. Gina was written all over this room. He could tell that this was all her. His eyes took in the blatant sensuality displayed. Everything in her room, down to the printed shoe-chair, brought intimacy and passion to his mind. Keith felt a huge bout of jealousy hit him at full force.

He gritted his teeth hard. He wanted to . . . He didn't know what. Coming here to Gina's home, and especially into her private quarters, had not been a good idea. All it did was make him realize how right he was about Gina. She had a passion hidden under her reserved demeanor that was begging to be released. Had Michael released it? Keith felt jealousy consume him at the thought.

As if a siren were beckoning him, he went to sit on Gina's bed. It was comfortable. Gina would probably be horrified if she found him here. Keith could not imagine too many men making it up there. She was way too private for that. This room told a lot about her. Keith leaned back on the sheets. He inhaled her scent. Lying on her bed, Keith knew he was exactly where he wanted to be . . .

Gina got off the phone with Michael feeling exasperated. He had been sorely disappointed that she declined his offer to come over for a movie night—and for seconds.

But . . . Keith.

Gina went into her living area and looked around for him, but he was nowhere to be found. "Keith?" She called out his name again, but didn't get a response. Frowning, Gina looked out of her window. His car was still there. Where could he have gone? She turned around slowly and looked at the staircase.

No . . . He would not have gone up there . . . into my bedroom?

Gina bounded up the stairs two at a time. She checked out the other two bedrooms, which turned up empty, and then raced toward her bedroom. She covered her mouth with her hands, not knowing what to expect. Had Keith mistakenly believed she'd invited him over to sleep with him? She hoped not . . . Gina wavered. She tapped her feet. *If he is waiting for me in the bed, I don't know if . . . I will say no . . .*

Gina took a deep breath, gathered her courage, and cracked her door open. She did not see Keith at first. Then Gina went all the way in.

A quiet laugh escaped her mouth. Here she was worried about saying no or saying yes or possibly sleeping with brothers, and the object of her worries was . . . sound asleep and snoring.

Gina didn't think to wake him. Instead, she did an about-face and decided to let Keith sleep. She went down the stairs into the kitchen to cook dinner.

He made it up here in your bed before Michael . . .

"Shut up!" Gina groaned to her inner voice. Sometimes she wished that she could just block out those traitorous thoughts. They were so annoying at times.

That's because we always tell you the truth . . .

Keith woke up at exactly 12:38 a.m. Befuddled, he looked around while he got his bearings. *Where am I?* His disorientation dissipated as it all came back to him. He slapped his forehead. He had fallen asleep on Gina's bed. He felt embarrassed but could not muster up one ounce of regret. This was the best he had slept in weeks.

He reached into his pocket and checked his cell. He had a voice mail. His phone had been on vibrate, and he'd been too knocked out to feel it. Eve had called to say she was at his place tonight. She hated to be alone in his mausoleum, as she called it. Keith returned the call to check on her, but it went straight to voice mail. She must be asleep.

He straightened Gina's covers and bounded down the stairs to find her. She was munching on popcorn and watching the *Matrix*. He knew he looked tousled and wrinkled. He could not have known that with his rumpled clothes and bare feet, he looked hot and appealing.

Gina gave him the once-over. Keith gulped and strove for normalcy.

"Hey, why didn't you wake me?" His voice was even deeper because of sleep, and he cleared his throat.

"Huh?" He realized that Gina hadn't registered what he'd said and grinned sheepishly. He pretended not to notice that she was still checking him out and was looking at his mouth like it was a piece of candy. Keith's smile faded. He would bet all the money he had that she was remembering when they'd almost kissed. He resisted the urge to ask her what she was thinking.

"Gina," Keith called her again. If she didn't stop looking at him, poking out those pretty lips of hers, he wouldn't be responsible for his actions. "Gina, I'm sorry I fell asleep. I must have been tired."

"It's okay. I didn't mind. You looked so comfortable that I didn't have the heart to wake you," Gina replied. She patted the couch, inviting him to join her.

Keith walked over to the couch and sat down. Gina took his hands and pulled until Keith's body turned toward her. As soon as their eyes met, the now-familiar tension between them began to rise. Gina broke the eye contact first.

"Keith, I cannot deny how attracted I am to you, but I . . ." she paused, unsure of what to say.

"I know, Gina. I would never try to hurt my brother, and I know you wouldn't either. But this . . ." Keith gestured his hands back and forth between them. "This feels right."

"It does," Gina confessed with a rueful grin. "I've never felt so strongly about someone I barely know. It's like we're connected somehow." She looked at Keith to see if he understood her point.

"I know," he agreed.

The two fell silent before Gina said, "Talk about meeting the right person at the wrong time!"

Keith commiserated.

"Keith, I only know that no matter what, I still want us to build on this friendship. I still want you in my life, even if it is just as a friend."

"I feel the same way too," Keith countered, feeling her sincerity. "I mean, it's as if I have known you all my life. I didn't know that it was possible to feel this way. I've only ever felt this way with Vanessa."

He saw Gina's eyebrow arch curiously at the mention of that name. Keith then surprised himself and told her all about Vanessa. He told her everything, including the anger that he held so close inside of his heart at her untimely death. Gina listened to him and let him express everything that seemed to have been inside him for ages. She held his head close and let him cry.

"Keith, I never imagined you would feel comfortable enough to divulge so much of your personal life. I feel honored that you would trust me to open up like that."

"Gina, I'm the one who needs to thank you. I had to open up to someone—and I am glad that it is you."

"Keith, you're so driven, and Michael told me how hard you work, and now I know why. You're trying to run from something for which there is no escaping, Keith. You can't run from your past."

Keith nodded, accepting her admonishment. He felt such relief talking to Gina. He never realized that he'd been carrying around all that baggage for all those years. He'd never expressed all those emotions to anyone, not even Michael.

"Gina, you're amazingly easy to talk to. You listened while I poured my heart out and gushed over another woman. Not too many women could do that, and I will be eternally grateful."

"It was nothing," she said shyly.

Keith saw her bend her head because of his profuse compliment. He put his finger under her chin and made sure she faced him. "Gina, this doesn't happen. I don't share my inner feelings with anyone. I told you things I've never mentioned to Michael. That is not 'nothing.'"

Gina nodded again, before saying, "It was like breathing, listening to you, Keith. That's how easy it was. It was like listening to a part of me. I don't know how else to verbalize it."

It was almost three a.m. when Keith pulled into his driveway. He had felt a great reluctance to go home. He would have stayed up with Gina all night if he could. But, he knew that he couldn't stay there and not make love to her. Eve probably would've had a fit too if he stayed out all night.

Eve barely stirred when Keith entered the room, and for that he was grateful. He didn't want to answer her prying questions, especially since he would have told her the truth.

Keith went over his and Gina's conversation in his mind. He still could not believe how open he had been with her. She was therapeutic for him. Picturing her in his mind, his heart expanded.

Keith closed his eyes, envisioning how she'd cradled his head against her and had tenderly wiped the tears from his eyes. He had not felt embarrassed when he broke down in front of her because Gina had handled that with finesse. She made it okay for him to be human and just cry. Not too many women could handle that.

He possessed such a forceful personality that he tended to stay away from people whenever he felt depressed. He would only end up bringing the other person down with him. Keith often ended up having to cheer the other person up. Gina, however, had wiped his tears away and soothed him so that Keith was uplifted. She was mentally equipped to handle him.

Keith could honestly say that he felt a thousand times better. Gina was good for him. She had missed her calling. She could be earning two hundred dollars per hour for what she had just done for him. He was glad to finally have someone that he could consider a true friend. He went into the bathroom to wash up and took a good look at the face staring back at him. Then abruptly, he looked away, not being able to handle what he had seen reflected there.

All night long the image taunted him. Gina's face taunted him. He tossed and turned. Keith got up the next morning to face himself again, secretly hoping that it would be gone. But it was still there. He still saw the face of a man who had fallen in love.

Chapter Sixteen

Terence entered his office and dropped to his knees. For the past couple of days, he had been reflecting on what Colleen had hurled at him about his mother. She hadn't spoken to him since then. Well, actually she did. But it was only if she had been spoken to. As he stood to his feet, he admitted that it wasn't the same. Colleen was behaving like a marionette, and he felt like the puppeteer pulling the strings. She moved and did everything he wanted, but it felt—practiced. Her heart wasn't into it. He could tell.

It wasn't the same. Terence slapped his knee and sighed. Somewhere inside him, he accepted that what his wife said was true. His mother was meddling in his affairs. It had been that way all his life, but his eyes were just now being opened. Before Colleen, Terence had always followed and done everything Francine told him to do. She told him that he'd make a good architect, and he'd done it. She told him that he should be a minister, and he was almost there. The only thing he'd ever refused to listen to her about was Colleen.

Terence loved Colleen. That was the truth. He knew too that he had hurt her significantly, and that he was still hurting her. But Terence didn't know how to stop hurting Colleen without upsetting his mother. He only knew that he didn't think he could handle it if Colleen left him.

Then tell your mother to mind her own business.

Terence straightened at that thought before he quickly rebuked it. He had to honor his mother. The Bible said so. Now, Terence felt guilty that he had even entertained such a rebellious thought. He bowed his head, clasped his hands, and prayed earnestly. "Lord, please take away these bad thoughts I have been having about my mother. Please forgive me for not honoring her with my thoughts. Lord, I seek your help with bridging the gap with Mom and Colleen. I really need them to like each other. Please, God," he begged, "don't take Colleen away from me. I know I don't deserve her and that I have not cherished her the way I should, but I honestly couldn't bear it if I lost her. Help me, Father, to make the best decision. Amen."

The next day Terence bought Colleen a lovely bracelet. It had a beautiful heart-shaped pink diamond encrusted on it. He showed it to his mother to see what she thought.

"Oh, Terence, I love it. I think it's dainty and just so pretty."

"Good," he said, pleased. "I wanted to get your blessing before I give it to Colleen."

"Colleen?" Francine's confusion was evident. "I thought it was for . . . Never mind." She wrapped her arms around herself in a protective gesture.

Terence rushed to her side. He grabbed his mother's hands. "What is it, Mom? What were you going to say?"

"Colleen does not deserve that bracelet after all the heartache she put you through disappearing all those days. You called me distraught, and frankly, I've never heard you sound so out of it before. Besides, you can never be too sure about anyone."

Something about her tone made Terence uneasy. "Mom, what are you implying? Just say it, will you? My mind is going into some dangerous territory. So now is not the time to be vague."

"Well," Francine played with the collar of her shirt. She arched her eyebrow. "I can't help but wonder if Colleen was with someone all those nights she went to," she formed quotations marks with her hands, "'cool off'" at the hotel. I just don't think she would be all by herself in a strange place and in a strange bed. Not even Gina, her best friend for almost fifteen years, knew where she was. Warning bells would be going off if it were me, son."

Terence stewed. He pondered the truth of his mother's insinuation. She was right. Gina hadn't known where Colleen was, and that was odd, because they were practically joined at the hip.

"Tea, dear?" Francine asked him.

Her saccharine tone did nothing to calm the war suddenly raging in his head. "No, no . . ." Terence sank into his mother's couch. *Who? Who was she with?*

Instantly, everything came together.

Felix! That must have been what they were talking about outside the church. The two of them had been plotting—their lovers' getaway. Imagine that he had actually believed Colleen when she told him that she didn't know the man.

Yet, they had been standing really close—planning their clandestine affair. Then Colleen had made sure she found a reason to start an argument so she could take off. The little manipulative tramp. "I don't believe her—that she would do something like this to me," Terence fumed. Visual images of Colleen and Felix entangled in the sheets reverberated in his mind, driving him past the point of reason. He closed his eyes, willing the images away.

Fiery anger surfaced. Thoughts plagued him of another man caressing and making love to his wife. Filled with rage, he tossed the delicate bracelet on his mother's coffee table in disgust. "I've got to go."

Terence jabbed his hands in his pockets to retrieve his keys and moved toward the door. How could Colleen come home and make love to him after she'd spent the night wrapped up in someone else's arms?

"Leaving so soon? I hope it's not because of what I said, because I would just feel really awful."

Terence stopped and turned to face his mother. She looked fretful. "No, Mom, you've done nothing wrong. All you're doing is looking out for me, and I am grateful to have you. I would've made a fool of myself if you hadn't shown me the light."

Colleen had a lot of explaining to do.

Terence was so enraged with jealousy that it distorted his ability to think and it made him irrational. He left in such a hurry to confront his wife that he missed the self-satisfied and smug expression written all over his mother's face.

Francine heard the door slam and smiled.

She picked up the bracelet and brought it closer to her face. She turned her hands this way and that while she examined it. "It's exquisite. My son has excellent taste." This was the kind of gift that came from a man who was truly in love.

Well, it was just the proper gift from a son to his mother.

Holding it in her hands, Francine wandered up the stairs to her bedroom to put it in her jewelry box. She'd wait awhile before debuting it in public. She had just the right dress to accentuate it when she went to church.

Chapter Seventeen

Colleen slowly eased up off the bathroom floor and got on all fours. She could barely move, and there was laborious effort just in that simple task. She used her hands to wipe her mouth, which was still covered in blood. At a snail's pace, she crawled over to the face basin and gripped the porcelain until she stood and gently washed her face.

Looking in the mirror, Colleen saw that her lips were swollen and bruised. Her long, curly hair was disheveled, and she looked awful. She started to cry again.

She could not believe that Terence had done this to her. He had come home that night in a terrible rage, accusing her of having an affair with Felix. Colleen had not even remembered who Felix was until Terence had shouted that he had seen them talking together outside the church.

She had started yelling back at him, even though she was terrified. This was the first time that she had actually heard Terence roar from rage, and it petrified her. Terence had rambled on and on about how she had played him for a fool. Then he just hauled off and slapped her across her mouth. Her head swung back sharply from the impact, and she got a serious case of whiplash.

Colleen had been too stunned to do anything as her mouth hung open. She could not believe what he had done. Then Terence had the audacity to start preaching at her, of all things. The nutcase spouted scriptures while her head pounded and she bled from her injury. "Thou shalt not commit adultery!" he'd screamed at the top of his lungs as he torturously pounded on her body like it was a punching bag.

Colleen had wailed, "You're demented and crazy," then seeing him advance, with terror-filled eyes, she'd raced into the bathroom.

She'd vomited and spat up blood, after which she lay on the floor and cried.

That had been an hour ago and still she remained confined in her escape room. What had she done to make Terence so mad at her? She racked her brain to recall her words to Felix and her body posture—anything that would clue her in on the logic behind the raging lunatic she'd encountered that day. But that was the dilemma; a raging lunatic had no logic. After all, Colleen had been home all day, and she hadn't even gone anywhere. How could Terence accuse her of cheating?

Colleen sank back down to the floor and put her head into her hands. She had to get out of here. She was married to a madman. "Lord, what is your will? Please tell me. Was Terence just the means to lead me back to you? Did I complicate things by falling in love and getting married?"

With grim determination, she slid over to the door and held on to the door handle. Pulling her body up, Colleen cracked the door and peered out. She was cautious because she was not sure if Terence would be waiting for her outside the door. But he was nowhere to be found. "Thank you, Lord."

In a frenzy, Colleen began throwing clothes into her suitcase. That they were costly designer garb was inconsequential. She had to get out of there. When she was done with her haphazard packing, Colleen ran down the stairs and into the kitchen. She had left her keys on the counter by the stove, but they were nowhere to be found. Frantic, she looked this way and that, hoping to spot the metal ring. Colleen felt panic rise within her, but she made herself calm down. She ran to pick up her purse and dug inside. "No!" Her wallet with all her money, credit cards, and bank cards were missing.

"Oh, God, no!" She put a fist in her mouth and sobbed.

"You're not going anywhere, Colleen."

Colleen turned around as soon as she heard his voice. Her husband walked over to her and grabbed her hair, before giving it a hard pull. He wrapped it around his fist like a corded robe. Colleen flinched with each hard tug, but she refused to cry out. She gritted her teeth. She would not let him see how much he was getting to her if it killed her.

"You're my wife, and I love you, Colleen," Terence said with calm determination.

He spoke with that eerie tone of voice again. That voice and the way that he sounded terrified her.

Suddenly, like a flash of lightning, her anger kicked in. No way was she going to let him do this to her. She wasn't one of *those* women. She wasn't going out like that.

Colleen hunched her shoulders and bunched her hands into a fist. Then summoning all the strength she possessed, she lifted her hand and punched Terence hard across the face.

"Awww!!" His head reeled back from the impact at a weird angle.

Colleen could see the shock fill his eyes, but she didn't care. Terence could not believe she'd done that. Colleen backed away feeling apprehensive about Terence's next move, but she wasn't sorry for defending herself. If he comes at me, I am going to fight with all my might, she told herself. David had killed a bear with his hands, and she would fight Terence if she had to, Colleen vowed.

Terence advanced toward her and Colleen continued her cautious retreat, but she was resolved. *I am going to hit him even harder and make him see stars!*

She felt the imposing wall behind her.

Cornered like a rat in a trap.

Whew! She expelled a breath and gathered her wits. Terence had just backed her against a wall. He stood about a foot away.

Here goes nothing. David had five stones. She had her five fingers on each hand, which she bunched into fists.

"J," she whispered. Colleen lifted her right fist and struck him hard.

"E." She found her voice.

His body bent from the impact. She put all her body weight into her hands and hit him again.

"S!" this time she shouted.

His hands shielded his head. Terence pleaded, "Don't . . . Please don't."

She raised her hand to swing it toward him again. He wasn't fighting back, but she didn't notice.

"U!" she screamed.

Terence's body folded, and he cried out, "No!"

Colleen was far gone. *Lord, give me strength.*

"S!" she howled.

Terence shocked her speechless. His body curled on the floor. She gave him a few hearty kicks for good measure. "Take that you . . . You sorry excuse for a human being . . . you worthless piece of—"

"Don't hit me! Please! I'll be a good boy, I promise! Don't hit me!"

Colleen's mouth fell open as her mind registered Terence's words. Her chest heaved from her heavy panting. She strove to catch her breath. She rubbed her hurting hands while eyeing the man prostrate on the floor. *What just happened?*

Terence remained huddled on the floor and wailed. "Don't hit me. Don't hit me," he begged. "I'll be a good boy. I promise." Sobbing uncontrollably, Terence continued to beg her not to hit him, and he kept saying that he would be better.

Colleen was dumbstruck. She didn't know what to think. Her heart started racing in concern. Terence's behavior mirrored that of a young child—one who'd suffered significant trauma.

She slowly stooped down until she was on the floor with him. Like she would a child, Colleen lifted Terence onto her lap. She'd seen grown men cry, but never like this—not with such unabashed fear. Not knowing what else to do, Colleen hushed him like he was a baby.

"Don't hurt me, please." Terence held on to her as if his life depended on it. Colleen could only hug him while her mind struggled to come to terms with what was transpiring before her. Something was going on with her husband, and she intended to find out what it was. She would not rest until she had an answer.

Chapter Eighteen

Someone was at her door.

Gina opened the door in an obvious haste to end its constant peal. "Colleen!" she exclaimed in surprise and moved out of the way to let her enter.

She waited while Gina quickly scanned her friend from head to toe to make sure that she was all right.

"What's the matter?" Gina asked with concern. She did not even attempt to disguise the worry in her voice. Colleen interpreted all the thoughts that were running through her friend's head as a result of her overactive imagination.

"I'm fine, Gigi," Colleen addressed her friend and hugged her reassuringly.

With the ease of a friend who knew her way around, Colleen sat on the love seat and patted on the seat, silently bidding Gina to sit by her. Gina quickly complied. Colleen could see that Gina's heart was literally racing. It had been ages since Colleen had appeared at her house unannounced.

Colleen took a huge breath, not sure of where to begin. She'd come to Gina's seeking refuge. She had wanted to voice exactly how she was feeling aloud to a sympathetic ear. But now, looking at her friend, Colleen was beginning to second-guess herself. Maybe coming there had not been a good idea. For the first time since her friendship with Gina, Colleen was reluctant to share this part of her life with her friend. She just didn't feel as if Gina would be able to understand.

Marrying Terence had bound her to him, not just physically, but it seemed as if it were psychological as well. Colleen hadn't been prepared for this emotion. It was new to her. She found that she had lost the words to fully confide in her friend. What happened between her and Terence was their business and God's. It was really no one else's. Not even her friend's.

Colleen saddened at the thought, but she felt surprisingly comfortable with her decision. It was time to draw the line between her husband and her friend.

Holding her body erect, she smiled at Gina. Several minutes had passed, and she still had not yet offered a single word of explanation. Colleen could see that Gina was doing everything in her power to be patient. She knew that it was killing her to stay silent this entire time. Colleen reached over and gave her friend an even longer, tighter hug. Gina returned the embrace with a reassuring squeeze.

"I . . . I just came by to see you . . . to get out . . ." Colleen began in a low voice.

"Okay," Gina responded.

Colleen could hear the uncertainty in her voice. For a split second, she felt the urge to appease her friend's curiosity, but Colleen stood her ground. She was not going to bring her friend into the mix. Especially since she had a pretty good idea of how Gina would react.

"I'm okay," Colleen said again. She released Gina from the hug. Then she put a smile on her face to convince her friend that she was indeed okay.

"Okay, I know you came here to tell me something, but looking at you, I can see that you've changed your mind. Whatever it was, I see you're going to keep it to yourself. I know I can't push you, but please just reassure me that I have nothing to worry about," Gina pleaded with her friend.

Colleen looked Gina in the eye and smiled. "You have nothing to worry about."

"You're scared. Admit it." Terence felt a bit apprehensive to go home and face his wife. He had no idea how Colleen would react to him. He also had no idea how he would react to her.

Honestly, he felt like a wuss . . . a big retard. Terence could not, for the life of him, explain how he had broken down in front of his wife in that manner last night. He could not believe that he'd started crying like a sissy and had begged her not to hit him. He was supposed to be the strong one—the man. How on earth could he have allowed himself to become so vulnerable toward someone else?

Terence had grappled with that question all day. It didn't matter that it had been his wife with whom he had become vulnerable. The fact that he still remained vulnerable and men just did not do that sort of thing. And he'd confided something to Colleen that he had shoved in the inner recesses of his mind ages ago. He thought he had buried those memories so deep down that there would be no bringing them back. Yet, they had resurfaced and Colleen had seen him at his weakest point.

He'd cried until his nose was stuffy and his throat sore. He'd clung to Colleen like she was a life jacket. If he hadn't been holding on to her, he felt like he would have sunk emotionally in a dire pit.

You have me. You can depend on me.

Recognizing God's voice, Terence sat and whispered in an awed tone, "Lord, do you still love me?" He asked the question, filled with doubt and disbelief. How could God still love him when he was like one of the biggest hypocrites out there? He was holding the Bible with one hand, and punching his wife with another.

As far as the east is from the west, that's how far I have removed your transgressions.

"God, would you do that for me?" Terence questioned aloud. Somehow, he just couldn't grasp the whole "wipe the slate clean and start over" concept. He didn't want to get off so easy. It just didn't seem fair after the pain he'd caused his wife.

Yet, Colleen had stayed with him, and had hushed him. He recalled the tears in her eyes that brimmed with sincerity as she said, "I love you, Terence. I forgive you. Tell me what happened."

Terence had opened his mouth, as he felt the story begging to come out, but all he could say was, "My mother hurt me. She hurt me as a child, Colleen."

"What did she do?"

"I . . . I can't talk about it now, but I will tell you. I promise. I just need you, Colleen. I don't want you to leave me, though I deserve it. I should never have put my hands on you."

"You're right. You shouldn't have." Colleen had agreed. He'd seen her contemplate something before she looked at him and said, "God is telling me that He brought us together. I can't promise you that I'll get past this overnight, but we can start by praying."

Then to his shame and amazement, his wife had prayed for him. She had cried out to God on his behalf. Then she'd held him until he had fallen asleep. Terence had awakened the next day embarrassed, and had left before she woke up.

Terence paced. He just did not know how to behave after bearing his soul like that. Would things just go back to normal? He closed his eyes and expelled a huge breath. Truth be told, it was a relief to talk about his experience with someone like his wife. Colleen was such a caring woman, and she was capable of so much. But she was also an old-fashioned woman. Maybe she would see him as a weak man now. Maybe she would use the information that he had shared with her against him.

Terence hit his forehead and grunted as another thought occurred to him. Colleen was sure to tell Gina about this. From what he knew, Colleen always told Gina everything.

Great! Now, there would be two women he would have to avoid.

He rubbed his forehead and squeezed his eyes tightly closed. He could feel a headache coming on. His secretary beeped him to inform that his mother was on the phone.

Overwhelmed, Terence shook his head. His mother was the last person that he wanted to talk to. Everything was just too fresh in his mind right now. "Tell her I already left for the day," he replied.

Then he stopped in surprise as a thought occurred. That was the first time he could remember ever turning away a call from his mother. He thought about that for a minute; then he smiled.

Francine hung up the phone and looked at her watch. Terence should have still been at work. *That's strange.* He always let her know when he was going to be somewhere else. His secretary had put her on hold saying that Terence was there. Then she'd returned with a cryptic, "He's unavailable," before abruptly ending the call.

Unless Terence was just not accepting any calls from her . . . *He wouldn't!*

Francine frowned in disgust. *Colleen!* She didn't even have to think twice about it. She knew that somehow, and in some way, that tart was connected to this! Imagine! Her own son refusing to talk to her!

Francine tapped her nails impatiently. Well, she would soon fix that. She was going to give Terence a piece of her mind the next time she saw him. They were scheduled to have lunch the very next day. Francine made up her mind that she would deal with him then.

The next day, Francine entered the restaurant pleased to see that her son was already there and waiting. He knew how much she abhorred tardiness. She lifted her chin, feeling assuaged when Terence got up to make sure she was settled in her chair and gave her the usual perfunctory kiss on the cheek.

She stiffened when she heard his huge sigh. Francine ignored him and spoke her mind. "Why didn't you take my call yesterday, because I know you were in the office?" she asked in an accusatory tone.

Terence did not even bother denying it, but he answered her truthfully. "I just did not feel like talking to anyone yesterday. I had a lot on my mind."

Francine was put off by his answer. "Well! I am not just anyone, Terence. I am your mother!"

"I know that," he said dryly. "You never let me forget it."

Francine stopped and stared at her son. His sarcasm was not lost on her. She did not appreciate his smart remark at all. "I would thank you to mind your manners with me, young man!" she warned. She lifted her eyebrows at him and waited for the usual apology. Unfortunately, none was forthcoming.

She saw Terence merely shrug dismissively before he picked up his menu and scanned its contents. "Are you ready to order?"

Francine was nonplussed at her son's odd behavior. What was going on here? She wisely decided to change tactics. "Are you all right?" she finally asked.

"Yes. Why?" he responded.

Before Francine could go on, Terence's cell phone rang and interrupted the conversation. Speculatively, she eyed him and observed his every move. It was Colleen. Ugh! She should have known! Francine dropped her napkin to show her displeasure.

"Colleen," Terence said, warmly. "What's up?"

"I just called to hear your voice." Terence's volume was loud enough for her to hear Colleen's responses. She frowned and tapped her nails on the table, hoping he would get the hint and get off the phone. To her dismay, he studiously ignored her.

"It's nice hearing from you," he answered.

Francine saw that his face was practically beaming, and she wrinkled her nose, not bothering to hide her displeasure. However, at that moment, Terence did not care about her feelings.

"Actually, I can't wait to see you later. We have to talk. I'm here having lunch with my mother, though. But, you know what I think? I'll cut out of work early to see you."

Francine harrumphed at this last statement, but Terence seemed content to just let her stew. She felt relieved when he finally ended the call and gave her his complete attention.

Francine saw the challenging glare that her son gave her. She supposed that he was waiting for her to make one of her customary cutting remarks about his wife. Now Francine was many things, but an idiot was not one of them. She knew that her son was in a funk and now was definitely not a good time to throw any insults. Judging by his behavior, Colleen must have given it to him real good last night because her son was sitting there, acting the fool. Francine was willing to bet that Colleen had even done *things* that *good* girls just didn't do. She just looked like that type.

Francine picked up her menu to order and let the moment pass. She put the charm on and pretty soon, she and her son were enjoying themselves immensely. But

Francine's resentment toward Colleen had now doubled. She felt threatened by the younger woman. Colleen was taking her place. Pretty soon, Terence would no longer even want to see her. *His own mother.*

Francine's fears were unfounded, but she didn't realize that she had no reason to feel that way. In her mind, she felt that the more love Terence showed Colleen, the less that would leave for her. She just could not afford to let that happen. She had to break those two up, by any means necessary, and she knew just how to do it. But, for now, she would bide her time.

Chapter Nineteen

Keith watched as Michael looked at his cell, and then sighed. Over Gina's head, he mouthed the question, "Karen?"

Keith pressed his lips together but didn't say anything. Gina turned her head toward Michael's direction. His brother needed to answer that phone. Keith observed the silent conversation taking place before him.

Gina looked at Michael with the question in her eyes, "Aren't you going to answer that?" Michael looked away, but Keith knew that his conscience was killing him.

The phone rang a second time. "Answer it," Keith commanded. He knew Gina wouldn't let that slide a second time.

Michael nodded. He uttered a quick, "Hello," before discreetly turning the volume on the phone down. Seeing Gina curve her body to listen in on Michael's conversation, Keith intervened. With a light tap, he captured Gina's attention so Michael could make his escape.

Michael gave his brother a look of undying gratitude. Keith returned with a look of his own telling Michael he would hear it later.

Gina's mind had followed Michael outside the room and onto the patio. He knew the best way to divert her. Keith dropped his voice. "I just wanted to thank you again for listening to me the other night."

Gina gave him her full attention then. "It was nothing. I consider the fact that you confided in me an honor," she stated. She had lowered her voice as well.

"Well, it meant a lot to me. I hope you realize that." Keith gave her a warm smile.

Gina beamed in return. "The food was delicious," she complimented.

He saw her search for something else to say, but she was obviously coming up short. He was also trying to keep his face from proclaiming his love for her.

Keith had called to invite Gina over to his house for dinner again. He had to see her. He wanted to see if what he was feeling was his imagination or a reality.

Gina had gladly accepted once she heard that Michael would also be there. Keith had told her that Michael was staying with him, since he lived closer to her than Michael did.

"Thank you," Keith answered with a smile. He could feel the ever-present tension building between the two of them. He knew she felt it too. There was no denying their mutual attraction. "I really invited you because I just needed to see you. It's been like forever."

"Forever? Keith, that's a gross exaggeration." Gina blushed and pulled her sweater closer.

He heard her husky laughter and glanced behind him. Michael was still on the phone. Keith was going to give his mule head of a brother an earful. He needed to shake Karen loose and hold on to Gina.

Speaking of holding on to something, Keith tenderly asked Gina, "Can I hug you?"

"You want a hug?" she repeated.

Keith snatched her to him. "Yes."

He felt her body curve into his and inhaled deeply. He could stay like this forever. Aerosmith's song came to mind. He hummed, "Don't wanna close my eyes . . ."

"Get your hands off my woman!" Michael boomed from behind them.

Ignoring Gina's harsh intake of breath and her attempts to pull away, Keith methodically turned to face his brother. He challenged, "And if I don't?"

Gina looked down to see that her cell phone was blinking, which meant that she had a message waiting. She would check it during her lunch hour the next period, she told herself as she continued her discussion. However, her actions hadn't gone unnoticed.

"You got a hot date, Ms. Price?" Mark, a particularly bright student asked. The entire class laughed and began making catcalls.

Gina laughed along with them before lifting her hands to silence them. "I won't know the answer to that question until . . ." She looked at her watch and waited a few seconds. "Now!" she said. The bell rang simultaneously with her declaration.

The students laughed again. They thought Ms. Price was so cool.

"He's a lucky man, Ms. Price," another student, Steve, said.

"Thank you," Gina replied graciously. She probably should have reprimanded Steve, but shoot, he was right. Besides, this was her best class. She loved the high school seniors because she could kid around with them, as long as they maintained their respect for her.

Gina waited patiently until the last student left her room before going into the back of her classroom where she had better reception. She checked her message. It was Keith. He said he wanted to see her. Gina could not help the wide grin that spread across her face. The sound of his voice was enough to brighten her day. She pressed her hands to her cheeks. Gina just knew her face was as bright as a lightbulb.

She looked at her watch. She had just enough time to return his call. "Hello?"

"Hi, I want to see you. I need a hug!"

"Remember the last time you asked for one? You and your brother almost came to blows."

"Say what?"

Gina heard Keith burst into laughter and embellished her tale. "Yes, imagine two grown men duking it out like that. You two were Neanderthals."

"You wouldn't be making jokes if that really happened, believe me. Michael and I rarely ever fought over anything as boys. But I have a feeling if we ever did, it would be catastrophic since we both have vicious tempers. Besides, he was joking, and you know it."

"I saw him punch you senseless." Gina crossed her fingers at her fib. Michael had actually given his brother a playful swat on the arm. He had no reason to doubt her or his brother.

"Gina, stop it! I'll see you later. Be ready."

She looked at her phone. Keith was so—straightforward.

To her surprise, it rang again. Two calls in one day. She picked up on the second ring. "Hi, Colleen," she said after seeing her best friend's name on the caller ID screen. "It's good hearing from you."

"Yeah," Colleen agreed. "It feels like ages instead of mere days."

Gina shared Colleen's sentiment. "I never once imagined that there would be a time when we would go this long without talking."

"Me either," Colleen said on a more serious note. "I guess . . . I don't know . . . I just know that I miss you."

Gina felt a pang. She realized that she also missed her longtime friend. Colleen was right. It didn't feel like days; it felt like ages. To Gina, it seemed as if there was so much going on with the two of them that they barely had the time to speak to each other.

"Well, I called to fix that," Colleen proposed. "How about a girls' night?"

Her eyebrows rose at that suggestion. That sounded like a good idea to her. Before Colleen got married, they had so many of those nights that it was as if they lived at each other's houses. But, Gina supposed marriage had changed things. They could still hang, but now they just had to plan. She could live with that.

"I love it!" Gina exclaimed.

"Good! Terence will be going on a spiritual retreat with the other ministers in the church, so you could come over here and spend the night with me."

"Sounds like a plan."

She heard the phone ring and Francine rushed to answer the call. She just knew it was Terence calling to check in on her before he went on the retreat. He would most assuredly be apologizing for his behavior at lunch the other day too. She took her own sweet time to answer the phone. Not for one second did she intend for her son to get the impression that she had missed him.

"Hello?" Francine injected a calm and relaxing tone, even though her heart was beating a mile a minute.

"Hello, Francine."

Francine frowned at the other end, recognizing Colleen's voice. She looked at the phone to make sure that she was hearing the right voice. "Hello, Colleen," Francine said. Her voice had cooled several degrees. She had no reason to even try to be friendly. Unless . . . "Is Terence all right?"

"Yes," Colleen responded. "Yes, he is. He just left actually, and asked me to call and check up on you to see if you needed anything."

Francine stood up straight. Her mouth popped open and closed like a fish. She was not hearing right. Terence had the audacity to leave without calling her first! Then, he had the nerve to have his wife call her, a woman that she could not stand? Francine was outraged. Her last shred of politeness disappeared. "I do not need anything from you, missy. *Nothing at all!*"

Francine banged the receiver into place. Her chest was heaving with something akin to hatred for Colleen. She closed her eyes as another emotion assailed her. She bit on her lips, trying not to acknowledge what she was feeling. But she had to. She was afraid. The moment she had been fighting tooth and nail was here. Another woman was slowly replacing her. Terence obviously didn't care for her anymore. It was as if Colleen was wiping away all the love her son had for her. Francine gulped and allowed the tears to run down her cheeks. She was losing her son. Her baby didn't need her anymore.

Francine sat there in her apartment feeling truly alone now. Turning her head, she looked all around her apartment and all that she could see were pictures of her son, outlining every aspect of his life—from birth, to infancy, to school, to graduation. The pictures, the memories were all there. Her eyes landed on the most recent addition to her collection. It was Terence and Colleen's wedding picture.

Francine got up and walked over to the mantle to pick up the picture. She held the frame in her hands and intently studied the picture like a hawk watching its prey. She felt the resentment build as she looked at Colleen's smiling face. *She* was happy, while Francine was absolutely miserable. Francine's hand flew to her throat. She honestly didn't know what to do without her son in her life. He was her shining achievement. He had always been.

Francine had gotten pregnant at fifteen. Not knowing what else to do, her parents had shipped her off to live with her aunt. All her friends and family had abandoned and ostracized her. She had felt so alone. Crying herself to sleep many nights, Francine had vowed she was going to love her son and give him everything she could, no matter what the cost. Doggedly, Francine had worked and attended GED classes throughout her entire pregnancy, but once the baby came, she had to quit her job. Her aunt was no help. She only made sure that Francine had a roof over her head. Francine had to feed and clothe herself and her young son all by herself.

That was how she had gotten involved with the church. Francine had started going because there was always someone willing to give her a free meal after the service or money for food. She'd gratefully used the money to buy Terence's Pampers and baby food. The government gave her aunt money for her rent and she did get some food stamps, but it was not enough.

Ensconced in her memories, Francine let the tears fall.

She remembered how she'd even gone back to her parents to beg them to take her in. They had refused. So, she had done the next best thing. She married Deacon Fisher Hayworth. He was not the best-looking man, and he was twenty years her elder, but Francine knew that he could provide for her and her son. In fact, Deacon, as she called him, owned his own business, so Francine never had to work another day in her life.

When Deacon died, he left everything to her and Terence, who he had adopted as his own. Terence had never known who his real father was. Francine had not seen any good in telling him the truth. She had transformed herself into a new, upright woman, and that was all her son needed to know.

And, she had been hard on Terence. She had pushed him. She'd disciplined him hard because she wanted him to be something. Francine wanted to prove to everybody who had cursed her and called her a slut that she was worth something, no matter how she had started out. And, she had. Terence had turned into a fine, young man. He'd never ever gone against her . . . until Colleen.

Francine heaved a huge sigh and pulled a tissue out of the box nearby. She wiped her face and swallowed. She replaced the picture of the happily married couple and turned. Wiping her hands on her skirt, Francine vowed she would fix that. Colleen wasn't going to take her son away from her.

Determinedly, Francine picked up the phone to make a call to the one woman who could.

Chapter Twenty

"A motorbike? I don't know. I've never ridden on one before." She eyed the helmet he held. He didn't miss her dubious expression.

Keith grinned. "I had a feeling. Don't worry, you'll be fine. Hop on."

"I'm not exactly dressed for . . ." She put the helmet on and hoisted onto his luxury bike. Her small arms encircled his waist. *Aah.*

"Hold on tight."

"Something tells me that's why you suggested it."

Keith felt her mold her body against his.

"When I came out of the building, you were the last person I expected to see. How did you know I was still here?"

Keith shrugged. Not for one minute would he admit to Gina that he'd waited outside her job for two hours. She'd think he was a stalker. He revved the bike to life. Before he pulled off, Gina screamed in his ear.

"Gina, relax. You'll be fine. I promise."

When she loosened her grip, he took off. Keith had bought the bike on impulse. He rode with skill and precision. He felt Gina rest her head against his. He should keep going. He had money in the bank. He should ride her out of town and never look back.

Keith pulled over, stopping in front of the park. He assisted Gina off the bike and unlocked the small compartment in the back of his bike. He retrieved papers for his court case. He wanted to go over the contents with Gina for the final time. They found a spot to work.

Along with the papers, he had brought them subs to eat while they worked. Keith interrogated her at length. He went over every single detail with a fine-tooth comb until he was satisfied. It was almost dark before he packed up the papers. "I've got everything I need. I don't think you'll have to take the stand, Gina."

Just then they both reached for the same sub. Their hands touched. Fire ignited.

Keith grabbed her hand and tugged, enjoying the feel as her body slammed against his. His breathing deepened. "Can I kiss you?"

She licked her lips. "I . . . We shouldn't . . ."

"Can I kiss you?" Keith bent his head. His body followed as he scooped her into his arms. Her feet dangled. Her face was mere inches from his. He repeated the question. "Can I kiss you?"

Gina shook her head. Her eyes pleaded for his understanding. "I want to, but I can't. We can't. Michael's your brother, Keith. Your brother."

Keith put her down. He raked his hands through her soft hair. "Don't you think I know that? You think this is easy for me?" Ugh. He buried his head into her hair and kissed it, luxuriating in the smell of vanilla. His hands took on a life of their own. He heard her groan and lifted her chin. He had to taste her.

He was too weak to resist.

But she was stronger. "No, Keith. I can't let you do this. We can't. I want to—believe me. But we can't."

Keith closed his eyes, and his ardor cooled. Then he pierced Gina with a torturous look. "You've bewitched me. What have you done to me? I sleep—I think of you. I eat—I think of you. At work—in the shower—everywhere I am—I.think.of.you."

Gina's breath caught, and her breathing became labored. She gripped his arm; then she spoke through clenched teeth. "I haven't bewitched you. It's you who has interfered with my good sense. With you, I want to just—" She backed away from him.

Oh no, he wasn't having that. "Just what?" Keith demanded. His arms stilled her. "Just want to what?"

"Open up . . . Give you all of me." She fiddled with her shirt.

Keith slumped. How he wanted that! He looked up to the heaven. *Lord, why can't I have her?*

God remained silent, but Gina voiced, "But, your brother is good to me. He doesn't deserve this from either of us." Defeated, Gina made her way onto the seat of his bike. "Take me back to my car. I've got to go home."

Keith complied. Gina was right. What had he been thinking trying to maul his brother's woman? "Gina, I hate making promises I won't keep. But I will do my best to stay away from you."

His promise didn't last twenty-four hours.

The next day, Keith walked out of the courtroom with a huge weight lifted off his shoulders. Payton Marshall was right behind him. Forcefully, she grabbed him and engulfed him in a huge bear hug. Tears streamed down her face as her body rocked with so much emotion she could barely contain it.

"Thank you so much," Payton said, unabashedly wiping her face.

Ever the gentleman, Keith reached into his pocket to retrieve his handkerchief, and judiciously handed it to her. She could keep it because he had several in his briefcase. Working these cases had taught him to be prepared for moments like these. He held Payton a little longer until she composed herself.

"You can keep it," he said gently when she attempted to returned the soiled linen.

"Thank you, again," Payton reiterated before finally going on her way. "I'm free!"

Keith listened to her yelling that to anyone who would listen. As he walked away, he let his smile loose. He felt like celebrating. He had done it. He had won the case.

Keith stopped. Who could he call?

He knew who he wanted to call.

He shouldn't.

He made a promise—sort of. One he needed to keep—kind of.

He couldn't.

A few minutes later, Keith pulled into Gina's driveway, anxious to see her. She came out of her house and closed the door. With her frilly yellow polka-dot dress, and a light coat tucked under her arm, she looked like a schoolgirl.

Keith greeted her with a broad smile and a kiss on the cheek. Gina returned his smile with a thousand-watt grin. They were glad to see each other again, although it had only been yesterday since they'd had their rendezvous at the park.

He waited until Gina fastened her seat belt and smiled when she rocked her legs in anticipation. She teased. "So I thought you were going to stay away. How long has it been—one whole day?"

"I have a good reason," Keith grinned.

"What's the occasion? I could feel your excitement on the phone."

Keith nodded. "I am excited. No, I take that back. I feel ecstatic!"

Gina's eyebrow arched. "Wow, you're in such a euphoric mood. Please explain."

"I won the Marshall case." Keith pumped both arms in the air, reveling in his triumph.

Gina let out an excited whoop. "I wish I'd been there."

"I did think I would have to call you in to take the stand," Keith said. "But that could've been hours, or days away, which is why I advised you to wait for my call."

"Yeah! Keith, you're a hero." She undid her seat belt, twisted her body, then reached over to give him a tight squeeze. His body tensed under her arms, but Keith decided that he was not going to move but welcomed her hold. He relaxed and returned the hug.

Gina soothed, "That's better." Pulling away, she faced him and said, "Keith, we're doing nothing wrong. It's okay for us to share an honest emotion."

Then how come Michael doesn't know that I'm with his girl tonight, and last night? Keith frowned at that silent question, but he refused to allow his conscience to bother him about this. He had just shared a meal with Gina. He didn't have anything to feel guilty about. "I agree with you, Gina, so don't you harbor any guilt either. After all, you're not cheating on Michael. We're just enjoying each other's company as friends. And, what almost happened yesterday is in the past. So, let's leave it there."

Keith released his grasp and started the vehicle. It purred to life. He knew he wasn't being 100-percent honest. From his peripheral vision, he could see Gina fidgeting—a sign she didn't buy his whole *friends'* spiel.

Keith drummed his fingers on the wheel. *Why was she the first person I called?* He'd had this compelling urge to share his news with Gina first—before Michael or Eve. They'd share his enthusiasm, but he just wanted to share this moment with Gina. No one else.

He glanced over at Gina, whose eyes were closed as she hummed along to the radio. Kashief Lindo's "Love Is Overdue" was playing on the air. Keith didn't know him, but Gina bobbed her head to the catchy reggae beat.

He was dying to ask if she'd tell Michael about their dates—er—meetings. Yet, he didn't. Her answer might lead to a conversation they didn't need to have.

Keith drove to his destination, content to listen to her sweet voice. He realized that she hadn't even asked where they were going. He knew that Gina mirrored his sentiments, and that it did not matter where they were, just as long they were together.

Still, he racked his brain to think of something to say, but he was all mush. It was probably better to remain silent than to say what he really wanted to say and do. Imagine her reaction if he pulled her into his arms and drew her closer to him for a kiss.

Whew. He needed a distraction. Another song was on. He knew this one. Keith turned up the volume on the radio and added his baritone with Gina's voice at certain parts.

"I'm surprised to hear that you have such a good singing voice," Gina complimented.

"Well, I often sing to the women in my bed. That's how I reel them in," he tossed out. He wiggled his eyebrows suggestively.

Gina laughed at that. "Keith, you are fine, and you know it. So you don't even have to utter a word to get with any woman."

Keith accepted her compliment, but deflected from providing a response. As he drove, he felt Gina's eyes on him. Was she checking him out?

From his peripheral view, he saw that she was. Keith gulped.

He strove to act normal, but it was extremely difficult not to let on that he felt Gina staring him up and down. He was also trying hard to control his very masculine response. She had no idea what she was doing to him. Her eyes felt like razors piercing his body and Keith was doing everything in his power not to pull over and crush her lips to his, to see if they were as sweet as they looked.

Unable to stand it anymore, Keith decided to relieve his tension by turning to look at her. A light blush grazed her cheeks when she realized she'd been caught. She quickly turned her head away to look out of the car window. Keith's humor kicked in and he said, "Like what you saw?"

She didn't even hesitate. "Yes."

"What are you thinking about?" He had stopped at the light and noticed that Gina was shaking her head like she had something on her mind.

She studied him. "I was trying to figure out exactly what it is about you that makes me think and feel things I have no business thinking or feeling."

Keith raised his eyebrows at Gina's blunt answer. He wasn't ready for her truth. His heart rate increased, and his insides warmed. An insistent car horn beeped, pulling Keith's attention back to the road. "How am I supposed to respond to that?" Keith demanded. He couldn't cross the line—break the unspoken man code. His hands were tied, and he couldn't say what was in his mind and heart. She had to know that, but she shrugged at his question, not even bothering to reply.

So, she was enjoying this. Her small smile made the little rascal inside him respond. "I mean, am I supposed to tell you now, that the very sight of you makes it difficult for me to breathe?"

Her intake of breath filled the car. She had no comeback.

Keith laughed. "I didn't think so. So I won't say it."

"You're having fun at my expense," Gina accused.

"No, I'm simply rising to the challenge. I never back down," Keith warned. "So, be careful what you say and be prepared to take it if you are dishing it."

"Okay," Gina surrendered, and waved an invisible flag. "Let's change the topic." Then he heard her say in a low voice, "I was just having a little fun."

"I know. But any sort of flirting between us is not an option. It's dangerous."

"Yeah, you're right," she agreed with a sullen tone.

"Stop pouting," Keith ordered.

"I'm not pouting," Gina defended with a huff. "I'm a grown woman and pouting is for children." She slapped his arm.

He laughed at her spunk. It was ridiculous how much he loved—er—*liked* this woman. He just wished there were something he could do about it. "Gina Price, I like you." I love you, he corrected to himself.

"I like you too, Keith Ward," Gina countered as she lowered her lashes.

Keith pulled up to Trattoria L'Incontro, an Italian restaurant in Astoria. Taking her hand, Keith led Gina into the beautiful establishment. Gina admired the open brick oven in the dining area. Neither of them noticed the stares and glances that they were getting from the other patrons as they were being seated. They only had eyes for each other.

Chapter Twenty-one

"You did what?" Colleen asked her friend, clearly appalled at Gina's news.

The two women were nestled under huge blankets in Colleen's living room. Even though it was only fall, it was cool enough that night to light the fireplace. So, Colleen and Gina decided to sip champagne and roast marshmallows.

Colleen added honey-roasted peanuts and chocolate-covered strawberries to their impromptu feast. Combine that with a movie from Blockbuster and they were set for the night.

They had just begun roasting the marshmallows in the fireplace when Gina told Colleen about Keith and her going on a celebration date.

Colleen continued. "You went out with Keith? Why? Why would you, when you're going out with Michael? What's going on with you? This is nothing like the Gina I know from way back."

"I know." Gina bit her lips. Colleen didn't miss the fact that Gina couldn't even look her in the eyes—a true sign of her wrongdoing. "But it's not like what you think. Keith and I are just—friends."

Who does she think she's fooling? "It's *exactly* what I think," Colleen went ballistic. She was now a married, saved woman so she was coming from a different perspective. "I can't believe that you would be two-timing a man with his own brother. Where is my sensible friend, the one that always walked a straight line? Can you find her and please bring her back?"

Gina lifted one hand with a warning. "Hold up. Ease up on your righteous tirade. You're right; I've never done anything remotely close to this before. I don't know what it is about that man . . ." Gina trailed off, not knowing what else to say.

Colleen, however, did. She had plenty of words for her friend. "Well, you'd better fix it," she commanded. "The man is about to become a father, and you're messing around with him. For obvious reasons, I have a problem with that! God said, the marriage bed should remain undefiled, Gina. But you would know that if you'd come to one of the Bible studies I keep inviting you to."

"Okay. Back it up. I told you that I feel badly already, but I have to talk about it. And who else do I have but you?"

Colleen softened at her friend's tortured look and released a breath to regain control. She was all Gina had, and she couldn't come off too strong or Gina would retaliate. "Listen, I'm not trying to come off as a self-righteous Christian who never did any wrong. You know I've made my share of mistakes with men. But I love you, and I just don't want to see anybody get hurt, Gigi—especially you. And that's precisely what's going to happen if you don't wise up to what you are doing. You're playing with fire, girl. Just be careful, that's all I'm saying." Colleen eyed the Bible. She wondered if she should ditch the movies and grab the olive oil instead. Her friend needed prayers.

To everything there is a time . . . Colleen gave an imperceptible nod at that verse. This was not the time for study. She had to be there for her friend, and she couldn't be judgmental about it. She gathered her thoughts as Gina snuggled under her blanket and popped another marshmallow in her mouth.

"You're right, girl. I don't know what is going on with me, either. I didn't tell Michael I went out with Keith, and that's why I think I feel so bad. I don't know why I'm hiding, when technically, Keith and I did nothing wrong."

"So, nothing happened," Colleen said, even though she was really asking a question.

"Nothing," Gina said. "We talked, we ate; and then he took me home."

"Well, okay," Colleen said, though she still felt a little unsure. "I guess."

But, for reasons unknown to her, Gina felt compelled to voice her feelings aloud. "But I would be lying if I didn't tell you that I like him. I like Keith a lot."

Colleen kept any further comments to herself. She was definitely surprised at her friend's actions. She would never expect Gina to be mixed up in any form of a love triangle, especially one involving brothers. She had always been too straitlaced for that. But then again, she never would've thought she'd still be with someone who'd abused her. So, who was she to talk? Colleen supposed the saying was true. Never say never.

"How's everything with Terence?" Gina asked.

Colleen recognized that Gina was trying to change the subject from herself. Her mentioning Terence was meant to distract her. It worked. She felt her face transform into a sappy smile. She just couldn't help it. "Everything's fine. Things were a little rocky for a minute there, but now, honestly, I never imagined that they could be this good. We spoke on the phone last night for hours. I miss him. I had no idea that I would miss him this much."

"Wow," Gina said, impressed. "You're beaming brighter than a thousand-watt bulb. I'm happy—and relieved—to hear that, Colleen."

The women hugged spontaneously.

"I'm just so happy for you, friend. How do you do it?" Gina looked at her with amazement.

"What?" Colleen asked curiously. Gina's mind moved a million miles a minute, and she conversation hopped, so she needed clarification.

"I don't know how you could just give, I mean, open up yourself like that to someone so freely," Gina explained. "That's the scariest thing for me to do. I mean, Michael is great, but I feel a huge block there that makes it impossible for me to put myself out there like that."

"Because you're commitment-shy—and too much of a cynic. You've been that way since I've known you. You have a hard time believing that somebody could just love you because you're you, and for no other reason."

Gina nodded in agreement. "You're so right. I do find relationships daunting."

"Gina, you're afraid to make yourself vulnerable to anybody, because you're too scared of getting hurt to even try."

"You're right," Gina acknowledged again. She whispered, "I am scared. I don't know how to give less than 100 percent of myself, and if I'm going to love somebody, then I'm going to love him with all of me. Honestly, I don't think there's a man out there who can handle that."

"But how are you going to know if you don't ever give anybody a chance? Take Michael, for example. You tell me that the man tells you that he loves you, and you clam up. You haven't even told him how you feel."

"Well," Gina said, a little defensively, "that's because I'm not too sure about my feelings. When I tell a man I love him, I have to know it without a shadow of a doubt before I say anything."

"I see your point," Colleen conceded and sighed. Sometimes talking to Gina was so draining. The girl was just too serious for her own good. "But if Michael is a good man, then give him a chance. You might just surprise yourself and find that he's the one."

When Gina got up to turn on the television and put in one of the videos in the DVD player, Colleen knew that move had just signaled the end of their discussion, and she let it go. She knew Gina well enough to know that Gina would mull about what she'd said. The girl thought nonstop, even in her sleep. She took the remote to press the MUTE button.

Gina looked askance at her.

"Gina, I do know someone who you can love freely without fear."

Seeing Gina was open, Colleen continued. "Jesus is that person, Gina. He is the only one who won't ever do you wrong. There's no perfect man out there, Gina. You have to know that."

Gina nodded but didn't respond. Instead, she picked up the remote and turned the volume on.

As the opening scene began, Colleen felt good that at least she'd gotten a moment to share Christ, if but for a second. Sometimes that's all it took for the seed to take root. She'd leave that to God. As far as dating, she hoped Gina would see that she had a valid point and that it made sense. She wanted to see her friend happy and settled with a decent man. Gina was a beautiful and caring person and could make such a great partner and wife. But she seemed to be the only person who was aware of that, and she sincerely doubted that even Gina herself knew it.

Colleen wished she could wave a magic wand and fix everything for her friend. But this was something she was powerless to do. Gina herself had to realize her own potential and worth, on her own.

For a brief second, she felt guilty. Had she shared enough of God?

You don't have to talk about me for people to know I exist. You just have to live.

Colleen knew that voice. She breathed in deeply and looked over at Gina. *Then what do I do, Lord? I don't want to feel like I'm not a real Christian.* She thought the question, but her heart pounded as she waited.

I don't need you to honor me with your lips, Colleen. I need you to honor me with your heart.

Instinctively, Colleen touched her heart. She was hearing from God while watching a secular movie? She creased her eyebrows. That was weird and surreal. "Thank you, Lord," she whispered.

"Huh?" Gina turned to face her. How could Gina remain completely unaware that the creator of the world was just speaking to her? Colleen wondered, but didn't voice the question, for Gina would've surely thought her cuckoo. Nevertheless, Colleen admitted, "I was just talking to God."

"Tell Him I said hello," Gina quickly replied.

Colleen took umbrage to her jest, but bit her tongue. Inside, she prayed earnestly. *"God, make Gina experience something so inconceivable that she has no choice but to trust you."* Colleen had no idea how her prayer would be answered. If she did, she would've prayed for something different.

Chapter Twenty-two

"Lord, I lift your name on high . . ." Francine sang and lifted her hands in the air. "I just love to sing your praises . . ." she hummed the rest. She was in such a good mood. Thanksgiving was fast approaching, and Francine had already prepared her huge shopping list and made arrangements with the butcher to get first pickings with the turkey. Yes, sirreee! Terence was going to lick his fingers this year. She'd found a new recipe on the Internet that she was about to try out. She dutifully washed her hands. "I'm so glad you're in my life . . . hmmm . . . hmmm . . ."

Francine wiped her hands on her apron and bent over to look under her sink. Where did she put her big sterling silver bowl? She rummaged around, not the least bit bothered by the clamming and banging, until she found what she wanted. "Aha! I found you!"

She always looked forward to Thanksgiving and enjoyed the early-morning preparations and time that such a huge meal required. For over two decades, Francine would be up before the crack of dawn to begin her feast. She painstakingly prepared every single dish—candied yams, baked mac and cheese, collard greens, rice and beans, potato salad, pot roast, and, of course, the turkey.

It was a lot of hard work, but Francine was methodical and always got everything done. Her strategy had always been to do the seasoning, mixing, and cutting the day before Thanksgiving. *Now where did I put my recipe for the candied yams?*

After looking here and there, she found it by the computer under the mouse. Francine was mulling over the ingredients when the telephone rang.

"Hello?" she answered the telephone distractedly.

"Mom?"

Francine smiled at her son's voice and said, "Hey, what's up? I'm just going over my usual Thanksgiving list for the big day. I'm actually about to try out a new recipe for my candied yams."

"Oh, sounds interesting . . ." She heard a light pause before Terence continued. "Well, ah, that's kind of what I'm calling you about."

"Yes?" Francine queried, quizzically.

"Well, the thing is . . ." Terence paused again. "The thing is that Colleen and I were thinking of doing things a little bit differently this year. You know, we figured that since you've always been slaving over the Thanksgiving meal, that we would take the burden off your hands this time."

Francine could not believe her ears. "What? Did I just hear you right? You figured? Figured what?" She had escalated to a yell, and by now, Francine was seeing red.

"Come on, Mom," Terence urged, "don't be like that. Colleen thought that you might need a break, and I agreed with her."

"Colleen thought!" Francine snapped. "Colleen thought! What right does that . . . that woman have to suggest anything?"

"She has every right," Terence said, sounding annoyed now. "She's my wife."

"Well, I tell you what," Francine shouted, "you and your wife can spend this Thanksgiving without me!"

"Mom," Terence urged, trying to smooth her ruffled feathers, "you know you don't mean that."

"Yes!" Francine hollered, "Yes, I do!"

"Well, okay then," Terence said, calmly, "if that's the way you want it, we will." And with that, Terence hung up the phone. Francine looked at the receiver in shock. Her son had just hung up the phone on her. She couldn't believe it. He'd never done anything like that before. Francine slowly put the receiver back on the hook.

Belatedly, she realized that she still held the recipe in her hands. In a fit of rage, Francine tore the paper into shreds and tossed the contents into her garbage can. "Where does she get off? Colleen thought . . . Imagine the gall . . . the nerve of that little . . ."

She would fix that little tart soon enough. If her plans went through, the *wife* was about to have a rude awakening. She would get that tramp for stealing her son away from her and turning him against her. She would fix things between them before her son's ordination service. That was for sure.

Michael swiped his card to enter his penthouse. It felt like ages since he had been home, instead of mere weeks. Thanksgiving was a few days away, and he wanted to make sure Karen had sufficient funds to tide her through the holidays. For the umpteenth time, he questioned his wisdom in letting her stay at his place. Keith pleaded with him to kick Karen to the curb or put her up in a hotel. He cautioned Michael several times that he was taking a big risk and predicted that this was all going to end badly. To Keith, Michael keeping her there didn't make any sense. But Michael didn't heed the warning.

He stepped inside and looked around. It was surprisingly clean. Karen must have finally learned how to clean up after herself, he thought. He doubted that, though. She had probably called housekeeping. Michael went into his bedroom and paused. "Oh no, she didn't!" Karen was slowly taking over his room, even though she had her own.

Michael sighed and walked over to his bed. It was un-made and various types of negligees hung over the chair. Methodically, he removed Karen's belongings out of his bedroom and back into hers. He had five bedrooms. Why she insisted in taking up his space was beyond him. He then made his bed and walked into his closet to retrieve more clothes to take back with him to Keith's house.

He'd left his laundry with the carryout service.

Michael glanced at his watch. He figured he had a good hour or two before Karen came home. He was not trying to run into her at all. He had been doing a good job so far of eluding her. But he just wanted her gone. He wanted to bring Gina into his home and had thwarted her hints long enough.

Michael walked into the kitchen and placed several hundred-dollar bills on the kitchen counter. *She could get a real good rental with that money*. Obstinate, Michael shooed away the thought. *Something is different*. He scrunched his nose and investigated. A minute or two later, he figured it out.

"Cows," he said aloud.

He looked around. Karen had added feminine touches everywhere. She had replaced his imported Italian floor mat with a cow-shaped mat. His top-of-the-line potholders, salt-and-pepper dispensers, were replaced with cow motifs. There was even a cow-shaped cookie jar and a cow-shaped refrigerator magnet.

Something else caught his eye. *What is that?* Michael hunched his body and crept over to the stove. He shook his head as recognition dawned. A cow-shaped kettle.

Michael decided to leave everything the way it was. *Maybe I should just give Karen this place. Naw*. It was prime real estate with an amazing view. New York City was all about location—and this was the crème de la crème.

He opened the blinds to see the city. Gina would love it up here. If she were here, he would make love to her while the city bustled beneath them. *I have to get Karen out of here! I want her gone!*

The problem was that he needed to keep things amicable between himself and Karen. Michael feared that Karen would do something crazy like commit suicide or tell Gina. He poured himself a drink and went to sit on his couch. Maybe he just needed to confront Karen and let her know that she had to leave. Maybe that was the best thing to do. Keith had warned him again that very morning to get rid of her before Gina found out. Michael closed his eyes, trying to figure out exactly how to do what he had to do.

A huge clap of thunder rolled across the sky. Michael jumped up off the couch in surprise, and then groaned when he saw Karen. This was just not what he wanted. What was she wearing? Karen was dressed in the sheerest, skimpiest nightgown he had ever seen. He was in serious trouble, he thought, as she purposefully advanced toward him.

She walked up to him and greeted him. "Hi, Mikey. You gave me a fright. It's been awhile since I've seen you."

"Hi, Karen, I must have overslept," Michael explained, stepping away from her.

Karen stepped forward again, not bothering to hide her desire.

Michael tried to get the image of how Karen was dressed out of his mind. He closed his eyes . . . and still saw her. He took two more steps backward. He could kick himself for falling asleep here. Now Karen was onto him like a leech about to suck his blood dry.

He hated his male reaction and felt like a mouse caught in a trap once Karen noted it. Michael quickly circled around her, but Karen grabbed onto his tie.

"Let me go, Karen," Michael dictated.

"Is that what you really want me to do?" she asked him seductively.

The old dog began to wag its tail. But Michael was not about to feed into that. He shrugged his body away from her. "Yes," he stated, firmly. "I want you to let me go."

Surprisingly, Karen released him. He sighed with relief.

"She must be something," Karen said, referring to Gina.

"She is," Michael agreed. "And that's why, even though you are . . . fine, I can't go there with you."

"Okay," Karen said. "I'll leave you be. But please don't rush off, okay? It's going to get real bad out there."

Another boom of thunder sounded through the room, validating her point. Michael looked outside the window and noted the darkened sky and heavy downpour. Still, he was skeptical. He knew from past experience not to be fooled by Karen's seemingly agreeable nature. She could be waiting to pounce on him.

"I'm not going to touch you, Mikey," Karen said in a convincing tone. "I really just do not want you getting hurt or something, because you were trying to escape me. Besides, I want to take the time to thank you for the job you got me and for the money you have been leaving for me. I'll be right back."

Michael relaxed, trusting her. Karen sounded sincere. He was going to give her the benefit of the doubt. As if to prove her words, she went into her room to change her outfit. This time she was fully covered from head to toe. He couldn't help the laugh from escaping his lips, but he felt relieved.

He saw her head into the kitchen to continue working on a meal. He sniffed. Something smelled good. She must have been back for a while.

"What're you cooking?" Michael asked. "By the way, the place is immaculate. Did you hire someone?"

"Chicken Alfredo," Karen replied as she placed the pot on the stove for the pasta to boil. "And to answer your second question, no, I didn't. I do know how to clean, you know. But, thanks, it feels good to come home to a clean place. Do you want some food? Don't worry, it's not poisoned."

That thought hadn't occurred to him, but the fact that she needed to point that out . . . "Sounds good," he voiced. He was hungry. He supposed there would be no harm done in staying overnight. This was his place, after all.

Karen came over and sat on the couch next to him. "Mikey, I met someone."

Michael's head drew back in surprise. "You did?"

"Yeah," Karen admitted shyly.

"So, why were you trying to make a move on me then?" he asked, more than a little peeved at her comment.

"Because," Karen replied, "I don't know. I've always had this thing for you, you know. And this thing with Arthur—that's his name—well, it's kind of new, and . . . I just met him about two weeks ago, and we've been talking."

"Has he been here?" Michael asked, dreading the answer. He didn't relish the thought of Karen entertaining some strange man in his place, and possibly, in his bed.

"No," Karen replied, with a blush. "It's nothing like that."

Something in her tone of voice told Michael that Karen really liked this guy. "You sound like you like him," he offered.

"I, ah, I think I do," Karen said. "But, I'm just not sure, Mikey. He's different." Karen paused, and then confessed. "I feel weird talking to you about this . . . considering."

"Don't," Michael assured her. "We might not be together anymore, but we can still talk as friends. Besides, I
prefer this to trying to pry you off me."

Karen laughed. "Am I really that bad?"

"Yes," Michael answered her, laughing. This moment
felt surreal. He had never had a conversation like this
with any of his ex-girlfriends.

"I don't mean to be," Karen assured him.

"Tell me more about Arthur," he asked. He'd noticed
some changes in Karen and was curious to find out if this
Arthur guy had something to do with it.

"Well," Karen began, with a relaxed demeanor, "he's
nothing like you. He's short and chubby and baldheaded."

Michael laughed and inquired, "Where did you meet
him?"

"At work. It was during my lunch hour, and I was
walking to the diner when I noticed this guy following
me. At first, I thought he was a creep, and I attacked him
with my purse."

"Wait a minute. No, you didn't." Michael interrupted.
Then, he counteracted his own words. "On second thought,
I believe it." He slapped his thigh and howled with laughter.

After a moment, Karen joined in. "I guess I deserve
that. Well, you know I'm crazy! So, I was getting ready to
kick some, you know what, when he started yelling that
he wasn't trying to do anything to me. He just wanted to
take me out to lunch. So I asked him, what're you following me like that for? And, that's when he said that he just
wanted to see where I planned to eat before coming over."

Karen stopped to take a breath. Michael used that moment to process her comments. When Karen was excited,
she spoke so fast that it was hard to hear everything that she
was saying.

"So, after that, he apologized, and you two started
talking," he deduced.

"Yeah," Karen confirmed. "He just asked me out today, and I told him I'd have to think about it, you know? But then you showed up, and . . ."

"Yeah," Michael said. Then he addressed her in a quiet tone. "Karen, if this guy sounds great, then move on, because I have. Gina is great, and I feel strongly about her."

Karen hunched her shoulders in disappointment; then she straightened. "That didn't hurt like I thought it would. Maybe I am over you, and I'm just holding on to the familiar. So I guess I should move out and give you back your space."

Michael smiled. Karen was growing up. He would have to congratulate this Arthur person if he ever laid eyes on him. A thought suddenly occurred to him. "Hang on!" Michael exclaimed, "Does Arthur have a last name?"

"Okay, don't laugh. Bugle. His last name is Bugle," Karen said.

Michael's mouth hung open.

"Dang. His name's not that bad," Karen defended.

"No, it's not that," Michael said. Then he began to laugh. "You have no clue, do you?"

"What?" Karen's brows rose. She opened her hands in question. "Will you just tell me?"

"Arthur Bugle is rich—filthy rich. You did good!" Michael slapped her on the back several times.

"Uh . . . I . . . I don't understand what you're saying." Karen eyes narrowed depicting her confusion.

"He is one of my company's top clients, and he definitely doesn't work in the building. Haven't you ever heard of *Arthur's Pickles*."

Karen's mouth formed an "O" as recognition dawned. Her eyes widened, and she was silenced by shock. She whispered, "Sugar, honey, iced tea . . . I didn't have a clue."

"Well, you'll have more than that soon," Michael promised her. His smile was for two reasons—she'd met someone, and he would soon have Karen out of his hair. Arthur would know how to handle her, though. He was sure of that. Arthur Bugle was more crafty and wily than Karen was. Michael chuckled. She had met her perfect match!

Karen finished cooking, and the two shared a meal, as friends.

Michael left the next morning feeling content. His steps were light, for a burden had been lifted off his shoulders. Karen had told him that she would be looking for her own place. She could move to the Arctic Circle for all he cared. Michael was just happy for her and for himself. Now he could finally have Gina spend the night. He'd taken her on a tour of his penthouse—and they'd dropped in a couple times—but they'd never stayed over.

Michael rubbed his hands. But that was about to change.

Finally, his life was looking on the up and up.

Chapter Twenty-three

Thanksgiving Day was beautiful. The sun was bright and clear in the sky and provided enough warmth for a lovely fall day. A light jacket was all that was needed. Gina and Michael pulled into Keith's driveway. The leaves were falling off the trees, and they left a hue of brown, yellow, and red colors that was breathtaking. Gina breathed in deeply to sniff in the smell of pinecones.

She was dressed in a purple form-fitting dress with a ruffled flare on the hemline. When she walked, she exposed a scintillating view of her slender thighs. She held back a smile, knowing Michael's eyes roamed her best attributes.

She knocked and turned the knob. Discovering it unlocked, she stepped in. An array of smells assailed her senses and her stomach rumbled. Her mouth watered from the delectable aromas, and she clenched her stomach to still the unbecoming noises.

"Something smells good, Bro!" Michael yelled from behind.

Keith came out of the kitchen with an apron wrapped around his waist. "Hi, Gina," he greeted with a warm hug and a kiss on the cheek.

Gina blushed from the close contact. *I see nothing has changed,* she said to herself. His proximity enticed her. Her body tingled. Her breath quickened. She hunched her shoulders to limit the physical contact.

Keith loosened his hold, and Gina stepped back.

Colleen and Terence arrived. She'd been overjoyed when Colleen agreed to share Thanksgiving dinner with them. It was almost like old times—Except for Terence, of course.

"Hi, Terence," Gina said, politely. Terence bent his tall body to place a kiss on her cheek. Gina kept her smile plastered on her face, but she couldn't help the small cringe.

Colleen grabbed her with an exuberant grin. Her taller frame overshadowed Gina's smaller one. Gina felt like she was standing between the Twin Towers before the tragedy. "It's good seeing you, girl."

"Same here," Gina returned.

Michael strolled over and he, Colleen, and Terence made small talk.

Gina tapped her feet as her mind wandered away from the conversation. She looked at Keith. Of their own accord, her feet trotted toward him. She was like a moth drawn to a flame.

Keith saw her approach and gave her the salad that he was holding. "How're you?" he inquired once she was in close proximity.

She felt her body shiver and fought the goose bumps rising on her flesh. He was hotness personified. "I'm okay," Gina replied with practiced nonchalance. "What about you?" Here she was making small talk when she'd much rather hug him and feel his body up close.

"I can't complain—and, might I add, you're wearing the 'you-know-what' out of that dress."

Gina glanced down and whispered a "Thank you." Goodness, she couldn't talk to him without blushing. Desperate to keep up the charade of nonsense conversation, she asked, "Is Eve coming?"

"Yeah, she is. She told me that she had a quick errand to run, so I'm expecting her back any minute." Keith played along, but growled. "Don't change the subject."

"That's nice," Gina said loud enough for Michael's benefit. She craned her neck in his direction, but he was still engaged with Colleen and Terence. Gina fiddled with her dress. She could not think of another appropriate thing to say at this point since she couldn't say what was on her mind.

Colleen looked in their direction. Gina figured she felt the need to play interference and walked over to them. She raised her right eyebrow at Gina, not fooled for an instant, but wisely decided to let it go.

Then Eve walked in. She looked flushed, slightly disheveled. Nothing like the diva she did the last time Gina met her.

Keith rushed to Eve's side in concern. He took both her hands in his. "Are you okay?"

"Yeah," Eve answered. She greeted everyone before making her excuses to run to the bathroom. By the time she returned, everyone was seated at the table and waiting for her.

Eve had an apologetic smile on her face. "I'm sorry to keep you waiting. The baby was acting up." Eve gave everyone a gracious smile.

"That's all right," Michael volunteered, and then turned to his friend. "Terence, would you like to say grace?"

Terence nodded his head and urged everyone to hold hands. Then he said a brief prayer of thanksgiving and blessed the food. At the end of his prayer, a warm air filled the room.

"You brought the Holy Ghost down in here, Preacher Man," Michael joked.

Everyone laughed and began to eat.

Keith, however, was concerned. For once, his mind was not on Gina. With his hand under his chin, he scrutinized

Eve. Something was up with her. Of late, she'd not been herself. Since she hadn't been forthcoming, he needed to ask. Normally, Eve would come to him, but now, he was positive that he would have to break the ice to find out what was going on.

Eve had been working longer hours. He could count on one hand the number of times that she had been over at his house the last few weeks, choosing, instead, to crash at her place. Keith ran his eyes over Eve's body. Physically, she seemed well.

Hmm . . . If there were something wrong with the baby, Eve would've told him. He watched her laughing at something that was said. He couldn't put his finger on it, but something was definitely up. Keith was determined to find out that very night.

When everyone left, Keith put the dinnerware and utensils in the dishwasher and soaked the pots in the sink. Normally, he would have washed everything then and there, but he wanted to confront Eve before she fell asleep. She was undressing when he walked into the room.

"Hey," Keith said.

Eve almost jumped out of her skin. She turned around and snatched a robe to cover up, her face a light rosy hue. "Keith! You scared the life out of me."

"I'm sorry. I just wanted to talk to you." He creased his brow in thought. Since when did Eve cover up around him? If anything, she was usually trying to undress around him. "Why'd you cover yourself?"

"I . . ." He interpreted her guilty look before Eve confessed, "I just felt funny about you seeing my big belly, that's all. I've gotten so big, I can barely see my feet."

"You're beautiful," Keith said, seeking to reassure her. Then he asked, "Is everything all right, Eve?"

"Honestly, I am quite unprepared for your show of concern. I am not sure how to answer you, because if I tell you the truth. you're going to be angry."

Keith observed that Eve began to wring her hands, which was a dead giveaway that something was indeed wrong. He sat down on the bed and transformed his features into one of absolute patience. He wanted Eve to feel as if he had all the time in the world for her. "You can tell me, Eve. I can't promise I won't be upset, but I won't upset a pregnant woman," he prompted.

Eve was still unsure. "I just don't know, Keith."

He saw her lip poke. "Try me," he urged with a calm tone.

"I know that look," Eve chuckled nervously. "You'll sit there and wait for hours until I spill my guts."

Keith didn't say anything to deny that she spoke the truth. He saw her gather her courage, walk over to him, and sat next to him on the king-sized bed.

"I've been seeing Bass," she blurted and placed her hand over his.

Keith removed it. "Bass?" He shook his head, stood, and ran his hands over his head. "How long?"

"About three weeks."

"I see," Keith said, becoming as closed and hard as a shell. "Well, that explains everything. The long hours . . . the sudden disappearances . . . I should've known." He walked out of the room.

Eve followed him into his office and plopped into the chair. "Is that all you're going to say? Your face is like granite. Have you no emotions?"

"What else do you expect me to say?" Keith asked.

"I don't know. But say something," Eve responded. She twisted her hands.

"Why should I waste my time on words when you know how I feel about the situation already?" He refused to bend.

"Well, at least let me explain," Eve offered. She didn't wait for an answer but rambled, "He called me out of the blue that day when I had the amniocentesis done. I remember, you'd just called me to check on me. Then my phone rang again. I thought it was you—but . . . He caught me off guard . . . But I thought that it was only fair for me to meet him, considering . . ."

Her words hung between them.

"Why didn't you tell me?" Keith asked.

"Because I knew exactly how you felt about the situation and Bass, and that's why I didn't say anything from the very start. But I was going to mention something to you."

"Have you slept with him?" That was what Keith really wanted to know.

Eve's face told it all. Keith wrinkled his nose and closed his eyes. Disgusted, he was trying hard not to release the bile turning over in his stomach. He opened his eyes to give her a contemptuous glare. "Your face is answer enough," Keith spat out. He could not believe her. "When you gave yourself to him, did you, for one second, think about the fact that the child you're carrying could be mine?"

"But it's not," Eve returned. "I've told you that."

"Well, we both agreed that we would wait until the baby was born to find out," he doggedly reminded her. "And, if you remember, that's why we haven't been sleeping together, or doing, or *saying* anything else."

Eve lowered her head in shame. She whispered, "I do love you, Keith, and I'm not going to apologize for saying that. I also was honest enough to tell you about Bass when I found out that I was pregnant, even though it made me look like a . . . terrible person." Eve's eyes filled with tears of self-remorse.

"I don't think you're a . . ." Keith sighed deeply. He needed to get a grip because she was pregnant and very fragile. He assured her, "I understand fully what it is like to have a love for someone that you just cannot shake. I also knew that you were in love with Bass when you met me, and I can accept that I was a rebound thing. What I cannot deal with is the fact that this baby could be mine, and we agreed to put everything on hold until we knew for sure."

"But I also told you that the possibility of you being the father was slim. We only had unprotected sex once," Eve explained. She held her hands out, but Keith wouldn't concede.

"Well, you agreed," Keith said. "But you just couldn't stay away from Bass as you promised. I mean, that's what caused this whole mess in the first place. Now, where has he been all this time, huh?"

Eve shifted her eyes away from him. "In Europe, on tour."

He snorted, "Bass hasn't changed. He, his guitar, and his you know what have probably been leaving his imprint all over Europe."

Eve gasped at his bluntness, but he wasn't taking it back. He'd meant every single word.

"Bass has changed," Eve refuted, shaking her head. She entreated him. "I'm telling you, Keith. Bass is different, and he's prepared to be a father to this baby, if it's his—Which, I'm sure, that it is." She felt the need to point that out.

Keith put both hands on his head and looked up at the ceiling. This was so complicated. He didn't know how he had even become entangled in such a scandalous position. He was about to be a father to a child who may not even be his. He wished that he had never gotten involved with Eve.

He'd met her through a mutual friend, and the two began dating. Eve told him all about Bass whose name was originally Trevor Browne. He changed it to Bass because he figured the name represented his true artistic nature.

Keith had heard him play the guitar, and Bass was admittedly good. But he was a dog when it came to women. That was why he hadn't expected Eve to fall under his spell again. But she had.

Keith had to give her credit, though. When she realized she was pregnant, she had confessed it to him right away. The only problem was that the time span between her sleeping with both him and Bass had been a short one. So, even though she and Bass were through, she was unsure of whom the father of her baby was. Bass had turned tail and ran at Eve's news. She had been heartbroken as a result.

Keith, however, had stuck around. He had even opened up his home and life to her, if not his heart, in order to help her through her pregnancy. He hadn't even told Michael the truth.

He had just gotten used to the idea of becoming a parent and had been softening toward Eve, and *bam*. Bass shows up to throw a monkey wrench into everything. For, Bass's sake, Keith prayed that Bass was the father of Eve's child—and not him. He clenched his fists.

Then Keith looked at Eve, and his heart won out. He could not be too hard on her. After all, he knew what it felt like to love someone even when you knew it would be bad for you. He was in love with his brother's woman. Life was just too complicated at times.

"Eve," Keith said, "just please know that I care, and I will be here for you, no matter what . . . Whether or not this child is mine."

"I love you, Keith," Eve returned. "You are truly a wonderful and caring man."

"Thank you," Keith replied, "I love you too, Eve. But we're not in love with each other, and we both know it. So, I really hope that Bass is the baby's father."

"Me, too," Eve stated dreamily. He watched her struggle to her feet, stomach first, knowing she was tired and ready for bed. "I'll see you."

"Good night," Keith said.

He watched Eve walk away, signifying the end of one messed-up melodrama in his life. Then his mind wandered to Gina. If he were not the father of Eve's baby, he didn't know how he was going to stay away from Gina. Right now, that possibility was the only thing keeping him at bay. Otherwise, he would be going head-to-head with Michael for her. This was the second time in his life he could say he felt strongly about a woman, and it was eating away at him that he couldn't have her.

Chapter Twenty-four

Terence and Colleen entered their home. They had enjoyed spending Thanksgiving with Gina and Michael. Keith and Eve were also a charming couple.

Colleen noticed that Terence was unusually quiet and voiced her concern.

Terence looked at her and said, "Yeah, I was just thinking about my mother and her being all alone tonight. It felt weird not being there with her."

"I told you to call her and sweet-talk her into still having us over," Colleen said, "because I certainly don't want her thinking that it's my fault."

"I know," Terence replied, "but it's more than that. My mother needs to respect you as my wife, and until she does that . . ."

"Thank you for that, Terence," Colleen said, "But how your mother feels about me doesn't bother me anymore—Okay, I do care. But I'm sure now of how you feel about me." She tilted her body toward his and kissed him on the cheek.

"Things have been great, haven't they?" Terence confirmed. He looked over at his wife. She was lovely. Terence knew that he had to say something about the incident that had taken place weeks ago. He had never really voiced his feelings aloud, but had just waited for things to fall into a normal routine.

"Colleen," he began, "I know that I've never really told you how sorry I was for hurting you, and I just wanted to take this time to tell you that I'm truly sorry. I also wanted to let you know that you're the best thing that has ever happened to me. You've changed my life and made me a better man."

Tears formed in her eyes. "Thank you, Terence. Your apology means a lot to me. I've wanted to talk with you about that night for so long, but I knew you were probably embarrassed about it, so I didn't push. But, we do need to talk about that night."

Terence knew that Colleen was right. He just didn't know where to begin. "Colleen, I have replayed that night over in my head so many times, it's not even funny. You are right, I was scared to talk to you about it," he stated. Then he corrected himself. "Well, not scared, really. I mostly felt vulnerable. Especially thinking about what Gina must think of me now."

"Gina?" Colleen gave him a quizzical look. "Gina is my friend, and her opinion matters, but she doesn't control my life. She just doesn't know about the physical abuse or your breakdown. But I did mention your controlling ways in the past. I want you to know I've never kept anything from her until now, and that's because I felt that God was telling me not to. She's not saved, and I don't want something like this being a stumbling block."

Terence heaved a huge sigh of relief. He knew Colleen would've confided in Gina but was grateful she hadn't disclosed everything. Still, he felt overwhelming embarrassment. "Colleen, I'm so relieved to hear you say that," he said. "I mean, I felt so funny being around her today. Like a big hypocrite. I'm about to be ordained as a minister, and I was so ashamed of what she might think about me."

"Well, she doesn't know everything. But, she's no dummy—and I may feel led to tell her at some point. But anything else that transpires between us will stay between us—unless my life is in danger, then all bets are off. You have my word on that."

"Thank you," Terence said, humbled. He didn't deserve this woman. He knew that for sure. He swallowed her in his arms, cherishing the second chance he'd been given. He grazed her cheek with light kisses before finding her mouth. His passions overtook him, and he deepened the kiss.

Ever since that night, Terence had changed in so many ways. He knew that tonight was the night that he would truly open up and tell Colleen everything. He had only confided a piece of the truth to her. Terence had only told Colleen that he'd been hurt as a little boy. But he had never gone into detail. Tonight, that was about to change.

The couple got undressed for bed, and Terence snuggled Colleen in the crook of his arms. He then opened up to go back in time to that horrible day in his life. "I was about six or seven years old, and I was in bed when I thought I heard my mother crying. So I went to investigate. All I did was ask my mother what was wrong when she started yelling at me. She shouted at the top of her lungs, 'It's all your fault. It's all your fault.' What's my fault? I wondered."

"Did she ever tell you?" Colleen bit in.

Terence shrugged—caught in his memory. "To this day, Colleen, I don't know what I did. But, I apologized. That didn't matter to her. She kept blaming me for something. I said to myself, my room was cleaned and my toys were all packed away. So, I started crying, and I begged my mother to stop crying. But she didn't want to hear it."

Colleen turned her body around until she met him eye to eye. Anger blazed. "Terence, don't say it."

Terence placed his hand over her lips. "Shh . . . Let me do this, Colleen. I've never told a soul, but I have to let this out."

Colleen nodded. Terence gathered his courage. "She scared me, Colleen. I'd never seen my mother that way before. I couldn't help it—I peed my pants. When she saw that, she called me stupid and she . . ."

Terence heard Colleen's bellow of outrage, but she said nothing. She pushed herself to a sitting position and reached over to turn on the lamp on the nightstand. When she patted her legs, Terence rested his head on her lap and continued. "She hit me. It was like she'd gone crazy because she pummeled my body with her fists." He couldn't help but cringe then.

"Oh my, goodness," Colleen found her tongue. She sobbed. "I can't believe she did that to you." Her anger was palpable.

"Hush . . . It's okay, Colleen. I'm over it now."

"What happened to you after that?"

Terence needed to see her face. He rose to a sitting position. "I figure that I must have been unconscious because I woke up in my bed. My mother had a cloth—I remember it was white with yellow ducks on it—well, she used that to wash my bruises. The next day, Colleen, she was so nice to me. She bought me candy and snacks. She told me it had all been a bad dream and told me it would never happen again. But it did. It became a pattern. She'd beat me one day, and then hug me the next."

Terence gulped. He held out his right arm. "Remember this birth mark?"

Colleen's eyes widened as the sordid truth sank in.

"My mother burned me with an iron."

"She should be in jail!"

Terence could see the venom in Colleen's eyes. Tears spilled.

His own eyes blurred. "No, she's my mother. Colleen, I'm not telling you this to excuse my actions because I know there is no justification for what I did to you. I just need you to know more about me and how I got this way. This is about me—not my mother." He needed her to understand that and felt better when he saw her nod. "I never told a soul about the abuse. As I got older, I thought

I'd put it all behind me. So, it wasn't until you hit me—and let me tell you, you pack a mean punch—that I had a rude awakening." He chuckled and scratched his chin at his slight jest. "But now that my past is hitting me in the face, it's like it's always there. I have been praying about it. But, Colleen, I think that I'm beginning to hate my mother."

Terence voiced that last comment in a hushed tone.

Colleen wiped the tears that had been running down her cheeks before pulling her body nearer to his to comfort him.

"Terence," Colleen said, "I know that you don't hate your mother, but she did a terrible thing. I think that you two just need to talk and bring everything out in the open."

"No," Terence returned, "I just don't think I can do that. Ever since I remembered, I find that I don't even want to talk to her. That's why I honestly didn't mind not going to her house this Thanksgiving. I would've felt like a hypocrite, smiling in her face, when I'm not sure how I feel about what she did to me."

"I understand," Colleen stated, "But you need to confront your mother. You can't keep these feelings buried inside. Your traumatic, dysfunctional childhood made you like a puppet on a string when it came to your mother. Terence, you need to let her know that you remember."

"But what if she denies everything?" Terence wondered. "Then it's my word against hers."

"I know you're not lying," Colleen persisted. "The way you broke down and begged me not to hit you was surreal. As I held you that night, all I could think was that something must have happened in your past to make you hit me. And now, I know why. Your mother abused you. She still has a tight control over you. It's like you're her pet, instead of her son. She's not letting that leash go."

He hated the metaphor she used, but it captured his relationship with his mother to a tee. "I hate to agree," Terence replied, "but you're right. My mother has dictated everything I have ever done in my life. It wasn't until you that things became different."

Terence shifted his body to face his wife and said, "You changed that, Colleen. You were the only thing that I truly wanted and fought her for."

Colleen offered Francine a pitiful defense. "Maybe your mother is just lonely. I think she devoted so much of herself to you that she finds it hard to believe that you're grown now and have your own life."

"I don't know," Terence said. He played with her chest and ogled her natural response. "I'm so glad that you've given me another chance, Colleen. I don't know what I'd ever do without you. My mother was like my best friend until you. But now, you're my best friend, and you're the best friend a person could ever have."

"You'll have to confront her one day, Terence," Colleen advised her husband. "You and your mother need to talk and deal with your past, or maybe seek professional counseling. You might find she's this way because she's never truly forgiven herself for what she did to you. You both need to resolve this as soon as possible."

"Hmm, hmm, I will, Miss Psychologist," Terence mumbled, somewhat distracted. His lips had found her delicious ear. He heard Colleen's sigh and continued on that trend. He knew she was still talking, but Terence wasn't really listening to what she had to say anymore. So he simply agreed with whatever she said.

That same night, Francine put away the leftovers in her refrigerator and began washing up the dirty dishes. She had actually had a decent time tonight with Bishop

Greenfield. Francine had invited him over and had cooked a smaller meal for two. They played cards and talked, so the evening had been enjoyable, even though Francine missed her son.

This was the first Thanksgiving that she had ever spent away from him. Bishop Greenfield urged her to call and make peace with Terence. For a split second, Francine considered calling Terence to apologize for her rash behavior. Then almost instantly, she decided against it. She was not about to let Terence know how much he affected her. She would freeze him out. He was the son, and *he* should be the one seeking her forgiveness. Not the other way around.

Chapter Twenty-five

"There you are. Working—as usual."

Michael leaned against the entrance to Keith's office and wagged his finger in his direction. Keith gave him a perfunctory "What's up?" nod before returning to his work. Undeterred, his brother entered his office with the speed of a whirlwind. He plopped down in the chair across from Keith's desk. His excitement was visible. Keith put down his pen and gave him his undivided attention.

"I just got off the phone with Karen. She's moving in with Arnold Bugle. Guess what? She is packing as we speak. Hallelujah! And I've got more good news. I went to Tiffany's and found the perfect ring."

Keith's heart froze. He picked up his pen with deliberate ease because he needed to grab hold of something. With a practiced calm he did not feel, Keith repeated, "Ring?"

"Yes, I bought a ring. I'm going to ask Gina to marry me."

Jealousy pierced his heart. He refused to believe what he was hearing. Michael was going to ask his Gina to marry him. "What?" he stammered, hoping that he hadn't heard right.

"I said," Michael repeated, with excitement, "I'm going to ask Gina to marry me this New Year's Eve. I plan to fly her to Paris and ask her on top of the Eiffel Tower."

He knew that he had to be happy for his brother, but he wasn't. How could he be when he was in love? "Isn't it a bit too soon for such grandiose plans? And isn't Paris hours ahead of us? How're you going to swing that?"

"I'm not worried about that," Michael said, dismissively waving his hands. "It'll all work itself out. That's what I have an executive secretary for—to make it happen, work out all the kinks. What I'm sure of is how I feel. When I'm with her, the earth shakes." Michael blushed at his poetic phrase.

Keith swiveled his chair so his back faced his brother. He needed a moment to compose himself. "What about Gina?" Keith asked as he turned around in slow motion. His insides ripped apart. Gina and Michael . . . Gina and Michael married, and with him as the best man. He would have to stand there and watch them tie the knot. Kiss. The whole nine yards. *I can't do it.*

You don't have a choice. Keith grappled with his conflicting emotions. Agitated, Keith jumped to his feet. His airways felt clogged, and he needed to walk. He saw Michael waver.

"Well, she hasn't really said much about how she feels, you know. Not in words, anyway. But I do know that she loves me. She's just one of those people who seems to have a hard time vocalizing her feelings."

Keith argued. "Maybe that's one good reason why you should wait."

"Yeah," Michael sounded unsure of himself now. "I really value your opinion, and you know women—you have that knack. Now that I'm thinking about it, Gina's never said how she felt. I'm not trying to buy a twenty-five thousand dollar engagement ring and face possible rejection, but I'm going to put myself out there. She's worth it."

Keith watched the myriad emotions sweep across his brother's face. He felt guilty. He knew that he'd thrown a monkey wrench in Michael's plans because of his own selfishness. He suppressed the feelings of turbulent jealousy whirling around his insides. Keith couldn't handle seeing a rock on Gina's hand. His mind needed time to assimilate. His heart was another story altogether. It would never recover.

However, Keith would stand by his brother's side—just not right now. It was too soon.

"But, you do think that Gina's the one for me, right?" Michael questioned, interrupting his thoughts. "I mean, I'm not making a mistake wanting her as my wife."

Keith spoke from his heart. He reached over and picked up the small box and studied the ring. Then he slid it across the desk to Michael's hands. "Any man would be happy to have a woman like Gina in his life." *Any man, like me.*

"Yeah," Michael joked, "Even you."

Keith gulped at his brother's jest. Had he just read his mind? If Michael only knew how close to the truth he was. "Yeah," Keith said halfheartedly, even though he felt miserable.

If only he'd gone with Michael to Terence's wedding. He would have met Gina first. He would be the one who was engaged. No, he would have eloped. There's no way he would have waited this long to claim her as his wife. Michael had shown more restraint than he would have.

"Life was meant for living. I love her so much that I'm going to put myself out there. Love means taking a chance. I'm going to ask her to marry me."

No matter how hard he tried, Keith couldn't conjure up genuine joy. He functioned and said and did the right things, but every day for eleven days, he waited for a phone call from Gina or Michael to share the good news.

Then Eve waited until the day before New Year's to drop her news that she was moving in with Bass. He felt relieved to close that chapter of his life, but that left him dateless to his firm's ball. Each year the partners threw an over-the-top celebration, and it was a tacit rule that you attended.

Gina. He could ask her. She wasn't engaged, yet.

Michael. His brother wouldn't go for that.

Keith considered several women who would gladly fill in. No. A sister might read too much into a simple date, and he liked being drama free.

Keith was torn. He didn't think Gina would turn him down—but Michael.

Never had anything, or anyone, made him question his loyalty. Plus, Michael planned to ask for her hand in marriage. To ask her out would thwart his brother's plans, and it would be a low blow—the lowest of the low.

But even knowing this wasn't enough to deter him. His heart was doing the talking. He just needed Gina, like he needed to breathe. He'd ask. Leave it up to her.

"Michael told me he has big plans for us, but we aren't leaving until near midnight. So, yes, I'll go with you, since he'll be settling his affairs he said. He did promise that we'd ring in the New Year together." Gina ended the call. She looked at her cell phone. What had she just done? How was she going to explain this to Michael? She twisted her lips and thought. Michael trusted her.

Usually, she was deserving of a man's trust. "But not this time, Michael," she confessed. This time she fell short. Her good sense evaporated when it came to Keith. She was putty. Her hormones spun out of control.

Even now, just thinking of him made her palms sweaty and her heart thump like a drum. Maybe she should call Keith and back out.

No.

She'd go with Keith. Michael wouldn't find out. Her telltale heart raced as her conscience raged war. Desire won out.

Thoughts she'd suppressed surfaced. She hadn't dared to think about Keith's lips pressed against hers. She touched her chest. Keith stirred up a secret passion within her that just excited her and made her feel so . . . so alive.

But, she cared for Michael. She'd slept with him more than once. But she held back. That secret part of her remained hidden—a part she didn't know how to release or express. Maybe if Keith wasn't in the picture, she would've been able to open up with Michael.

Maybe. Maybe not.

Her cell buzzed.

"Gina, I think I can move up our meeting time tomorrow because I really want to be there to kiss you when the clock hits twelve."

"No!" Realizing her too strong reaction, Gina mellowed out. "I mean, I've got beauty appointments, ugh, and . . ." She couldn't continue the deceit.

Michael chortled. "Okay, I understand. Our plans stand. I can't wait for tomorrow, baby." She heard him kiss her through the phone.

That was so unlike him. Gina laughed. "See you then."

Gina knew Michael was in love with her. He said it often enough. He dropped not-so-subtle hints about settling down, and his persistence increased.

Michael was a good man. She couldn't lose him.

She would keep her date with Keith. It was time to explore these feelings and put them in proper perspective. She and Michael had something good. She sizzled for Keith, but that attraction would fade.

Wouldn't it?

Chapter Twenty-six

Ugh! Please. Get a room.

If they were going to maul each other like that in public, then they should've just stayed home. Francine looked out of her window and spied her son and his wife making out—hugging and kissing like lovebirds.

She grimaced in disgust at their public display; then she turned away from the window and folded her arms.

That girl was turning her son into a sick sex-starved puppy. Maybe Colleen was addicted to it and was now dragging her son down that immoral and unseemly road. He was going to be appointed as a minister in February, and that hussy had him behaving like a commoner in broad daylight!

Francine wouldn't be surprised if they did "it" in the daytime, all the time. Colleen didn't appear to have any shame about her. But, Francine plastered a smile on her face as she saw the couple finally emerge from their car. She could be civil to the gal, especially since she had a surprise due any minute.

She suffered a brief moment of doubt . . . until they entered her home.

"Hey, Mom. Thanks for having us."

The paltry greeting her son gave her was reason enough to stiffen her backbone. Where was the usual bouquet of flowers and New Year's gift? Last year, she'd gotten tickets to see *The Color Purple* on Broadway.

But this year, she was looking at her bare hands. Well, she wasn't having it. She would go ahead with her plans and would prove Colleen a fraud. Colleen could never love Terence more than his own mother.

Well, Colleen and Terence's love and marriage were about to suffer a major shakedown and Francine would be right there to help her son pick up the pieces, as any good mother would.

Gina and Keith entered the hall together. They made a dynamic couple. She noticed how all the other women were checking Keith out, and she subconsciously claimed her turf by moving closer to him.

Gina looked at Keith and realized that he had caught on to what she had done. He didn't say anything but tentatively reached out to take her hand. She put her hand in his and felt the heat of some envious glares. She had no right staking a claim on Keith when he was now free to play the field. Keith had told her about Eve's leaving to be with Bass.

Gina privately thought that Eve was out of her mind— or blind—or stupid. Keith was gorgeous. He had the mannerisms, etiquette, and drive, to match his good looks. She didn't understand how another woman could just pass that up.

Gina looked at Keith. The brother was just plain fine. He filled out his tuxedo as if it were sewn onto him. When she first saw him, she'd forgotten how to breathe. If she were prone to drooling, she would have. But instead, she had gulped and prayed that she would make it through the night without doing something dumb like making a pass at her man's brother.

***

Keith liked the feel of Gina's hand in his. He too was staking his claim. He had noticed a few men who were checking out Gina's generous assets outlined in the gown that she was wearing. It was black and silky, and she was wearing a pair of shoes that highlighted her pretty little purple toes. Those shoes should have been patented for exclusive use in the privacy of her home. They were just too hot for words.

Keith imagined Gina dressed in those shoes in her bedroom, and he felt a huge pang of envy. Michael was going to take a trip to paradise tonight. Keith closed his eyes to bring his jealousy under control. He vowed that he would enjoy this night with Gina; then he would let her go. He had to. Michael wanted to marry her.

Keith knew that he needed to jump out there and start dating again. That would divert him. Then he felt Gina close her fingers around his, and he turned to her with a smile. He was kidding himself.

They found their places and sat down to eat some of the appetizers. The deejay was very good. He had started to spin some slow jams and the air filled with thoughts of love and romance. Keith led her to the dance floor.

She asked, "Do you think this is a good idea?"

Keith put two of his fingers over her lips to silence her. He didn't want to question anything tonight. He merely wanted to ride these sensations as far as he could. He drew her close and reveled in the feel of her in his arms. She felt so small and yet so right. Keith drew in her scent and bent over to nuzzle the top of her head. Gina's body arched into his, and she moved in tune with him. Keith closed his eyes and began humming along to the music.

Gina was so close to Keith that she could feel him breathing in and out. When he started humming to the music, the sounds reverberated through her body. Gina could feel herself responding to him and the atmosphere. Tonight was a night for people in love. The deejay transitioned into another slow jam. Gina and Keith continued moving.

As their bodies got used to each other, they adjusted into an even more intimate position. One of the other lawyers in Keith's firm tried to cut in, but Keith turned him down flat.

Gina was shocked but flattered. "That wasn't nice," she chided.

"I'm not known for being nice," Keith countered. "He can have you when I'm done and that may never happen. That's what Rafael gets for trying to interrupt my groove."

"That's chauvinistic!" Gina said, with a laugh. Keith was so blunt at times.

"I didn't say that I wasn't chauvinistic either," Keith replied. Then he drew Gina back into his embrace. He moved his hips suggestively that left no doubt in Gina's mind that he was feeling the same way that she was.

They continued dancing until the music died down. Then they returned to their seats in a sweat. Moments later, the bosses began an overview of the year and the progress that had been made.

Keith was awarded with a plaque for his hard work for the year, particularly on the Marshall case. He received a standing ovation.

Gina's chest swelled with pride for him, knowing that Keith had been surprised. He clearly was not expecting the award, and he stumbled through the appropriate thank-you speech.

She was glad to have been there to share this moment with him. She knew it had to feel good to be recognized and admired by so many of the other professionals in his field. Keith came over to her and placed the plaque in her hands. He was beaming.

"Vanessa would've been proud of you," Gina said softly, smiling from ear to ear.

"Thank you. Hearing you say that means a lot to me."

She checked her phone and saw that she'd missed a call from Michael. However, instead of leaving a message, he'd sent her a text. Honey, something's come up. A small emergency. Need another hour or so. Gina exhaled with relief and quickly replied with a No prob. Take your time. If she were honest with herself, she would admit that she'd barely given Michael a second thought. She was glad for the extra time with Keith.

"Everything all right?" Keith nudged her shoulder.

"Oh yeah," Gina nodded. "Michael needs more time for this big surprise he's planned."

"Oh," he smiled.

Just then, the music blared. This time, the deejay was playing jams like the Cha, Cha, Cha, and the Electric Slide.

"Ready for round two?" Keith asked.

"I'm more than ready," she purred.

Gina and Keith joined in with the crowd. They stayed on the dance floor getting down to every type of music the deejay threw at them. When the calypso and reggae came on, Keith held Gina's leg, gyrating his hips as close to her as he could. Gina surprised him with a few tantalizing moves of her own.

Before they knew it, it was time for the countdown. Gina suddenly felt a little nervous. She hadn't thought about it. The *kiss* that usually followed the countdown. The two looked at each other as time seemed to stand still. They could hear people shouting "Eight! Seven! Six! . . . One!" Gina and Keith shouted, "Happy New Year!!"

"You only live once!" Impulsively, Keith grabbed her and crushed his lips against hers.

Gina felt powerless to resist. She thirsted for it. He started kissing her as if he were a man who had been starving for days. Helpless to resist, she opened her mouth. Keith devoured her, exploring every hidden recess of that delicious cavern.

Gina challenged him when she returned his kiss with every bit of passion that she possessed.

Keith moaned and moved closer.

Gina pulled away, breaking contact. "Whew," she exhaled.

The crowd around them was still cheering, kissing, and celebrating.

Gina and Keith looked at each other mesmerized at what they had just done and what they had shared. The kiss had been a scorcher and a shock to both of their senses. They had both fantasized about it but never for one second imagined that it would feel like that.

Gina's tongue came out of her mouth to lick her lips. She stepped back and blinked several times. "I c . . . I can't do this," she stammered.

"I know. You're right."

"We'd better go," Gina said.

"Yeah."

"I feel like Cinderella," Gina exclaimed. Inside, she was dying . . . dreading the night to end.

"I know what you mean. It's midnight and now I have to return you back to your rightful owner."

"Partner," Gina corrected.

"Yeah," Keith conceded. "You missed your calling because nothing ever passes you by."

"Except you."

Chapter Twenty-seven

Arrghh—when will he learn?

Michael couldn't for the life of him figure out why Karen would choose New Year's Eve to return to his place. She claimed she needed to get something she'd left behind, which sounded convenient *and* suspicious to him—especially since she knew about his big plans for Gina. The woman was plain diabolical.

Why didn't he keep his big mouth closed? But when she'd called him earlier that day to wish him a Happy New Year, suffering from a case of verbal diarrhea—he'd blabbed about asking Gina to marry him.

As soon as he said that, Karen had been adamant that she had to get her forgotten item—one she refused to divulge even at his insistence. Why he'd given her permission was beyond him.

He had just gotten ready to leave Keith's when Karen called, screaming, at about nine p.m. "Mikey, you've got to hurry up and get over here."

Hearing her frantic tone, he asked, "What happened?"

"I went into the bathroom to get my—ah—item, and when I reached up, somehow I pulled too hard and broke the showerhead."

Uh-oh. He didn't need this now. "Why didn't you call me? What did you need to get?"

"I didn't want to bug you; besides, I thought I could fix it myself. But, I think I damaged the entire thing. Mikey, hurry! There's water everywhere."

Michael had rushed over to his place to find his bathroom in an unmentionable state. *Will this woman never fail to cost me money?* "Why are you doing this to me?"

Water was flowing everywhere. He attempted to reach up to stop the flow and had only managed to get both him and Karen soaking wet.

"Great. Just great!" Michael ran to the kitchen, opened the miscellaneous drawer, and hunted for some duct tape. "Bingo." He snatched the huge roll. He had to use almost the entire thing to stop the water from running. Karen had already used up a roll of paper towels to stuff the hole. It was a huge mess.

"What did you have to get that was so important?" he lashed out.

"This." Karen held up the tiny piece of underwear. "On a whim, I'd left it wrapped around the showerhead for Gina to see. But then I had second thoughts, and we'd come too far for me to resort to a childish prank. Especially since I'm with Arthur, and well . . ." Karen stopped. She gave him a sheepish look, holding up the "item" for him to see. "Sorry. Old habits die hard."

With a deep groan, Michael picked up his cell and called for a plumber. He didn't even bother to answer her. He couldn't even be mad. She was trying to atone for her stupid stunt, but, as usual, at his expense. He rolled his eyes.

Together they waited for almost two hours for a plumber to arrive to try to fix the damage. He'd told her to leave, but Karen's attack of conscience made her stay put. She wouldn't budge. "Not until it's all fixed again," she'd declared.

Hiring a plumber on New Year's Eve was no easy feat, but the front-desk clerk knew someone. He looked at his watch. The hours had just flown by. He'd finally had to text Gina to tell her he would be late.

Lucky for him, she'd been real cool about it. Not many women were as understanding as she was. He couldn't resist eyeing the time again. He sure hoped he made it out of this mess before Gina arrived. He and Karen were still wrapped up in huge bathrobes waiting for their clothes to dry. He didn't think to put on more suitable clothes. Besides, he had practically moved everything he owned to his brother's house.

Michael sighed, not knowing how he always managed to get himself into these kinds of jams. Karen put the television on, and the two listened to the countdown and rang in the New Year. She reached over, pecked him on the cheek, and said, "Happy New Year, Mikey. Please believe that I'm sorry."

Michael relented. "It's okay, Karen. I know you didn't do this on purpose." He hugged her in return and opened a bottle of champagne, resolute to make the best of a bad situation. They even shared another glass with the plumber.

At precisely one twenty-three a.m., the plumber proclaimed the job finished. Michael investigated the shower and was amazed to see everything looked as good as new. He could barely tell that it had been completely unhinged a few hours ago.

Michael gave the plumber a hefty tip and walked him to the door. *One down and one to go!* He was extremely hopeful. He began to spread out the trappings for his romantic rendezvous.

"Let me at least help you," Karen offered. Once she helped him get everything ready, she gathered her things to take off to meet Arthur, who was now waiting downstairs.

Michael hugged her. "Good luck. I wish you happiness." *Now, get out of here,* he thought.

Karen bid him a warm "Good-bye" and opened the door.

She came face to face with Gina.

"Who was that?" Gina asked Michael with a dangerous glint in her eye.

He looked at her with a comical expression of disbelief. "Why didn't you call?" He blurted out the first thought that came to his mind.

"I did. Now answer the question." Gina tapped her feet.

"That was Karen," Michael answered lamely. He saw the look on Gina's face. Apparently that answer wasn't good enough. He sighed, knowing that he would have to give Gina a more in-depth explanation. He went to pour himself another glass of champagne and began talking. He told Gina about Karen needing a place to stay and how he'd agreed to let her live there until she got back on her feet. He made sure to point out that she'd moved out. He couldn't surmise her reaction, so he just kept talking.

Gina remained silent until he had finished his story. "So, that's why you've never invited me to spend the night here," she affirmed.

Her calm tone put Michael at ease. "Yeah—well, no, at first, yes—but, I was mostly at Keith's house."

Gina pointed her finger as she paraphrased, "So, let me see if I have this right. Your girlfriend—no, excuse me, ex-girlfriend who moved out, came by tonight—on New Year's Eve, I might add—to get something, broke your showerhead—and, blah-blah-blah."

Underneath her calm demeanor was a seriously ticked-off woman.

"Yeah," he answered.

To Gina, he looked and sounded like a buffoon. "I just want to know one thing. Since you've met me, have you slept with her?"

"Ahh . . . Once. I did once, and it never happened again after that because I—"

Gina lifted her hand. "Save it." She gathered her coat and quickly plucked her cell phone out of her coat pocket and speed dialed Keith to see how far away he was. A thought occurred to her. Gina quickly disconnected the call. Keith was Michael's brother. She couldn't call him. He probably knew all along. All this time, he must have known and had said nothing.

Gina headed through the door and ran down the hallway.

"You're leaving!" Michael shouted the obvious.

"You finally caught on!" Gina shouted back and pressed the elevator button. Thank goodness the elevator was right there and opened up for her instantly. Michael was now fast on her heels. Gina didn't hesitate. She just jumped right in.

As the door closed in Michael's face, she showed him the crude finger. That summed up all that she had to say to him. She never planned to rest eyes on Michael Ward ever again.

Gina caught a cab to her house. She paid the driver and entered her home. She could see her message button beeping but determinedly ignored it. Gina looked at her cell and saw that Michael had called quite a few times. She noticed that there was even a phone call from Keith's cell phone.

But for once she was able to ignore it. At this time, Gina did not want to hear anything from either one of them. On the ride over she had started to wonder if the two of them had been in cahoots all along. Maybe she was part of some sick bet between them, and they each wanted to see who could bag her first. Maybe she was all a game to them. She honestly didn't know what to think.

Gina could feel herself begin to defrost and hurt was taking center stage. She sniffed her nose several times and kept her lips tightly closed to keep from crying. She felt betrayed by Michael and Keith. She'd given each of them her trust and a piece of her heart and this was what she had been dished.

Imagine, that for once in her life, she had bought the reformed dog story—hook, line, and sinker. When had her natural-born cynicism disappeared? She had been too busy being taken in by their magnetism to think straight.

She sighed, sat down, and miserably looked down at her dress. This was indeed a Cinderella night because her Prince Charming had just turned into a huge pumpkin, and the other brother was definitely a rat.

Her doorbell rang.

Concerned, she peered through her curtains to see Keith standing on her doorstep. He saw her. She knew that he saw her, but Gina had already decided that she was not going to answer the door. Stubbornly, she let it ring.

Stubbornly, Keith kept up the insistent peal. "I'll keep pressing it until you let me in," Keith said through the door.

Fine. Gina went and opened the door. He used his body width to ensure that she let him in. The big oaf. She had to step aside so that he could fit in her doorway. She was too angry for words.

Once he had some room to work with, Keith barged into her home. He took off his coat and sat on her sofa. Gina sat down, but she did not utter a single word.

Keith could feel the heat emanating from Gina's upright body. She was way past angry. "Michael called me, and I knew that I had to come by. I couldn't sleep until I knew for sure that you were okay.

Gina raised her eyebrows to let him know that she was okay. She still did not speak.

Keith sighed, knowing that this was going to be hard. But still he pressed on. "Gina, I know that you're understandably angry at both of us, but I just wanted you to know that Michael really does love you. He wasn't trying to play you at all. That whole thing with Karen is way in the past, and things between them were over, just the way that he said."

Gina's hissing teeth let Keith know that she was not impressed with his or Michael's explanations. Michael had called him upset, to the point of tears. Keith did all that he could to calm him down. He had been overwrought at the thought of losing Gina. It was only when Keith assured him that he would try to get through to Gina that Michael had simmered down.

Keith knew that of the two of them, he had a better chance of getting in her house than his brother did. So far, that was all he had managed to do. Gina was a suppressed mass of extreme anger.

"Gina," Keith said softly. He dropped his voice, hoping that his tone would help in soothing her ruffled feathers. "You know how I feel about you. I wouldn't lie to you about this." He saw that she had involuntarily leaned closer to hear him. So he continued, "Gina, I am in love with you. I only have your best interest at heart. I wouldn't have let my brother near you if I didn't think that he had genuine feelings for you. It's hard for me to admit this, but Michael even talked of marriage."

Gina's mouth dropped open.

Okay, now she seemed a little more receptive. He dared to reach out his hands to touch her. He had to make some sort of physical contact with her. His heart was breaking to see her so hurt and confused. "I know that you probably don't want to believe me," Keith said with such gentleness that she finally made eye contact with him. He could see the tears in her eyes that she allowed to fall.

"But if you don't know anything, you must know that I love you, Gina. I wouldn't lie to you. I wouldn't hurt you.

Believe me, the way I feel about you, I would not have let my own brother deceive you. He loves you, babe. We both do."

Gina reached her hands over to caress Keith's cheeks. He leaned in and gave a tight hug. She relaxed against him.

"I love you too, Keith," Gina whispered. To Keith, that admission had come from her soul. It had been torn from her very being.

Keith tensed at her declaration and withdrew from the hug. "Gina, what're you saying?"

"I said," Gina gulped, "I love you, Keith, and I know that you wouldn't hurt me. Tonight made me realize that I've got to stop kidding myself. I want you, Keith. I guess I should be glad that Karen was there, because I wasn't ready to talk to Michael about marriage. Not tonight. Not after the kiss we shared."

"I know," Keith soothed. He drew her close to him and gently rested his chin on her head. This time her hair spelled like apricots. "Gina, the way I'm feeling now, I know I've got no business being here. If I was a loyal brother, then I would leave right now. But my heart has a mind of its own. And it's overjoyed that you love me." As he spoke he shifted, until he was whispering in her ear.

Gina confessed, "I feel so guilty."

"I know," Keith comforted her by rubbing her shoulders. "Imagine how I must feel. But, Gina, we cannot continue like this. We have to do something about it. We have to make a decision tonight."

"What kind of a decision?" Gina hedged and pulled out of his arms. She addressed him with troubled eyes. "I'm horrified at the thought of hurting Michael in any way, even though he's hurt me. Basically, I would be helping to destroy a strong bond between you and your brother."

Keith's heart spoke for him. "I know the ramifications, but you are a risk I'm willing to take. I'd like to hope that, in time, Michael will find it in his heart to forgive me. But the way I feel about you, I'm willing to take that chance. Are you?"

Gina looked into Keith's eyes. *What would she decide?* He wished he could read her mind.

Then she lifted her chin. "I can't deny the passion you ignite within me. But, I love Michael too, and I can't bear the thought of hurting him."

Keith groaned. He kissed her. Endearments poured from his heart to his lips. Their ardent kisses increased as they engaged in a passion-filled tango.

You know you should stop. Don't do this, Keith.

No . . . No . . . For once in my life—

Keith blocked every single negative thought out of his mind. His love outweighed every rational thought. He unleashed all of his pent-up emotions, confident that Gina would be able to handle them. Without breaking the kiss, Keith picked her up in his powerful arms and carried her up the stairs to her bedroom. He entered Gina's room and gently placed her to stand, so that he could look at her.

"Gina, are you sure about this?" Keith wanted to make sure because there would be no stopping him from this point.

Gina nodded her head and unzipped her dress.

Keith just stared at her, taking in everything that he had only previously imagined. She was a vision. He reached out his hands to touch her shoulders and to draw her closer to him. Placing a kiss on her neck, he promised, "I'm going to love you with everything I have to give. All night long."

Chapter Twenty-eight

She clicked her heels three times . . .

Colleen was ready to go home. Francine had been unbearably nice to her, and it had been ingratiating. She had had to grit her teeth to keep from being catty. Francine had been as sweet as sugar in her presence, which aroused her suspicions. The old bat was up to something.

Whatever it was, she knew she wouldn't like it. If she was a gambling woman, she'd bet all the money in her purse on that.

Then, at about eleven thirty p.m., the doorbell rang.

Colleen wondered who would be coming to Francine's house at such a late hour. Francine jumped up and rushed to answer the door.

Curious, Colleen looked at Terence to see if he had a clue. He shrugged, signifying that he had no idea who the mystery guest was that his mother had expected.

Francine entered with a woman close on her heels. Terence's indrawn breath made her focus on him. His eyes were widened with shocked recognition.

Colleen leaned forward to get a better glimpse of the woman. She was breathtakingly beautiful . . . a tall, majestic, dark-skinned beauty.

In her element, Francine didn't even acknowledge Colleen. She addressed her son, "Terence, you remember Dana White, don't you?"

"Terence!" Dana squealed with a distinct Jamaican accent and jumped into his arms. "It's been a long time since I've seen you."

Terence visibly paled at the younger woman's exuberant greeting. He extricated himself from her arms and said, "Hi, Dana."

Dana flung her arms around his neck. "Aren't you glad to see me?"

Colleen was tired of being the fly on the wall. "Terence, aren't you going to introduce us?" She asked the question with her eyebrows raised in inquiry. For some reason, her heart began to pound. Dana was probably an old girlfriend. Colleen fiddled with her ring finger—for solace. She wouldn't get jealous, not her. She who has the ring has the power.

"Uh, yes," Terence stammered, again dodging out of Dana's arms. "Dana, this is my wife, Colleen."

"Wife?" Dana exclaimed. She stood up with her arms akimbo. "You never told me you had a wife."

Dana was acting as if Terence was her man. Colleen's heart hammered as she grappled to figure out the scene unfolding before her eyes. She stole a glance at Francine who remained quiet.

"When you came to Jamaica, you never mentioned a wife to me."

"Wait a minute," Colleen interjected. She addressed her husband. "Terence, I thought that you've only been to Jamaica once and that was with me on our honeymoon."

"Colleen," Terence beseeched her, "give me a chance to explain—"

Dana cut him off, "And, perhaps you need to explain that to me too."

Colleen trounced over to the other woman and got up in her face. "My husband owes you no explanation."

Dana backed up, but she didn't back down. "Yes . . . Yes, him do. After all, he was the one who approached me and sweet-talked me into giving him some; then he just up and disappeared. If his mother hadn't found me, I don't know what I would've done. I mean, I thought it was love at first sight."

Colleen was at a loss for words. Was this woman saying that she and Terence had slept together? Colleen foamed at the mouth, but she sought to remain in control. She tapped her feet and counted to ten. That didn't work. *Lord, I need you. I need you, now.* "Terence, aren't you going to say something?" Colleen's voice escalated.

Wait a minute. Her brain caught up with Dana's words. The ugly truth sank in.

"Is this woman saying that you slept with her on our honeymoon?" Colleen screamed at the mute man standing before her. She shook her head in denial. "That couldn't be right."

Colleen kept her eyes pinned on Terence. He was going to give her some answers. He broke contact first and pointed at Francine, who gloated. He accused her, "You did this! You just couldn't stand to see me finally happy! I confided something to you and you . . ."

"So, it's true," Colleen broke in with a sob. She marched over to him and slapped him hard. Riled, she grabbed onto his shirt. "You hypocrite! You're slime. Claiming to be a man of God. I can't believe you would do this. You're like a dog returning to his vomit—" Colleen looked at him with contempt. Through gritted teeth, she snarled, "I have no words for you," before stepping back.

"Is it me she calling vomit?" Dana piped in and jumped into Colleen's face.

Colleen stopped her cold. "You'd better get out of my face, or you'll be picking your teeth up off the floor." She knew she was saved, but she meant every word. It was eye for an eye time, and she wasn't going to turn the other cheek—except to slap it. Wisely, Dana retreated to a chair in the far corner.

Francine found her voice and ranted, "Keep your trampy paws off my son, you . . . You ingrate."

Colleen sneered at her mother-in-law, but didn't bother to dignify her with a response. Spent, her tears flowing like a dam that had broken loose, Colleen clamped her jaws shut, but her resolve broke. "I loved you. I trusted you. I gave you the best of me." She held her hands out toward him, "And this is how you repay me. I just don't believe it."

Terence took her hands in his and said, "Baby, let me explain."

"No." Colleen shook out of his grasp. "I don't want to hear anything from you. In fact, I don't ever want to lay eyes on you again." Her nose and eyes were now running. Colleen could barely see through her tears, but she knew that she had to get out of there.

Francine watched her with a self-satisfied smile on her face.

"I hope you're happy, you old witch. You finally got what you wanted," Colleen's grief slurred her words. She told Dana, "You're welcome to him, 'cause I don't deal with swine."

Colleen grabbed her bag and flung the door open. She broke her heel on one of the steps and uttered a minor expletive in frustration. Searching for her keys to Terence's car, she unlocked the car door and jumped in. Instead of starting the car, though, Colleen cried from heartache.

From the corner of her eye, Colleen saw Terence coming out of the house. He had her coat in his hands and took the steps two at a time. She did not hesitate. In one fluid motion, she started the car and pressed on the gas.

In her haste, she almost ran a stop sign. The tires screeched as she jammed on the brakes. She heard her phone buzz. Looking at the lighted screen, she saw Terence's grinning face.

She pressed the button to roll down the windows. In one fluid move, she tossed the phone out the window. It landed on the concrete with a satisfying smash.

Chapter Twenty-nine

Terence watched Colleen's car skid and the tires swerve. His heart leapt into his throat, and he clutched his chest. If something happened to her, Terence knew that he would never forgive himself. But he was powerless to stop her. Instead, he prayed, "Lord, please protect her. Don't let anything happen to her." He watched, rooted to the spot, until her car sped out of view.

What have I done? He put his head in his hands and dropped to the ground. He had just lost the only thing that had ever mattered to him.

Colleen had endured a lot at his hands, but asking her to overlook this would simply be asking too much. He let out a huge cry of agony and defeat. He had lost his wife for good this time, and there wasn't anything that he could do about it.

A loud crack filled the air. It was followed by many more popping sounds. Terence looked up at the fireworks and heard all the shouts and festivities as people rang in the New Year.

"Happy New Year, Colleen," Terence brokenly whispered into the air. No, he couldn't let it go down this way.

He still had to try.

He called Colleen and left several messages on her cell phone. He didn't know how long he'd been standing outside his mother's house before he accepted that she wasn't coming back. Defeated, Terence called a cab.

A hand touched his arm. He flinched. "Don't you think you've done enough?"

Francine clutched her chest. "I just wanted to offer you a ride home."

"No, thanks. I called a cab." He cut his eyes at her as he waited. He tapped his feet trying to stay warm as he shivered from the cold.

"You can wait inside."

"I suggest you get away from me, because it's taking everything within me not to strangle you and that woman with my bare hands." He didn't even deign to look at her. His mother spun on her heels and ran inside the house.

Frozen, he said, "Thank you, Lord."

When he made it home, he uttered a low "Hallelujah" when he saw his car in the driveway. Colleen's car was also still there. He sought her out. He saw piles of neatly folded clothes. Some were on the bed, and some were in opened suitcases. Terence panicked at the thought of her leaving, until he realized that it was his clothes that she was packing. "Colleen, please don't do this. Sweetheart, listen to me."

She simply continued her methodical packing without even acknowledging his presence. When she was finished, Colleen had placed all of the things that she could fit into his car until it overflowed with suitcases.

"I love you, Colleen." Terence spoke and declared his love for her until he was blue in the face, and still, his wife hadn't offered a single response. She was like a robot.

Colleen left the room and went into the garage to get his golf clubs and other paraphernalia he had stored in there. Terence didn't even bother to try to stop her. He was reluctant to admit it, but he was actually afraid that Colleen might snap and do something crazy if he interfered with her plans.

Once she was finished, Colleen didn't even glance his way. She simply went up to what was now her room and locked the door. Terence still did not leave. He stood outside the bedroom door wondering if he should use his key, but he was scared of how Colleen might react. For a brief second, he even considered breaking the door down, but he thought better of it. His wife could be a hellcat when riled, and he wasn't even trying to prick her temper in any way.

Then Terence heard what sounded like muffled sobs coming through the door. "Colleen, honey, please let me in," he begged. He banged his head on the door in defeat. His heart started breaking at the sound of Colleen's abject sorrow. Terence knew that she was past listening to any excuses or explanations that he had to give. So he said nothing. He simply left.

Terence checked into a hotel not too far from where he worked. "How am I supposed to go to work tomorrow? I can't manage without her."

His cell phone rang and hope flared in his chest. Colleen.

Quickly, he looked at the caller ID. His shoulders hunched with defeat once he saw his mother's digits looking back at him. He cut his phone off midring. Then, all his hurt, pain, and sorrow catapulted into a huge ball of rage. His chest heaved. He rocked back and forth, stewing. This was all her fault. She meddled too much. Well, he'd had enough.

Terence grabbed his keys and jumped into his car. He was going to give his mother a piece of his mind. A tongue-lashing she deserved. Face-to-face!

The sun had just risen in the sky when Terence swerved in front of his mother's house and screeched to an abrupt halt. His mother had just wrecked his life completely, and he deserved to know why.

Terence pressed on the doorbell until she answered the door. Her eyes dilated in surprise, but she wisely stepped aside. He pushed past but paused when he saw Dana was still there.

His eyes scanned the scene before him—the tea cups and other breakfast items. From the looks of things, the two of them were entertaining, carrying on as if they hadn't smashed his joy to smithereens.

He bunched his fists as fire blew from his nostrils. Terence zoned in on Dana. "Get out."

She didn't move. Well, he was going to toss her out the door on her—

"Dana, could you please walk to the corner store and get me a few items? My son and I need some private time to talk," Francine interjected. She stepped over to the counter, picked up a small notepad and pen, and scribbled a list of miscellaneous items. Francine reached for her Vera Bradley purse—a gift from him—hanging on the back of the chair and retrieved several twenty-dollar bills.

Dana took the list and cash and rudely shoved past Terence. "I ought to scratch your eyes out for the way you're treating me. I am Miss Jamaica, and I left my country and a lot of willing men to come see you."

Terence curled his lips in contempt but by now had calmed enough not to dignify her with a response. As soon as he heard the front door slam, Terence rounded on his mother, "What in God's name were you thinking when you invited that woman here?"

"What do you mean what I was thinking? You were the one who told me about your little escapade," Francine accused. She pointed her index finger at him. "You were the one who got yourself into this mess. Not me."

Terence acquiesced. "Yes, Mother. I did it. I fooled around with another woman while I was on my honeymoon, and stupidly, I called my own mother for guidance and some much-needed advice. Exposing me like this is how you repay me for trusting you?"

"You gave me the ammunition," Francine stubbornly replied without any sign of remorse. "I simply decided to use it."

"On your own son," Terence said miserably. "Mother, how could you? You destroyed my marriage to a wonderful woman."

"A harlot is more like it," Francine scoffed. "Terence, you're about to become a minister, which is your lifelong dream. I did what I thought was in your best interest. Colleen would never have made a good minister's wife."

"And Dana will?" Terence asked with disbelief.

"Of course not," Francine retorted. "That woman would be outrageous. She was only the tool I used to get the job done. Nothing else."

"Listen to you," Terence said with disgust. "Mother, you would use anyone and anything to get what you want. It's always about you and what you want. You would even attack me, your own son, to get your way."

"That's not how it is," Francine denied with a huff. "Terence, you're upset, and you're obviously not thinking straight. You used to agree with me that Colleen was not a pastor's wife."

"Used to, Mother," Terence rebutted. "As in *not anymore*. Colleen's perfect for me. She completes me. She helped me come to terms with a lot of things, Mother. She made me free to be me."

"Free? That woman had you in bondage," Francine countered, spitefully.

"No!" Terence shouted, which was uncharacteristic of him. He was always in control, but he was past the breaking point. He saw his mother's head whip backward in shock.

Francine shouted back. "Listen to you now. This is what Colleen is doing to you. She's changing my good little boy into a raving maniac."

Terence grabbed his mother's arms. "No, Mother, Colleen didn't do anything. You did!"

"Me?" He saw Francine clutch her heart. "What did I do?"

Terence released his mother and took a deep breath. He strove to conquer his swirling emotions and to bring himself under control. He had to be able to carry on a rational conversation with his mother. "Let me start over," Terence said calmly. "Mother, I'm going to be totally honest with you. I don't want to be a minister because deep down, I know that I'm not minister material. I cheated on my wife on my honeymoon, for heaven's sake. Does that sound like someone who should be in a leadership position and in God's church? A minister must be blameless."

"Well," Francine insisted, "it was all *her* fault. I put the blame on her shoulders. She drove you to do that. It wasn't your fault."

"Yes, Mother," Terence said, "it was. It was entirely my fault. I was the dirty snake who cheated on a good woman for no reason." Terence sat down having spent a lot of energy. "I was just a coward to let you continually condemn Colleen for my horrible actions. I'm going to contact the bishop later and let him know of my resignation."

"No!" Francine cried. She pleaded with her son, "Don't do that! After all my hard work, you can't back out now. I didn't raise you to be a quitter."

"Are you listening to yourself?" Terence somberly asked his mother. "The pastoral position was *your* dream, not mine. Mother, don't you think it's time for you to take some accountability for *your* actions?"

"What do you mean?" Francine asked, feeling totally lost.

"Well, for starters," Terence answered, "you can take responsibility for what you did to me all those years ago, Mother."

Caught off guard, Francine held her chest and stumbled into the chair. His statement had come from left field and had dropped her on her rear end. She felt as if she'd been sucker punched.

Before she could say anything, Terence recounted all the events from his childhood, and Francine was forced to relive every hideous moment. When Terence was finished, he looked at her expectantly. She knew that he wanted—no—needed—her to confirm and confess. But she couldn't. She couldn't come face-to-face with the person she once was. Francine had done a lot to transform herself, and she wasn't ready to expose herself and divulge anything from her past. If she confirmed his stories as fact, Terence would only have more questions. Questions that she wasn't ready to answer.

So Francine denied everything. "Terence, that story you've concocted is all a figment of your overactive imagination. Or maybe that woman helped you conjure up such a spiteful and hateful story against me."

Terence studied her intently, and she resisted the urge to squirm. She wasn't admitting to anything. He looked her in the eyes. "You know what I just realized? You're not lying to me. You're lying to yourself. You need to believe that you're squeaky clean and innocent, because then, you can hold onto your condescension, putting on airs, and justifying your selfish and nasty actions."

Francine couldn't respond to his sentiment. Instead, she reminded him, "I'm your mother, and no one has ever loved you the way that I have."

She felt his keen disappointment. "Mom, there is no hope for you. You don't want to change. Because if you expect me to believe that you really love me after all your evil machinations, then you're seriously deluded."

Terence left Francine shaken and filled with doubts. She now knew that she had lost her son. She belatedly realized that she hadn't lost him before, when he and Colleen had gotten married. No, it was not until that very moment that she had truly lost Terence. She felt bereft, as if there were now a hole where her heart used to be. His marriage had not precipitated this feeling. Her own selfish and stupid pride had done it.

Francine placed her head in her hands and sobbed.

Chapter Thirty

Here it is.

In a hurry last night, Keith had left his cell phone in its charger. Michael must have been blowing up his phone. He glanced at the clock. It was a little past seven a.m.

He had done well on his word and had made love to Gina throughout the night. He'd left her satiated and asleep. Michael had been the sole reason he'd torn himself from the comfort of her arms.

What was he going to tell his brother? Now that the light of day was setting in, Keith was experiencing second thoughts. He felt guilt that bore down on his shoulders.

He'd never done anything like this before in his life. But he had done it. He had betrayed his very own flesh and blood.

Michael would be beyond hurt, of that there was no doubt. Eventually, his brother might find it in his heart to forgive him, but Keith didn't know if he'd be able to forgive himself.

He looked at the picture he had on the mantle of both he and his brother. He studied the picture intensely. Michael had such a look of absolute love and trust on his face, and he had destroyed that.

Keith bent his head. He reached into his back pocket and took out a picture of Gina that he'd swiped earlier from her coffee table. They had shared an unforgettable night. He looked back and forth between both pictures, indecisive and unsure. "What do I do?"

He loved Gina, of that there was no doubt. She was like water to him. He just had to have her. But what was the price he had to pay?

He felt an urgent need to call his brother. Just to hear his voice. He called Michael's cell phone. It was ringing. Someone answered his telephone.

There was so much chaos on the other end that it took a few minutes for Keith to decipher what was being said. He finally made out that the other person on the end was saying something about a bad accident . . . "A man was driving . . . he crashed into a stop sign . . . was now unconscious . . . Long Island Jewish . . ."

Keith put the pieces together in his mind. *Oh my God! Michael!*

He speed dialed Gina and told her what happened. He then called his mother in Atlanta. She would be on the next flight.

It took a half hour to get from his house to the emergency room at Long Island Jewish. Frantic with worry, he cursed himself with every filthy name that he could think of. If his brother died, he knew that he would never be able to live with himself. He prayed and begged God to spare Michael's life.

When Geraldine "Gerry" Ward entered Michael's hospital room, Keith's arms were wrapped around Gina.

"Keith!"

Keith tensed, recognizing the voice. He broke contact with Gina. *"Mom!"* Then in two swift strides, he ran over to his mother and picked her up and swung her in a huge embrace. She released all her fright with two great sobs before regaining her composure.

Gina retrieved some tissues for Keith's mother, handed them to her, and went over to the window to give them a moment together.

"How is he?" Geraldine asked with a shaky voice.

"He's better than he looks," Keith said. "At least that's what the doctor told us. But come meet Gina."

Keith led his mother over to Gina and performed the necessary introductions. His mother took stock of the other woman.

"I wish that when we had finally met, it would have been under better circumstances," Gerry entreated, putting her hand out.

"Me too," Gina responded tearfully.

Gerry turned toward Michael and cried, "He looks horrible. His face is so puffy that I barely recognize him."

"I know, Mom. Michael's been unconscious since they brought him in and has remained in that state. It's been five hours. The doctors said that he had suffered a tremendous blow to his head because he had not been wearing a seat belt."

Michael was always a safe driver but must have been too consumed with losing Gina to think straight.

Keith left his mother's side and went to stand by the window. Guilt whipped him. He didn't think he could continue living if his brother died. It would be his fault. He'd let his feelings for Gina block out all rational thought and behavior, and he was about to pay a huge price.

He saw Gina left the room and excused himself to join her. His long legs moved with speed to catch up to her. He hugged her tightly, knowing that she was the only other person who could truly understand the torturous emotions raging through his body.

Gina and Keith consoled each other and went into an empty room away from prying eyes and ears. They sat on the bed. Memories assailed them at the same time. Keith stifled a curse word and moved away to lean against the wall, burying his head in his hands.

"I . . ." Gina began. Keith turned to look at her. She stopped and closed her eyes. Then she continued, as tears streamed down her face, "I feel so . . . so . . . On my way here, I couldn't help it. I had to pull over to the side of the road to vomit."

In two strides, Keith was in front of her. He fell to the floor and placed his head in Gina's lap. He felt her place one of her hands on his head and another stroked his cheek in comfort. "I can't lose him," he wailed. He released his pain and soaked Gina's denim skirt with his tears.

"I know," Gina soothed. "Keith, listen to me." She gently lifted his head and made him look at her. Again, she closed her eyes. Keith knew it was because she couldn't look at his guilt-ridden face and bleak eyes, for they reflected the emotions she faced. "It never happened," she whispered. "Do you hear me?"

He shook his head, not understanding. "What are you saying?"

"It never happened," Gina's eyes popped open and pinned him with their intensity. She frantically commanded, "Say it."

Keith looked at the woman that he loved. How could he begin to deny what he felt for her in his heart? "I love you," he said.

"I know you do," Gina replied. She grabbed his face in her hands to capture his attention. "But look what happened. Look what happened. Ugh!" Abruptly, she released him.

He knew that Gina was right. Michael was possibly on his deathbed. It wasn't the time for selfishness. It was time for sacrifice. He hung his head in defeat. Then Keith rose to his knees and cradled Gina's face in his hands. "How can you ask me to do this?" he whispered. "How can you ask me to deny what's in my very core?" He sobbed, but didn't wait for an answer. Instead, he kissed her with passion, telling her good-bye.

Their tears flowed, but this time it was for the love that they knew that they could never have. Not now. A life hung in the balance.

Keith gathered the courage to pull away. His heart ached as if it were being ripped out of his chest. But he knew that it was for the best. He was audacious to even kiss her at a time like this.

Michael needed Gina. She would pull him back to consciousness. He was sure of it. "It never happened," Keith repeated her words, letting her know that he would go along with her demand. Heart-wrenching pain inflicted his very soul.

Gina nodded and stood. She brushed at her skirt and pulled at her white blouse to smooth out the wrinkles. Without another word, she exited into the hall. This time, Keith let her go.

He remained where he was until his mother found him. He felt broken and bruised and sore. He'd just fought the battle of his life, and he'd lost. "Keith, what is it?" she asked. Holding his raw emotions at bay, he snatched his mother and cradled himself in her arms. For a brief moment, he savored the comfort only a mother could give before releasing her to give her a shaky smile.

"There's more going on here, isn't there? I see distress written all over your face. Michael will be all right," Gerry soothed. "God's not ready for him yet." She looked around. "Where did Gina go? I thought she was with you."

He knew that she had seen the two of them embracing when she first entered the room. His mother had put two and two together. Keith looked at his mother with a wide stare. He knew that she knew, but she didn't mention it. Thank God she had obviously decided to take pity on him and let things rest.

It never happened . . . It never happened . . . Keith echoed that sentiment over and over in his mind. He would keep doing it until his heart believed it.

Gina ran into the ladies' room and into one of the stalls. She had barely locked the door before the dam loosed and the tears exploded. She cried and cried. She cried for Michael. She cried for Keith. Mostly, she cried for herself. She had finally known love, only to lose it in a twist of fate. Yet, she knew that she'd made the right decision. This way, she would always be able to live with herself.

She pulled herself together and returned to Michael's bedside. She took his hands into hers. "Michael Ward, this is not the way to get me to forgive you," Gina reprimanded. "Almost killing yourself . . . I am so mad at you." Then she belied her words by sniffling. "Oh, Michael, I love you," she said. "I love you, I love you. Did you hear me? Don't you dare *die.*"

She turned around to look at Keith, having heard the door open. "I'm sorry," Gina said. There was no way he hadn't heard her telling Michael that she loved him.

Keith swiped at his eyes. "Don't be," he urged. Then he changed the subject. "My mother went to get some coffee. Do you want anything?"

"No," Gina answered, shaking her head. "Thank you. But I couldn't swallow anything right now."

"Gina," he said, "I feel tacky saying this right now, but . . ."

She tensed but waited for him to go on.

"I'm sorry about a lot of things, but I'm not sorry about the way that I feel. For just a brief moment, I was allowed to rediscover love, and for that, I will *never* be sorry."

His words stayed with her.

All through the night, Gina tossed and turned on the couch in the waiting area, pondering his departing comment. At about four o'clock in the morning, she decided to use the complimentary phone provided in the room to check her messages since her cell had long died.

There were three from Colleen. Gina made a mental note to call her back as soon as possible. She just couldn't leave Michael's side yet. She hung up the phone and returned to Michael's room.

Keith and his mom were engaged in deep discussion. His mother was urging him to leave and to take Gina home.

"I'll be all right." Gerry waved her hands to ward off any more objections from her son. "Take Gina home so she can shower and change. Make sure she eats something as well. Then get yourself a shower. You two need some rest. Come back in a couple of hours. If anything changes, I'll call."

"Come on. There's no use arguing with my mother once she's made up her mind." Without realizing it, Keith took Gina's hand, and they left the room. He led her out to the parking lot and opened his car door for her. Dazed, Gina let him take over because she was exhausted and hunger pangs bit at her stomach.

When he pulled up to her house, she remembered what had happened between them just hours ago. "Oh, God," Gina cried. She put her fist in her mouth to contain her emotions. "It's all coming back to me. While we were . . . were . . . He was probably on his way here. This is all my fault."

Keith gripped her shoulders. "Gina! Stop it." He commanded forcefully. "This was not your fault. It wasn't my fault either."

Gina's expression showed that she did not believe him at all.

Keith reminded her, "Let's not forget about Michael's part in all this, okay? He deceived you by not telling you about Karen. That's why you were not with him."

He could see that he was not getting through to her. Gina was too consumed with self-recrimination to think rationally. "Listen, stop blaming yourself. If you want to blame anybody, blame me. I never should have said anything to you about how I feel . . . I should have left you alone."

"No." Gina said.

Keith released her. The two looked at each other. There was no use denying it. The love they shared was still a strong force.

"I'm glad you didn't leave me alone," Gina murmured. "How else could I have ever known what—" She stopped, regained her composure, and with an emphatic shake of the head, stated, "It never happened."

Keith cursed. "Yes, it did." He grabbed Gina and kissed her until she responded. Her body curved into his. Having proven his point, Keith pushed her away from him. "Say anything you want, Gina," he huffed, "but don't say that. It did happen, and it was . . . I don't even have the right word for how good it was. But I'm not going to stand here and let you dismiss it."

"How could you?" Gina asked. "How could you say this to me while your brother could be on his deathbed?"

"Because it's true," Keith insisted. "It's the *truth*. We can't run from the truth."

"Tell me," she pleaded, "what do you want me to do?"

"I don't expect you and me to ever be—not anymore. But I don't ever want you to regret what happened between us, and I don't want you to forget it either."

"So, what do you want?" She held her hand out with confusion.

"I don't know," Keith said, emitting a huge sigh. "I heard you tell Michael that you loved him, and I'm okay with that. I can even understand if you stay with him after all this because that's the type of woman that you are. I just don't want . . ."

"I won't ever forget what we shared, and I know how I feel about you," Gina said softly. "But considering a man almost lost his life because of me, I feel I owe Michael this. I've got to give him another chance."

"I know. I totally understand."

"This is awkward. But, let's at least agree that while we'll never regret what happened between us, we'll never allow it to happen again. We'll never allow ourselves to be put in that situation again."

Keith nodded in agreement. "I can live with that. Can you?"

Chapter Thirty-one

Terence called Bishop Greenfield and informed him that he'd decided to withdraw his candidacy for the ministerial position. The bishop was saddened at the news. "Terence, you're making a rash decision. Take some time and reconsider."

But Terence was adamant, and he convinced the bishop that he would not change his mind.

Bishop Greenfield stubbornly repeated, "Wait a few days to think it through completely, and then give me a call. If you feel the same way, then I'll accept your decision. In the meantime, I'll be praying for you."

Terence agreed to the bishop's terms, but knew that he was not about to change his mind. His heart was not in it, especially since it would be without his wife by his side. Bereft, he took a few days off work to get his mind together.

He looked a sorry mess. It had been three days since New Year's Eve, and he was still wearing the same clothes. He had not showered or shaved. The only thing he had done was pray. He had been on his knees practically the entire night, repenting and begging God to allow Colleen to give him another chance. "Lord, if you just soften Colleen's heart, I will never ever hurt her again."

When he wasn't praying, Terence was calling Colleen and leaving messages on her cell and their answering machine. Each time, his heartfelt pleas got even longer and even more poignant. But Colleen had not returned his calls. He didn't even know if she was at home. She could be anywhere. Her cell phone was turned off. Terence could only continue to pray and hope for a divine intervention. He needed God's help. Now.

Francine opened the door to a familiar face.

"Hello, Sister Francine," came the formal greeting.

"Hello, Bishop Greenfield," Francine responded and let him in.

"I'm here about Terence," he said. "For the first time since I've known you, I am truly mad at you. You have some explaining to do."

"Oh?" Francine asked with an air of innocence.

"Surely, you know that he's resigned," the bishop informed her. "I'm not falling for that innocent act. Not today."

Francine held up her hand. "Whoa . . . Yes, I know." It was no use trying to deny it.

"What did you do?"

"Me?" Bewildered, Francine took a step back at this belligerent tone. Was he trying to blame this all on her? She looked slyly at the bishop, wondering if Terence had told him anything from his childhood or . . . Boy, the secrets were too numerous to count.

Then she dismissed the thought. Terence was not the type to talk about his personal business to just anybody.

"Yes, you," Greenfield replied. "It's no use trying to pretend, Francine. I know you're behind this, or you have an idea of what's going on."

Francine sat down with hunched shoulders. She couldn't lie to him. Besides, Bishop Greenfield was the only person still talking to her, and she needed someone to talk to. She no longer had Terence. Francine shocked herself by confessing how she'd interfered with Terence and Colleen's marriage because she'd felt he'd chosen Colleen over her. "I was afraid to be alone," she explained. "But, I went too far." Francine gathered her courage and told about how she'd invited Dana to drive a wedge between the couple.

Bishop Greenfield leaned forward. Fury emanated from every fiber of his being. "I don't believe you," he spat out. "How could you do something like that? I can't believe that you did something so malicious and cruel to your own son."

Francine was not prepared for his anger and put her hand to her throat. She had never seen him act this way toward her before. "I . . . I . . ."

"I had no idea you were so selfish!" Greenfield huffed. "That is not how God wants you to be. That's not how *I* want you to be."

Francine's eyebrows shot up at his last statement. He had made it personal. She retaliated. "I'm not answerable to you, Bishop. Only God."

"Yes! Yes, you *are* answerable to me!" he returned heatedly.

Francine gasped. She was appalled at his harsh tone. He was sounding more like her man than her pastor. Francine was unsure of how to deal with this stranger before her. He had always been so kind and good to her. What on earth had she done to deserve this? "Why? Why am I answerable to you?" Francine asked the last question without an ounce of respect. She was going to give it as he was dishing it.

"Because I have been in love with you for the past ten years. That's why," the bishop panted. Then he got quiet as he realized what he had just revealed.

Francine's mouth hung open, dumbfounded by his confession. "I had no idea." She hadn't seen this coming.

"That's because you were too busy minding your son's business to realize it," he said and jumped to his feet. "Now, I'm not even sure what I ever saw in you. I was in love with a figment of my imagination. Because the person I fancied myself in love with would never purposely destroy two lives because of jealousy. It's time you let your son go and for you to live your own life. Woman, get a life!"

With that last statement, Greenfield stormed out of Francine's house. Francine wasn't even given a chance to make a comeback. She was too struck down to reply.

She moped around the house. She prayed to God for strength but knew what she had to do. Thus, the reason she was standing outside Colleen and Terence's home. She bunched her shirt in her hands before catching herself. Smoothing the wrinkles and patting her hair, Francine supposed she was as ready as she would ever be.

She gathered her courage and walked up the small flight of stairs. Nervously, she pressed the little round button and waited. She saw Colleen peer through the window and prayed for the younger woman to open the door. She wouldn't blame Colleen if she didn't let her inside. But Francine knew that this was something that she had to do.

She waved when Colleen looked through the windows a second time. Francine knew Colleen wished she would disappear into thin air, but she dug her heels into the ground. She wasn't going anywhere, and if she had to stand outside all day, she would.

She expelled a relieved sigh when Colleen opened the door, albeit with evident reluctance.

Francine nodded at the young woman and entered with a light, "Hello, Colleen. Thanks for letting me in."

Colleen assessed her with shock.

Francine touched her hair self-consciously. She knew she must look a hot mess because she wasn't wearing any makeup and her nails were unkempt.

Colleen plowed her hands through her own hair. She didn't look like a beauty queen at the moment, either. "I'll be right back," she said.

"I'll be here," Francine answered and took a seat. She hoped Colleen took the moment to drag a comb through her hair.

Truthfully, Francine was glad for the brief reprieve. She used that time to gather her thoughts. Groveling did not come easy for her, but she knew that this was the time for it. She had come to try to make amends.

Lionel had been so mad at her, and she couldn't have that. Francine blushed at the thought of using the bishop's first name. But ever since his declaration the other day, she had begun to privately think of him as Lionel. She whispered the name aloud. Francine supposed that she could get used to it. She hadn't had the nerve to call him since he'd stormed out of her house. She knew that there was no point in calling him without first fixing things.

Colleen returned. Francine could see that she had made an effort to make herself presentable for she smelled the distinct minty toothpaste, signaling that she'd just brushed her teeth. She'd also changed her robe into a jogging suit.

Francine gathered her courage and started talking. "Colleen, I came here to apologize because I am a fool . . ."

Francine talked until her mouth felt parched. When she took her leave, she wasn't sure how much progress she'd made, but there was more to do. At least Colleen had listened.

For the second time that day, she stood outside another door. This would be the more difficult of the two, but she couldn't back down now. "Get it together," she upbraided herself. Warily, she hit the knocker.

Terence answered the door. "What do you want?"

For an instant, Francine was caught off guard. But she barged her way in anyway. "I want to talk to you," she declared. Colleen had been the one to give her Terence's hotel and room number. She had obtained it from one of the several messages he had left on the answering machine.

"You and I have nothing to talk to about," Terence shouted in her face and turned to leave.

"Colleen told me where you were," Francine replied, ignoring his tirade. He whipped around at the mention of his wife's name. Aha! Open sesame . . . He sat down and curiosity blazed in his eyes.

"I went to see her today," Francine explained as she settled further into the chair. "I knew I owed her a big apology."

Terence's eyebrows shot up at her confession. He gave her a speculative look. "Why the sudden change of heart?"

"I realized how wrong and how selfish I was," Francine admitted.

"What new stunt is this you're trying to pull?"

Francine heaved. "Don't narrow your eyes at me, all suspicious and stuff. I'm not pulling anything. Can't a woman just be sorry for her actions?"

"Not you," Terence jibed. "You've never been sorry for anything you did a day in your life."

"Well, I am," Francine countered. "I'm sorry, Terence."

Terence stood up, looked her dead in the eye and said, "It's too late for sorry. My marriage is over, Mother. There's nothing you can do or say to salvage that now. Colleen made it perfectly clear that she wants nothing more to do with me—ever."

Francine opened her mouth, but words failed.

Terence, however, didn't have that problem. He slapped his head and gave a cackle. "Oh, let me guess. Bishop Greenfield told you, didn't he? That's why you're so penitent all of a sudden. Well, Mother, if you came here thinking this sorry song is going to change my mind, well, think again."

"No!" Francine denied, vehemently shaking her head. It was like he was going to misread everything she did or said. How was she to get through to him? "That's not why I'm here."

"Oh, so, the bishop didn't tell you anything?" Terence spat out.

"Yes!" Francine answered, "But—"

"But nothing!" he interjected harshly. "I think you should leave, Mother. You've done enough for a lifetime."

Anger infused her spine. Her hands shook. Terence was not even giving her a chance to explain. She shouted, "When I said that I was sorry, I wasn't talking about your marriage, Terence. I was talking about . . ." Francine paused, gulped, and gathered her courage. "I was talking about other personal matters between you and me, and I came here to explain."

Terence looked at her.

Francine met him look for look. They kept that position for what felt like forever.

Then Terence said, "Okay, tell me."

Francine hung her head in shame. *Here goes nothing.* "Let me tell you a story of a little girl. Her name was Francine, and she got pregnant by some sweet-talking, light-skinned, wavy-haired loser, so her parents kicked her out. She was only fourteen, and she was a disgrace to her family. So, anyway, this girl, Francine, was sent to live with her aunt. She had the baby, but she had to work and go to school. Things were hard, and she begged and begged her parents to let her come back home. But they wouldn't let her return no matter how she pleaded. Francine decided she'd show them by making sure that her child turned out to be something. He wasn't going to be trash. This made Francine especially hard on her son. Then one day, Francine got a phone call."

She stopped, not sure of how to continue. She could barely conceal the agony she felt. Shaking her head, she tried to stem the harsh pain. No, she had to do this. She had to go there. Francine clutched her stomach as memories assailed her. She felt herself cracking as she lost what semblance of control she had left.

"Go on, Mom. Tell me."

Comforted by the friendly tone in her son's voice, Francine lifted her hand to touch his face for a brief second. His gentleness gave her the courage to press on. However, she couldn't look him in the eye. "Well, I got a phone call, you see. And it was my mother. She called to tell me that my father had died. I started crying. I wanted to go to my father's funeral, and my mother wouldn't let me." Francine cried again as the awful recollections resurfaced.

Francine regressed to that time in her life. She had never wanted to go back there, but she knew she must. For her son's sake, and for her own.

"It's okay, Mother," Terence interrupted and used his hand to wipe her small face. "I can't bear to see you so broken. I don't want this, Mother."

He got her some napkins and a glass of water. But she'd come too far to turn back now. "I have got to do this," Francine said as she wiped her tears. "So, my mother was adamant. She said that my father would turn over in his grave if I showed up at his funeral; then she hung up on me. Once she did that, Terence, I swear, I think I just lost it. I used to spank you before, and I know I was hard on you, but it was nothing like this. You weren't as young as you thought, either. Terence, you were actually nine years old when this happened. I only remembered that I started yelling at you and blaming you. I put the blame on your shoulders when I shouldn't have. The only thing you tried to do was comfort me, and you put your arms around me, and I . . ." Francine started crying.

"I . . . I don't know," Francine said, caught up in the past. "I just started hitting you, and even then, you were trying to hug me. But I continued to reject you. Finally, I shrugged you off of me, but I did it too hard, and you fell . . . and you . . . hit your head." Terence hugged his mother as she cried.

"I swear," Francine wailed, "I didn't mean to, Terence. I didn't know that you were unconscious. I picked you up, and you wouldn't wake up. You wouldn't wake up. Oh, God, I cried and cried, and I started praying. I couldn't afford to lose the only precious thing I had in my life. You were the only thing I had done right all my life. I begged God not to let you go and to send you back to me. I swore I would be different, but I wasn't. Instead, I continued to hurt you. I—I have no excuse. But you're all I have, and I just can't seem to let you go."

"Mom, it wasn't all bad, you know." Terence embraced her.

"Yes," Francine agreed. She held his face in her hands. "But, I took it too far, honey. I held on to you so hard that I couldn't let you go. I didn't give you and Colleen the chance you deserved because of my own selfishness. I transferred all of my fears and doubts right onto her and made her the bad guy. I know it's a lot to ask, son. But can you ever find it in your heart to forgive me for ruining the best thing that ever happened to you?"

"It wasn't easy, but I've forgiven you as God continues to forgive me," Terence said. "I just wanted you to tell me the truth. That's all. If anything, I have more respect for you now than I ever did before. This explains a lot to me about why you were the way that you were all throughout my high school and college days."

"Thank you, son," Francine patted his arm. "But I have literally ruined your life because of my past mistakes. I was just too stubborn to see it."

"It's never too late," Terence said. He met her eyes. "And for the record, I ruined my marriage, not you."

"I tried talking to Colleen. I apologized for everything that I did, and I explained how I realized that I was just afraid of losing you."

"And?" He sounded hopeful.

"Well," Francine replied, "she listened, but she didn't say anything to me. Not that she would anyway."

"I called her so many times," Terence said, dejectedly, "that if I picked up the telephone my fingers would automatically dial the numbers."

"Well, son," Francine admonished, getting to her feet, "you just have to give her time. She knows where you are, and she has your number. Colleen will contact you, all in good time."

"For once, I really hope you're right," Terence declared. Then he stood and spontaneously enfolded his mother in a generous bear hug.

Francine smiled, but her eyes held sadness.

"Thank you," Terence said, wholeheartedly. "Thanks for everything."

"I owed it to you to finally tell the truth. So, now you know how imperfect your mother was," Francine mocked herself.

"You were perfect for me, Mom," Terence stated lovingly. "Look how I turned out. I could be dead or in jail. Instead, I'm alive and I have an education and a good job."

"Get back to work, son," Francine advised.

"I think I will," Terence agreed. He took his mother's hands in his and prayed. He praised God for the healing that had taken place that day. He asked God to remove all the hurt and pain of the past once and for all.

Francine listened to her son's intense prayer and said one of her own. "Lord, please soften Colleen's heart."

Chapter Thirty-two

Colleen pulled into the parking lot of Long Island Jewish Hospital. Gina had called her to tell her the horrible news about Michael. He'd been in the hospital since New Year's. That had managed to snap Colleen out of her stupor.

She had been like a zombie the last five days. Now she, like many others who hear about things like this, had started contemplating on how short life truly was. Colleen was grateful to be alive no matter what she was going through. She got on the elevator and headed for Michael's private room.

Gina had taken off from work, of course, but Colleen could not imagine how her friend would look. When Gina rushed toward her, Colleen noticed that Gina's face looked gaunt and her eyes had dark shadows under them. To Colleen, Gina looked like she'd lost weight.

It took some effort, but Colleen pried Gina out of Michael's room. His mother and Keith were in there with him. They promised Gina that if anything changed, she'd be the first to know. Behind her back, Keith gave Colleen a thumbs-up sign. Evidently, they must have been trying to get Gina to take a break, but she probably stubbornly refused.

"Have you been eating?"

"What?" Gina asked. "I don't know. I've been too busy crying . . . throwing up . . . and worrying to find time to eat." Gina turned her head to look back into Michael's room.

Colleen firmly held onto her hand. "You're not going back in there. Not yet. You're coming with me to the cafeteria to eat something, even if I have to spoon-feed you myself."

Gina must have been too tired to argue with her. She tightened her grasp and led Gina to the cafeteria and over to the table nearest to the ordering station. Once Gina was seated, Colleen ordered her friend some soup and crackers and a salad for herself. She needed sustenance, too. She had probably lost a pound or two herself.

"Well," Colleen began, setting the tray down in front of Gina, "it's been awhile since you and I have seen each other. Pity it had to be under these circumstances."

"Yeah," Gina responded distractedly.

Colleen watched her pick up the spoon and swirl it around in her soup, too agitated to eat. She had to do something. "Luckily," Colleen said, "I can always provide a source of diversion."

"What do you mean? What's wrong?" Gina straightened and asked with concern.

Gina was definitely focused on her now. "Terence and I are through. I packed his bags myself a few days ago," Colleen confided, feeling her lips quiver. Her heart still ached over Terence's betrayal.

Gina touched her on the cheek. That small human contact reached her, deep down inside. Tears pricked at her eyes. She blinked. But the tears wouldn't be contained. She dabbed her eyes with a napkin. "I thought I had cried enough about this already."

Gina picked up her spoon and took a gulp of the soup. "Tell me, friend. What happened?"

Colleen was surprised that Gina had not said anything nasty at that news. But she was glad about it; Colleen didn't think she could've tolerated any *I told you so,* right now. "It happened on New Year's. We went over to his mother's house, as you know. And Francine was so nice to me that I was suspicious about it, you know?" Colleen informed her friend.

Gina nodded her on.

"Well, when the doorbell rang, I knew the real deal. This . . . This tart came waltzing in there . . . Her name's Dana." Colleen slurred Dana's name like it was the bubonic plague.

"No," Gina said with disbelief. "I hope you are not about to say what I think you're going to say."

"Yes!" Colleen confirmed, taking in Gina's head swirl. "Dana headed straight to Terence and started talking about what a fine time they'd had back in Jamaica."

"Wait a minute," Gina interrupted. "When did Terence go to Jamaica?"

"On our honeymoon," Colleen supplied. She waited for Gina to react as the atrocious implications sank in.

Stumped, Gina shook her head. "He didn't. Tell me Terence didn't do this while you were on your honeymoon." Her eyes were huge and wide. "That's low—even for him."

"He did," Colleen confirmed.

Gina jumped to her feet and hugged her friend in commiseration. "I can't think of anything more reprehensible than that."

"Aren't you going to say anything else?" Colleen prodded. She tilted her head at her friend. Gina wasn't spewing nasty insults and snide remarks, and for once, Colleen would've let her. Welcomed it even.

"What did he say?" Gina asked.

Colleen slid out of her grasp, and they both sat and returned to their food. "He said that he wanted to have a chance to explain. But I wasn't trying to hear anything coming out of his lying lips. I had enough of him. So . . . I packed his clothes and sent him on his way."

"Are you sure you did the right thing?" Gina slurped her soup.

Colleen looked at Gina as if she had antennas sticking out of her head when she asked that question. "What do you mean am I sure? Didn't you hear a word I just said?"

"Yes, I heard," Gina replied. "But you guys are married. That's a whole different ball game. You should've at least heard the man out before coming to a decision."

"Excuse me?" Colleen was dumbfounded. "Eat your food because hunger must've impaired your judgment. This can't be my friend of over fifteen years talking like this. I'm confused, Gina. I thought you, more than anybody else, would be jumping up and down at this news."

"Yeah . . . well," Gina hedged, "that was before I saw you two together. The man is so in love, he can't even think straight. You both looked smitten to me. Seeing you guys made me start thinking, who am I to judge or say anything about true love?"

Colleen didn't utter a single word. She wondered if Gina needed to see a psychiatrist or had been invaded by aliens. "Who is this person I'm talking to?" Maybe her friend had a split personality.

"Trust me," Gina chuckled, "it's me, and I'm in my right mind. I just started seeing things a little differently, that's all."

"Since when? Okay, Gina, fess up. What's going on with you?" Colleen turned the tables "You've done a complete one-eighty."

"I guess I've learned that everything is not cast in stone," Gina surmised, touching her chin in thought. "Sometimes you just have to carve your own way."

Colleen didn't have a clue what Gina was talking about. "Are you saying that I should forgive Terence and just pretend that nothing happened?"

"I'm not saying or telling you anything like that. All I'm saying is that you two have to take control of your own destiny, no matter what anyone might think."Colleen thought about what Gina was saying. She supposed that there was some truth in it. However, Colleen wouldn't have minded talking with her old cynical friend, the one who'd be trashing Terence for his dastardly deeds. But it seemed as if a new Gina had taken her place.

"Listen," Gina reiterated, "I just want you to know that whatever you decide to do, I'm going to support you. That's all. If you find that you can't live without Terence, then talk about it with him. Go to counseling or something. Just be happy, girl."

"Thanks . . . I guess," Colleen said, "but my mind is already made up. Terence is history."

The two women parted ways after that. Colleen walked away feeling even more confused than ever. She had expected Gina to be her staunch ally; instead, it seemed as if Gina was telling her to forgive. Colleen contemplated the irony of Gina ministering to her, though she was the one who was in church. Her friend had actually given her some food for thought. Colleen just wasn't sure if she had it in her to forgive Terence or even hear him out.

Colleen's heart felt like a block of ice. Francine's apology hadn't even chipped the surface. She was at a different place. She was tired of being trusting and letting men have their way with her. It was her own insecurity that had caused her to marry Terence within four months of meeting him. The aggravation that she was going through was no picnic. Colleen realized too late that it was not enough to get married. It took much more to *stay* married. It took more than she had. She dragged her feet, not anxious to return to an empty home.

***

Gina hurried back to Michael's bedside, who, thankfully, had been transferred from ICU to a private room. He'd had some spleen damage and major internal injuries but had come through the surgery with flying colors. He'd need a couple months of therapy, but Michael was expected to be back to his old self in no time. All he had to do now was wake up.

She thought about how she'd called Terence low and felt like a hypocrite. There was something even lower than what he had done, and that was what she had done. She had *slept* with her boyfriend's brother. How could she be hard on Terence when she herself was grimy?

She was relieved that Colleen hadn't pressed her about her own relationship. She had no idea how she would have begun to tell Colleen the whole sordid tale. She still needed some time to sort things out in her own mind and come to grips with what she'd done.

Chapter Thirty-three

Keith sat with Michael, appreciating the quiet time. A nurse had convinced his mother to get some sleep in one of the empty rooms. He took Michael's hand in his and talked.

He recounted all the mischief they'd gotten into and the pranks they'd pulled as boys. He spoke about all the good times they'd had. Keith spoke until his mouth was dry. He had to believe that his brother was still there, listening to his every word. He was told that people in this comatose state could recall conversations when they awakened.

Keith hoped that something would bring Michael back. For some reason, his brother seemed content to remain in that state. Keith was worried about that. He knew that the longer his brother stayed in the coma, the greater the chance of his regressing or becoming a vegetable. Keith couldn't bear it if that happened. The sooner Michael awakened the better.

Keith turned around as Gina entered the room. He couldn't help but look at her. His eyes bespoke of his love for her.

Gina saw it and mouthed, "Stop."

Keith cut his eyes at her, not even bothering to respond. How was he to stop what he was feeling in his heart? Frustrated beyond belief because he couldn't make his brother wake up and because he couldn't have Gina, Keith got up and left the room.

Gina was a little taken at Keith's abrupt departure, but she resolved that she would let him go cool off and sat down next to Michael.

"I love you," Gina said, silently willing Michael to come back to her. "Oh, Michael," she exclaimed, "come back to me, so I can make everything right!" She held onto Michael's hand and placed her head into his lap.

"Why are you crying, Gina?"

"Because, I just wish that you'd wake up and tell me again how you—" Gina stopped and sat up. Her eyes widened, and she started hyperventilating. He's awake! He's awake! She looked into Michael's eyes. They were opened and glued intently on her face.

"Michael! Michael!" Gina screamed with heartfelt joy. She jumped on top of him and stretched out completely. Then Gina kissed him with all the passion that she could muster like there was no tomorrow.

Keith heard Gina's outburst and ran into the room. He saw Gina kissing his brother like a woman dying of starvation. Quickly he raced to get his mother.

When they returned, Michael's room was filled with doctors and nurses. Gina was standing off to the side, beaming and crying at the same time. Gerry ran over to her, and the two women hugged, and laughed, and cried.

Keith whispered a silent prayer of thanks. Soon, all three were ushered out into the hall while the doctors and nurses examined every inch of Michael's body. Then the psychologist came to speak to Michael.

The police were also notified of Michael's recovery. Pretty soon, the place was like a zoo. Keith handled the cops himself.

It had been a week since he'd woken up from his coma, and Michael was way past ready to go home. The doctors wanted to keep him longer for more observations and tests, but he wasn't having it. A part of him felt that if he didn't have the resources to afford his private room and perks, they'd have shipped him out already. Hopefully, he would be heading home tomorrow.

As he lay there, Michael reflected on his life. He couldn't believe he'd been reckless and drove himself into the embankment on the bridge. He didn't know how he had allowed a woman to get to him like that. But the woman in question was no ordinary woman. He looked at Gina, who was busy reading a magazine. She looked beautiful.

Michael asked Gina to retrieve the pants he'd been wearing the day of the accident from the armoire. She went to do his bidding, then returned to her seat by the window. He reached into his pants pocket and pulled out the small box. He opened it to peer inside. It made a small creaking sound, but Gina didn't even look up from her article.

It was still there. The ring. Michael breathed a sigh of relief.

Should he wait? No, life was just too short. He had tried to conjure up a right moment before and that hadn't worked. It had turned into a complete and utter disaster. No, there was never a right moment. Michael had to seize any available opportunity.

A sharp pain shot through his head. Michael harrumphed and held onto his cranium. Immediately, Gina rushed to his side in concern.

Michael shooed her back to her chair as the pain gradually lessened. The doctors had decreased his medication. He had to expect the pain. Michael actually welcomed it. It helped him remember that he was alive. God had been good to him.

Michael closed his eyes and allowed his mind to wander at will. Bits and pieces of little snippets of conversations from Gina and Keith came back to him. He had trouble piecing it altogether. Then he dismissed them. If he were meant to know something, he'd eventually find out. That was his policy. "Gina," Michael croaked.

"Yes?" Gina answered.

She filled a glass with water and handed it to him to drink. The doctors had told him he needed to remain hydrated. Once he'd quenched his thirst, Michael asked the million-dollar question. "Will you marry me?"

"Yes, Michael," Gina said, after hesitating. "Of course, I'll marry you."

Michael took the ring out of the box and placed it on Gina's ring finger on her left hand. Then he pulled her in toward him to seal it with a kiss. He felt Gina returned his kiss with equal gusto before she pulled away. "I love you, Gina," Michael stated, simply.

"I know, Michael. I love you too. I just wish that this tragedy didn't happen to make me realize that."

Michael did not give Gina a chance to think. "I want to get married as soon as possible, Gina. Is that all right by you?"

"Yes, Michael. That's fine," she agreed with an amiable tone.

"Gina?" Michael took her face in his. Something wasn't right. He could feel it, but he just couldn't put his finger on it. "Are you okay?"

"Yes," Gina chuckled. "Why is it that you men become concerned when a woman just gives in?"

Somehow her reactions seemed somewhat forced. "I guess," Michael capitulated, with a little hesitation, still trying to read her. "I was prepared for you to fight me tooth and nail and figured that I would have to drag you down to the altar."

"Well, now you don't have to," Gina said. Then she excused herself. "I've got to hit the ladies' room."

Michael let her go without any further comments. He looked at the empty doorway. He couldn't shake the feeling that something was wrong. Gina just seemed too—agreeable. No, agreeable was not the right word. It was more like she was resigned. She didn't seem overly excited or jubilant. Just resigned. That didn't sit well with him at all.

Gina entered the stall and plopped her head against the door. She berated herself for how she had acted. A great man had just asked her to marry him and had given her a sizable rock to prove it. Gina looked at the ring. It was exquisite.

She closed her eyes and gulped hard. She did not deserve this. Maybe she should tell Michael the truth. But Gina shook her head. She knew that she couldn't do that. She couldn't hurt him in that way.

Gina prepped herself. She was going to go back into the room and show Michael how happy she was. She had not responded at all like a woman in love. She ordered herself not to be so stiff and show a little more enthusiasm. She was going to be a married woman soon.

Gina resolutely quelled all the feelings of guilt and pushed them to the back of her mind. She pushed all of the love that she still felt for Keith way down in the inner recesses of her heart. Gina closed her eyes and brought Michael to her mind. She did love him, and she would spend the rest of her life devoted to him or she'd die trying.

It was mid-January when Gina finally returned to work. She had more than enough sick time to cover her days so she wasn't worried, but she'd missed her students. She proudly sported her rock on her hand. News spread like lightning in the teacher's lounge. Most of her coworkers came up to her to inquire about Michael and to offer heartfelt congratulations.

She faked her excitement until she felt some glimmer of enthusiasm. She called Colleen and told her the big news. She made sure her tone bespoke a blissful happiness at her impending nuptials. Colleen demanded that they get together for dinner that very night. She agreed, knowing that tonight would be the big show-and-tell.

Colleen did not give Gina a chance to ring the doorbell. The door flew open before her fingers even touched the small device. She entered with a huge grin and her left hand swooping in the air. She hoped Colleen would be too thrilled to question her closely.

"Let me see it!" Colleen demanded, grabbing Gina's hand. "Whoop whoop." She let out a shrill whistle. "Tell me everything," she squealed. "I mean, I cannot imagine you getting married and all that. That is so exciting, I mean . . . So, I guess you figured out which brother you really loved, huh?"

"Well," Gina hedged, trying to remain cool. She shifted her eyes away from Colleen. "There's a little more to it than that. Colleen, I found out that when we first started dating, Michael had a one-night stand with his old girlfriend Karen. Then he had her living at his place until she got on her feet. Well, he never told me, and I found out by accident. I was so livid that I broke it off with him and took a cab home. Well . . . then . . ." Gina wrung her fingers together. Then in one breath, like she was getting the world off her shoulders, she said, "Keith came over, and told me he loved me, and . . . We slept together. We were going to tell Michael and let the chips fall where they may, but then we heard about Michael's accident. So, we ended it. And, now . . ."

"You're marrying Michael?" Colleen finished with a deadpan tone and a resigned expression.

"Yes."

Colleen looked unsure. "So, all that hoopla you came in here with was just a front." She gripped Gina's hand and led her to the couch. "Gina, remember all the things that you were saying to me the other day? What happened to being true to yourself and love? I know you, and you don't sleep around. You wouldn't have given yourself to Keith if you didn't have genuine feelings for him."

"I *am* being true to myself," Gina protested. She hoped Colleen would stop because she wasn't trying to have second thoughts. She was resolved to do this.

"I don't think so. It sounded to me like you really felt something for Keith. I'm not sure that those feelings are something that you can easily dismiss like that."

"I didn't dismiss them," Gina countered. "I just made a decision between two men that I really care about."

Colleen wasn't convinced. "Gina, you seem sure that you can turn your back on your feelings for Keith. Are you positive this is the right thing to do? I mean, it's obvious that Keith is the one that you love. You're drawn to him like a magnet. Gigi, think twice about this."

But Gina's mind was closed. Colleen wished she would heed her warning. Instead, Gina changed the subject. "So, have you called Terence?"

"No," Colleen shifted. She was now in the hot seat.

"Now, who's denying her heart?"

Colleen sighed. "I don't know, Gina. I just need more time to sort this all out."

"Look at us," Gina moved her hand between them. "The two of us have finally found love."

"Yeah," Colleen gave an unladylike snort, "and now we've both experienced heartache."

***

"Michael's made so much progress that I imagine it'll be time for me to go home, soon. I can't believe it's the end of February already. Where did the time go? Well, right after the wedding I'm out of your hair. I was going to fly home and come back, but Michael convinced me to stay." Gerry amended. "April is a great time of the year for a wedding, don't you think?" In one swoop, she flicked her hair out of her face and pierced her gaze on Keith.

Since Michael had left the hospital, he'd been recovering at Keith's home. Gerry had stayed to take care of him and was now helping with the shotgun wedding arrangements. This meant Gina had been around, too. Everywhere. Anywhere he went, it seemed she was there. His home that had seemed so large before, now felt small. Keith's solution was to keep himself busy and scarce. He worked at the office until past midnight at times, and when he was home, he retreated to his room or his office. Work was the excuse he used, but he knew it was all about Gina. He avoided her as much as he could.

She did the same too. She didn't make eye contact. Instead, she waved or uttered a quick, "Hi," before going into Michael's room. He couldn't be near her and not have her.

Keith couldn't verbalize any of this to his mother, so he merely said, "Mom, it's been great having you here. Trust me, you're not an imposition at all," intending to head to the office. He was within feet of the front door when his mother grabbed his hand. Looking into her knowing eyes, he knew that the moment he'd been avoiding had arrived.

"I know how you feel about her," Gerry stated softly.

She said it so matter-of-factly that Keith did not even bother to deny it. Actually, it would be a welcome relief to finally talk about his emotions. "You also know the obvious reason why I can't have her," Keith declared, flicking at imaginary lint on his pants, knowing he sounded downcast and forlorn.

Gerry tried to comfort her son. "I cannot imagine how you must feel, but I just want you to know that I love you."

"I know." Keith patted his mother on the arm. "Michael loves her, Mom, and I know that Gina loves him too."

"But does she love him the way that she should? Michael is talking marriage here. I hope that Gina isn't sacrificing herself because she feels that she has to be with him."

"She genuinely loves him, Mom," Keith reassured his mother. "I can only wish them happiness and be happy for them."

"You're a good son and wonderful brother," Gerry said. "Someday, whether you believe it or not, you'll get lucky in love."

Keith did not bother to answer his mother. He already knew this was it for him. He could only treasure the wonderful experience that he and Gina had intimately shared. Hopefully, that memory would ease some of the pain of his heart and carry him through a lifetime.

He nixed the idea of leaving and went into his home office, where he poured himself a strong drink. He swallowed the contents in one swig. Then Keith poured himself another drink. He knew he had to pull himself out of this stupor.

Michael and Gina's wedding was only about a month away. He'd used that time to gather his wits and stand with his brother. Michael asked him to be his best man, which was no surprise.

Keith picked up the phone to call Gina. Then he stopped himself middial. He couldn't call her. What was he going to say? *Don't marry Michael. You're making a big mistake. Marry me instead.*

Chapter Thirty-four

Terence unlocked his hotel door to see both his mother and the bishop standing in the hallway. There was only one reason why they both would be here, he thought. He braced himself. Maybe they figured that together, they could convince him to change his mind about taking the ministerial position. Well, they were both about to be very disappointed because he was not about to change his mind.

Terence let them in and politely offered them something to drink. They both declined. He could feel an excited air about them, and he became curious.

"We got married," the bishop announced without preamble.

"Married?" Terence asked. He looked from one to the other in amazement. He hadn't even known that they'd been dating or anything.

"It was a spur-of-the-moment thing," Francine explained nervously. "When you get to be our age, you sometimes learn that you just have to jump."

"I see that," Terence said. He still couldn't believe it. His mother married. So, did that make the bishop his father?

"Please say that you approve," Francine begged. She wrung her hands in doubt. The bishop grabbed her hands to offer his moral support.

"Of course," Terence said. "This is good news. I could actually use some right now. Wow." His mother was married.

Francine jumped up and impulsively kissed her son with delight. "Thanks, son. I hesitated to say anything to you, considering your own situation."

"Mom, please." Terence waved off her concern. "I'm not so selfish that I can't be happy for you. You deserve it, and I couldn't have asked for a better stepdad!"

Bishop gave Terence a hug. "Keep your chin up, son. I'm praying for you. Trust that God will work everything out for the best."

"I know," Terence affirmed, with a gusto he did not feel. He watched his mother and the bishop acting like two doves as they left arm-in-arm. Terence missed that feeling. He sat down and thought about Colleen. For the millionth time, Terence wished that he could kick himself for doing such a stupid thing. He didn't even know why he had done it, and he was sickened by his own heartless stupidity.

He understood if Colleen never wanted to see his face again because he was having a hard time looking at it himself.

Terence sighed. He thought back to his honeymoon. He and Colleen had been at the beach and all the girls had been eyeing his ring. They were young, hot-blooded, and beautiful girls. One, in particular, seemed to have set her sights on him.

Dana had approached him and had made her intentions known. He had told her he was visiting the island on his honeymoon. That was why he had been caught off guard when Dana had stood in his mother's house and lied about that. She had come onto him strong, saying, "If I were your wife, I'd know better than leave you alone for even a few seconds."

As a man, Terence had been flattered and reacted to having a woman that close. He was stupid enough to allow

Dana to lure him into a secluded place. Colleen had been in their suite taking a shower, and she was none the wiser.

Terence remembered how he'd protested when Dana had kissed him. At first, he had kissed her in return, but then he had pulled away. However, Dana was not shy. She had other plans.

It was all a blur after that. The next thing he knew, they were both naked. Then, fate stepped in. Terence hadn't been able to perform. It had been so embarrassing, but he took that as a sign. He had wished Dana farewell after getting her word that she would never tell a soul what had really happened. In a state of panic, Terence had called his mother and gave her a rundown of what had occurred.

Naturally, Francine assumed that he and Dana had sealed the deal. He had omitted that pertinent part of the story. He preferred everybody thinking that they had slept together. It was the more manly option. He supposed that Dana preferred it that way too. The younger woman prided herself on her capabilities and irresistibility, so it wouldn't do for her to tell the truth either.

When he had confessed everything to his mother, Francine dismissed it and told him to put the incident out of his mind. He had hung up the phone, grateful that God hadn't allowed his flesh to take over. He knew in his heart of hearts that he loved Colleen.

After he had returned to the suite and taken his shower, he'd been glad to find Colleen had fallen asleep. Relieved, he had fallen to his knees and uttered a prayer of thankfulness. He'd also made a vow that he would never put himself in such a compromising position again.

Not once did he imagine that his mother would use that information for her own selfish purposes. He didn't even know how his mother had found Dana. But it might not have been that hard, since he knew that he had told his mother she was a former Miss Jamaica.

He had even forgotten about what had almost happened with Dana until she showed up, lying through her surgically perfected teeth. She could have told his mother the truth. He figured that Dana had her own selfish reasons, like getting a free trip to New York. His mother told him that she was still there. She hadn't returned home on her due date, and he was willing to bet that she was in the arms of some other wimp.

Now, he wished he hadn't allowed his pride to get in the way. That was the only thing stopping him from confronting Colleen. It was so silly that he didn't want Colleen knowing he'd been incapable of performing.

He felt like it would make him seem less in her eyes. Colleen hadn't even given him a chance to explain anyway. She was done with him, and he knew that she meant it. She was fed up, and there was nothing he could do about it unless he told her the embarrassing truth. He would too, if he thought that it would make a difference. He shook his head. Colleen wouldn't want him now, even if he were the last man on earth. He didn't think there was a prayer on earth that could change that.

Michael took a cab to Gina's house. He had stopped by his place to get the last of his clothes and to check on things. He and Gina agreed that he would move into her house while they hunted for their own.

The front clerk had given him a note from Karen. She wrote that she was blissfully happy with Arthur. Arthur was planning on taking her on a cruise to the Caribbean. He felt good that things were obviously going well for the couple. He honestly wished the best for Karen. She deserved to find happiness as he had with Gina. Karen had also given him her new phone number. He paid her a courtesy call but was relieved to get an answering machine. He left a quick message about his upcoming marriage before bidding her good-bye for good. He deleted her number after that.

Michael tipped the driver and used the key Gina had given him to enter her home. She was due in any minute, and he intended to be there.

Tonight they were going over their wedding plans. He strode into the kitchen and started preparing a meal. He wasn't as good of a cook as his brother, but he knew enough to get by. Michael felt confident that everything was going to be all right.

Suddenly he paused.

Everything was going to be all right.

"So I can make everything all right." Gina had uttered those very words right before he had awakened. He was sure about that. Michael thought and thought. What did Gina mean by that?

Her words puzzled him throughout the entire evening. It wasn't really what she had said as much as it was the way she'd said it.

He tried to recall the exact tone and inflection in her voice when she made that declaration. But Michael found that it was still too fuzzy for him to figure out. Sheepishly, he grinned and touched his bandaged head. Maybe the bang had softened him and had brought out this new sensitive side. He couldn't believe that he was dissecting Gina's words like this. However, he was definitely going to ask her about it as soon as her feet stepped through that door.

That was exactly what he did.

Gina hadn't even taken her coat off when Michael bombarded her with the question. She wasn't prepared for it, and Gina was willing to bet that he wasn't prepared for the truth. "I don't remember now," she looked him in the eyes as she lied. "I must have been talking about everything with you and Karen. I guess I wanted you to know that Keith had explained everything to me."

She maintained eye contact until Michael looked away first, determined not to let him see just how rattled she was on the inside. Had her answer satisfied him?

She quickly excused herself to go wash up while Michael set the table for five.

Gina had called Michael to tell him that Colleen was coming by to help with the wedding plans. She needed her friend there for two main reasons: she needed help with the wedding, and she wanted to get Colleen out of the house. Her friend needed some fresh air. Gina hadn't known Colleen to be such a hermit. But, she supposed love could do that to you. Love will make you do things that you never thought you would. She could testify.

Keith came across her mind for the hundredth time that day. She wondered how he was doing. She would find out that night.

Michael had asked if he could invite Keith and Gerry. Of course, she'd replied with a sugary, "Yes, what a great idea, Michael." She couldn't very well say yes to Gerry and no to Keith.

Gina groaned. She didn't know how she was going to get through this night—planning a wedding with one man when she was in love with another.

That didn't sound right. Gina quickly rectified her thinking. She was in love with Michael. She just had a thing for Keith. Yes. That sounded much better.

Colleen arrived first. To Gina, Colleen looked much better than she did the other day. That was a start. She would quiz her about Terence later.

She hoped those two somehow would work things out. A year ago, she never would have felt that way. A lot had changed since then. She was less about black and white. Gina had discovered that there were shades of gray.

Terence and Colleen were in love with each other. Gina did not doubt that for a New York minute. The man just had some serious issues but, shoot, there wasn't much better than him around.

Keith showed up alone. His mother pleaded a headache. To Gina, he looked haggard and beaten, and she could tell that he had not been eating or sleeping. He looked like he needed a shave too.

"Wow, Bro," Michael shot out, "you look like some old lady ran you over with her car."

"Well," Keith countered, addressing his brother, "the girls seem to like it."

"Yeah, I'm sure," Michael conceded. "But I don't know why they are so smitten with that ugly face." Michael playfully punched Keith on the arm.

Gina turned away at that comment. She didn't like what Keith said one bit, and she didn't want it to show. Keith wasn't lying, though. He still looked good in a rugged sort of way.

Keith greeted Gina and Colleen amiably and sat down at the dinner table. Everyone dug in to eat.

On the sly, Colleen checked Keith out. She could see what Gina saw in him. He oozed with masculinity and raw charisma that would make any woman drool. She could appreciate that even though she herself was not attracted to him. She could, however, fully understand Gina's predicament. Colleen saw Gina bravely trying to remain unaffected and unmoved by Keith's presence, and to someone who didn't know her, it seemed as if she'd succeeded. Colleen knew better, though. Her friend was about to come apart at the seams. Thankfully, Michael was oblivious to the underlying tension.

It only took an hour to finalize all the plans. Gina and Michael would tie the knot in a simple and private ceremony at Keith's house. There would only be about fifty guests. Terence was also invited.

She almost choked on her wine when she heard that, but she had to be gracious about it. It wasn't her wedding, and besides, she had to get used to the idea that she was going to see him sometimes.

Terence had sent her a bouquet of roses and chocolates for Valentine's Day, accompanied by a note asking her if he could come by. He was still living in the hotel. Colleen had refused to even respond. Instead, she'd stomped the life out of the roses and thrown them in the trash. The chocolates found themselves in the garbage disposal. She relished the crushing sound as they met their fate. It was childish, but as God says, there were times to be like a child. She figured that was as good a time as any.

But, now she had to be a grown-up. Colleen decided that she would not raise a stink about Terence attending the nuptials. She had sufficient time to prep herself. She was going to look good enough to eat that day. Gina was giving her carte blanche on the dress, and she was going to make sure that she looked smoking hot without overshadowing the bride, of course. Looking at Gina, she doubted that she could.

Keith allowed most of the details to go over his head. He caught a whiff of what Gina was wearing. That was the same perfume that she had on the night that they had been together. He knew it because it was doing things to his insides. *This is ridiculous,* Keith scolded himself. He was going to have to get this woman out of his system. He couldn't bear to stick around and see Gina with Michael. He needed some distance to get his feelings under control.

"I'm going to move away," Keith heard himself declare out of the blue. Why had he said that? Moving would be a nightmare—he had cases—and the firm wouldn't let him just leave like that. Plus, he'd have to take the bar in Georgia to practice. But he kept his reality to himself.

"Move?" Michael asked. The wedding plans came to an abrupt halt. "Why?"

"I think I need a change," Keith declared.

"A change from what?" Michael persisted.

Keith didn't answer that question. "Moving near to Mom sounds good too. One of us needs to look out for her." Though he addressed Michael, his eyes were glued to Gina. He dissected her response to his bombshell. Though she hadn't uttered a word, he'd seen her face go white at his announcement. Gina cared if he left. That knowledge gave him a small degree of comfort, because it took everything in him to sit here and go over her wedding plans to someone else.

"Atlanta is nice," Michael broke in with a speculative gleam in his eye. He gave Gina a nudge. "Maybe we . . ."

Keith interrupted, knowing what was coming next. He held his hands up and said, "Don't even suggest it, Michael. You don't have to follow me. Besides, you have Gina to consider now."

"Gina's a teacher. She can move anywhere. Right, Gina?" Michael obstinately continued.

"Yes," Gina breathed out in a gasp of air. She held her chest and pressed her lips together.

"Say what? Are you trying to take my friend away from me already?" Colleen chimed in. She called Keith's bluff. "Besides, Keith, you're an attorney; you can't just up and move like that." Colleen shook her head, before shifting gears. "Listen, nobody's moving yet so, let's get back to the wedding plans, okay?"

***

Colleen cornered Gina for a private conversation as soon as the opportunity arose. The brothers were involved in some conversation about the tuxes. She touched Gina's arm. "Girl, are you all right?" Colleen asked with concern.

"Yeah," Gina nodded repeatedly. Then she threw her hands in the air. "No. I don't know. I can't believe Keith! Imagine that I had to sit there and remain silent, pretending to be cool when all I wanted to do was scream or shake him. The man is just plain infuriating." Her shoulders slumped.

"Listen," Colleen whispered conspiratorially, "you don't have to go through with this, you know. It's not too late to back out."

"Yes, it is," Gina declined. She looked around to make sure they were indeed alone. "I couldn't do that to Michael. The man almost died because of me!"

"Well, he didn't!" Colleen said. She lowered her body closer to Gina's. "Just run off with Keith because you both look like you're going to die without each other. It's heartbreaking to watch, actually."

"I can't!" Gina said, grabbing Colleen's hand for support. "Keith's his brother, for crying out loud. I can't do that to Keith. He'd lose his brother because of me."

Colleen gave up because what Gina said made sense. "Girl, you need to send this story to *General Hospital*. 'Cause I don't know."

Gina could only laugh. "It would be a juicy, twisted love triangle if I wasn't the one going through it." Gina looked over at Keith.

Keith just happened to look over at Gina while she was looking at him and he lost his train of thought. The moment was bittersweet.

I love you, Gina communicated.

I love you more, Keith returned.

Michael glanced to see what had caught his brother's attention. He saw him looking at Gina and piped up, "Don't worry, Keith," Michael said, "I'm sure about her. She's the right one for me." Michael had mistaken the look on Keith's face.

"Yes, I suppose that you're right," Keith said quietly. He looked at his brother wondering if Michael knew something. But Michael's face was without guile. Wisely, Keith kept silent. He looked back at Gina, but she had already turned away. *I can't do this,* Keith thought. *I can't just let her walk away. Gina!* He screamed on the inside, and his heart raged. *Why didn't I meet you first?*

"I know I'm right," Michael returned, confidently, unaware of Keith's inward struggle. Then, unknowingly, he prophesied, "Trust me, Keith, you would feel the same way I do, if you had met her first."

Chapter Thirty-five

All through the month of March, leading up to the wedding, Gina went along with the scheme of things, but her heart counted the days—the hours—the minutes until Keith left. Gina's mind became consumed with Keith's possible departure. How *could* he leave her? How was she going to handle it? He couldn't leave. She wouldn't see him. Not see Keith anymore! She couldn't handle that. And, so it went on all day, while she pretended to be in pre-wedding bliss. The pretense of being happy was wearing her down. Frankly, it grated on her nerves. She had been on edge and snappy with her students, and that was totally out of character.

Then all of a sudden, it was April 7th, two days before her wedding day, and her final day at work before her honeymoon. Keith was at her house.

She'd broken down and called him, demanding that he meet her to talk. She had to confront these feelings. She felt like she was about to drown in her misery. She had to convince him to stay.

Keith had been waiting for her. His motorcycle was in her driveway. "Why are you leaving?" Gina demanded angrily while she juggled opening the door with her books and purse in hand.

"You know why," Keith answered. He grabbed the keys and unlocked her door.

"But, you can't do this . . ." Gina stammered and barged inside. She dropped everything by the front door. "What about your brother, your job—"

"My brother will be fine, and I can do this job any-where," Keith interjected. He followed on her heels. He swung her around and asked her a question. "Shouldn't you be saying what about *you,* Gina? Isn't that what this phone call is really about? Admit it."

Gina snorted, but she didn't answer. She folded her arms and gave him a mutinous glance.

Keith continued, "Just admit that you'll miss me if I leave. At least give me that much."

"Okay, yes, yes, I'll miss you," Gina caved. "But why are you going?"

"Because I can't live here with you married to my brother. That's why. I know I won't be able to handle it," Keith retorted.

Gina didn't know what to say to that because she wasn't handling it any better. But . . . She *was* going to miss Keith something fierce. To keep herself busy, she went into the kitchen, knowing Keith would be right behind her. Gina put on a tea kettle and took out a couple of mugs. She whipped around to face him. "I guess I understand. But I had hoped that I would at least get to see you . . . or something."

"Well, I can't do that, Gina. It's not fair of you to ask me to either." He dropped his voice as he ventured into deep waters. "Unless you want to come with me."

He came up behind her and pulled her against him.

Yes! Gina's heart cried. *No!* Her mind fought. Her chest moved up and down from her rapid breathing. Michael would be devastated, and what would she look like? Be-cause of her, he'd crashed his car, ending up in a coma. No, she couldn't chance that. One near-death encounter was enough. She wasn't psychologically prepared to handle anything else. "I can't," Gina replied in a dull and defeated tone. She leaned against the counter.

"I had hoped . . . But, I guess there is nothing else left for us to say." Keith moved away from her, and she felt bereft at the lack of sudden heat. When Gina turned, he had already left the kitchen and was by her front door. Her heart rebelled. Her feet propelled her forward. Every fiber of her being was now in red alert. On the verge of hysteria, she screamed, "Stop! No. Keith. Don't go. Don't. go."

He stopped. When he turned to face her, she held out her arms.

Gina and Colleen were spending the night with Gerry, at Keith's house. Michael and Keith had let them in before disappearing for parts unknown. Gina had hugged Michael with great exuberance, and Keith—well, it was best that she avoided any further contact with him.

She went and knocked on Gerry's bedroom door where she'd stowed the wedding dress because of the superl arge closet. Gina entered when she heard a cheerful, "Come in."

Gerry held Gina's gown in her hands. Gina saw her run her hands gingerly over the beads and laces. "I just came to see if you need anything." Gina greeted her future mother-in-law with a kiss on the cheek.

"I suppose you'll need this." Gerry had a winsome smile on her face. She turned and gently rested the gown across the middle of the queen-sized bed. Then she perched on the foot of the bed and patted the space next to her. After a slight hesitation, Gina took Gerry's invitation.

Gerry began, "Gina, your gown is lovely. It fits you like a second skin, and I have no doubt you will make a beautiful bride."

Gina beamed. "Thank you."

Then Gerry dropped a bombshell.

"But I was wondering about you. Gina, are you marrying my son because he nearly died?"

Feeling trapped, Gina uttered an inarticulate "Huh?" Her mind raced. Had she done or said anything amiss?

Had she betrayed herself somehow? "Have I done anything to cause you concern, Gerry?" Her heart pounded.

"No, dear," Gerry said. "Please, call me, Mom. You've done all the right things, but you're trying too hard at being happy. Are you truly happy, Gina?"

Gina gulped. She felt like guilt was written all over her face. Had Keith said something? No, Gerry had seen firsthand the intimate exchanges between her and Keith. You'd have to be blind—or Michael—not to see it. "Yes, Gerry—I mean, Mom. I love your son." Gina fidgeted uncomfortably, hoping this would be the end of it. She was having a hard time lying to Gerry, and she was this close to confessing.

Gerry appeared to accept her answer, or maybe she wanted to be positive that Gina was sure because she didn't let the matter rest. Instead, she took Gina's hand and covered it with her own. "I just don't want you marrying because of some mistaken notion that you have to, child. You know, it's hard for a mother to know her child is hurting, no matter the age."

Gina looked at their joined hands and tried to decipher those vague words. Was Gerry referring to Keith just now? She didn't know how to respond without implicating herself. She didn't know how much the other woman knew. So Gina just nodded her head. Then, feeling compelled to say something, Gina declared, "I love your son so much. I'm sure of it."

Yeah, but which son?

"Okay," Gerry tabled the discussion and patted Gina's hand reassuringly. But she added, "Just know it's not too late, until the papers are signed. I won't think any less of you if you changed your mind, and Michael would get over it."

Why would she say that? Gina pondered that for a minute. "I'm not going to change my mind," Gina assured Gerry. "I'm going to marry Michael."

It rained the next day. Gina felt gloomy as she looked outside her window. She hoped that the sun came out before her nuptials. She tried to keep her chin up. She was not about to be superstitious and start thinking that God was trying to tell her something.

"This isn't a good sign," Colleen said, coming to stand over at the window.

"Shut up," Gina warned her friend. "I don't want to hear any of that superstitious mumbo jumbo."

Colleen relented with a snort. "I'd be a fine one to say anything. The weather was perfect on my wedding day, and look how things turned out."

Gina held her friend's hand and reminded Colleen, "You know he's coming today, right?"

"I know," Colleen said.

"You all right with that?" Gina asked, seeking reassurance, again. She'd already asked Colleen the same thing numerous times, and Colleen always gave the same response.

"Do I have a choice?"

"Michael felt he had to invite him since Terence had invited him to his wedding and that's where he met me." Gina repeated the same explanation for the umpteenth time.

"I know," Colleen smiled. "Don't worry about me. I'll be fine. Just enjoy your big day. It's about you, today."

"It is about me," Gina agreed. "I can't believe I'm getting married!"

"I can't believe it either," Colleen said, feeling happy for her friend. "I hope your marriage lasts longer and turns out better than mine." She knew it was tactless, but she intended to give Terence the annulment papers today. She was going to see him, and this was as good a time as any to get the job done. That way, she would be free and clear to go on with her life from this day forward. "Now, let's review. You have something blue . . ."

"Yes, the garter belt," Gina nodded.

"And something new, supplied by yours truly," Colleen posed, batting her lashes for fun.

Gina giggled and clutched the pearls. Then she added, "And Michael's mother gave me her wedding veil so that's something old. I forgot about something borrowed!"

Just then, Keith entered.

Colleen must have seen Keith's expression for she made an excuse to give them some measure of privacy. Gina was grateful, especially when Colleen stalled Gerry, who had been on her way down the stairs.

"Oh my goodness. Gina, you're absolutely stunning. A vision." His words were complimentary, but his face said he wished he was the groom.

Gina blushed. Keith's eyes said all that he couldn't say. Suddenly, the day seemed brighter, and Gina felt like a bride. "You clean up real good too, Keith," Gina understated. Keith looked far past fine. He was like a soap hunk. Then she asked, "Do you have something that I can borrow? I have something new, something old, and something blue." She couldn't believe that she was participating in such a wedding tradition, but it was fun.

Keith tapped his nose in thought before reaching into his tuxedo pocket to lend her his monogrammed handkerchief.

Gina extended her hand. Their fingers sizzled where they made contact. Her smile froze. Keith was looking at her as if he were entranced. "Thanks, Keith," Gina breathed, trying to pretend she didn't feel the tension rise between them. "That means a lot to me."

"Well," Keith said, stiffening his spine, "let's get this show on the road. My brother's a veritable mess."

She moved past him, but his hand shot out to detain her.

Keith begged with a tortured voice, "Please. Don't wear that perfume again. That's my perfume. It brings back too many memories."

Gina hesitated. "It's become my favorite perfume. It just makes me feel closer to . . ." She stopped. "Okay, I . . . I won't," she promised. She felt a pang, knowing that small request signaled the beginning of the end of the road for them.

"It's not the end, Gina. It's a . . . something new." He drew her to him and placed his lips against hers. "Hmm . . . Your lips are so soft. This should be our day." Gina didn't resist. Within seconds, he released her from his grasp.

She had other plans. In a sudden swift move, she grabbed his head and went on her tiptoes. With panicked passion, she planted her lips on his. Keith groaned and opened his mouth to give her better access.

Who knew how long they stood engaged in their stolen kiss before a discreet cough came from behind them. The couple sprang apart and turned to the intruder who had interrupted—saved them. Keith used the back of his hand to wipe his lips.

"Colleen, this isn't what it . . ." Gina exhaled, horrified that she had just kissed another man on her wedding day. Who did that?

Colleen grabbed her and shook her. "What are you doing?"

"*Nothing.*" Gina answered defensively. She gestured with her hands for Colleen to keep her voice down.

"That's what you call nothing?" Colleen said but continued her tirade in an outraged whisper. "This is ridiculous. Your fiancé is in the next room, and your future mother-in-law is upstairs. Either one of them could have seen you just now."

"You don't understand." Gina wrung her fingers. "We were just saying good-bye."

"You couldn't have used words?" Colleen responded. She put one of her hands over her head as if she were about to swoon. "I can't take all this drama, girl." She looked up to heaven and prayed, "Lord, please give me strength."

Gerry walked down the stairs, effectively ending the discussion between the two friends.

Keith seized the moment and excused himself under the pretext of finding his brother. Gina composed herself and smoothed her gown. She looked straight ahead and refused to make eye contact with Colleen even as her body felt the after effects of Keith's searing kiss.

Maybe this was a sign.

Nope. Gina composed herself. She'd come too far to back out now. She was going through with this. She had made up her mind that she was going to marry Michael and live happily ever after. No telltale heart was going to interfere with what she felt was right.

Colleen pinched her to get her attention. Gina stubbornly ignored her. She eventually gave up, but threatened, "Just cause, Gina. Don't forget that."

Would she stop the ceremony?

All through the ritual, Gina wondered if that moment would come. She needn't have worried. In a matter of minutes, she'd pledged her heart and body to Michael. To everyone, it sounded sincere, and like she meant every word.

But Gina knew that her soul belonged elsewhere. It was impossibly entwined with the man standing a mere foot away. Once the vows were exchanged, she emitted a huge sigh of relief. She had done it.

Gina smiled at Colleen with gratitude for not ruining Michael's day. When the preacher had asked the important question about whether anyone had just cause as to why she and Michael shouldn't be married, she had waited with bated breath for those few seconds, half-expecting and hoping Keith would interrupt. But he had remained frozen in his stance. She definitely anticipated a passionate interruption from Colleen. But Colleen had proven to be a friend to the end, and the moment passed.

Colleen was furious at herself. She should have dropped a dime. She should have spoken up and said something. She should have yelled that Gina and Michael did not belong together. Yet, she hadn't. Who was she to interfere in somebody else's relationship? At least Gina was walking into this one with her eyes wide open. She, on the other hand, had walked into her marriage with her head in the clouds. It had all been about Terence. Colleen had been too far gone to think straight.

"Hello, Colleen."

Speaking of the devil, she thought. Colleen turned around and greeted her soon-to-be ex-husband. "Hi, Terence." She only returned the greeting because there were a couple of nosy people looking their way.

"You look ravishing," Terence complimented.

"Thank you," Colleen answered nonchalantly. But on the inside, she experienced a great sense of feminine satisfaction and was pleased. Colleen had picked out this red dress. It was superhot with a split that did not end.

Gerry had almost had another baby when she saw it. She told Colleen that the dress did not look like something a matron of honor should wear. Gina had jumped to her defense. She was tickled at Colleen's choice and had supported it. So, Colleen wore it. She looked good, and she knew it.

She gave Terence a look that said, "This is what you've lost. Look and weep."

Chapter Thirty-six

"Can we talk?"

Colleen seemed agreeable and followed Terence into the parlor. Seeing her just magnified how much he really loved her, and how much he had lost.

Terence had no idea how to even try to get her back. He'd been looking forward to the wedding because he knew that Colleen would be here. He had prayed and fasted and repented to God, but Colleen was another matter. She just wouldn't bend.

Even Gina had been cordial to him as well. Terence could see the pity in her eyes, and he hated it immensely.

"Colleen," he began, "seeing you here today, and at a wedding, no less, made me reminiscent of our own special day. I just wanted to let you know that I still love you and want to be with you. Do you think you can find it in your heart to give me another chance?"

Colleen snorted. "No, I have no intention of taking you back, Terence. I have endured too much with you. You are nothing but a wife-beater and a womanizer. I don't know what I ever saw in you in the first place."

Terence sputtered at her vehement response. "Are you saying that you never loved me?" His heart rate increased, anticipating her answer.

"*Love?*" Colleen spat and wrinkled her face in disgust. "You're a fine one to talk about love, Terence Hayworth. I doubt you even know the meaning of the word."

Terence looked at Colleen. He couldn't believe that she was speaking to him like that. Where was his sweet-natured wife? Troubled, he asked, "Did I do this to you, Colleen, huh? Did I turn you into this cold, unfeeling person standing before me?"

"Yes!" Colleen spat. "You did. Congratulations, Terence. Consider the rose-colored glasses officially broken. I hope you're proud of yourself."

"I hope you're proud of yourself." Terence threw her words back at her with disgust and began to walk away.

Colleen stopped him. "Wait," she said. Then she went into the dining area and over to the wall unit, where she had placed the manila envelope. She crooked her finger to make sure Terence followed. They went outside into the garden and out of earshot.

Silently, she handed it to him and stated, "Consider yourself served." She walked off with her head held high.

Terence creased his brows in confusion. He tore open the envelope and snarled when he saw what was inside. He quickly perused the documents.

Colleen wasn't even filing for a divorce. She wanted an annulment. In other words, she wanted to erase the memory of him from her life. Forever. Terence crumpled the papers and stormed after Colleen. She was not going to eliminate him from her life like that! Who did she think she was?

Terence found Colleen talking and laughing with two men as if she hadn't just driven a pole into his heart. Anger assailed his entire being. Jealousy flooded through his pores.

He had reached his boiling point. Colleen was over there flirting as if she didn't have a care in the world, while he felt as if the entire world had caved in on him. Terence couldn't take it any more.

He dragged her back out to the garden. From the corner of his eye, he saw Gina and Michael follow him. Colleen almost tripped over her gown, but he was past the point of caring. He would have his say. Once they were at a distance, Terence yelled. "You're not going to erase me out your life, Colleen. I didn't sleep with her. I couldn't even . . . I couldn't perform." His shoulders hunched with that admission.

Colleen merely looked at him as if he'd sprouted horns.

"Did you hear me, woman? I said *nothing* happened." Terence was so riled that he was not thinking rationally. That was not the sort of announcement that one would make public—if ever.

His words sank in, and Colleen's mouth hung open. She turned her head and pointed to Gina and Michael who most assuredly had heard his admission.

He felt compelled to address them. "I'm sorry you had to hear this, and believe me, I'm mortified, but I'm desperate." He looked at Colleen whose face was as ice. "I'm sorry."

She turned her back to him and folded her arms.

He wished she'd scream or do something. But she hadn't.

Terence left immediately after that to lick his wounds. He spent the weekend in a slump, appalled at his uncontrollable behavior. What had possessed him to put himself on blast like that? He replayed the whole debacle in his mind. He hung his head. He had made a fool of himself and put his manhood on the line for a woman who didn't even want him anymore. "Lord, is there any end to my humiliation?"

Terence knew that it was time to say good-bye. He hadn't intended for things to go this way. Yet, he accepted that his actions had led to the downfall of his marriage. Colleen was right; he was a wife-beater and a womanizer, and he didn't deserve a woman like her. It was time he recognized that and moved on.

Terence opened his briefcase and retrieved his notepad and pen. He was going to write Colleen an apology letter and ask for another copy of the annulment papers to sign.

With a heavy heart, Terence started writing. Just as he was almost done, he heard the clank on the hotel door.

Terence opened the door to find Colleen standing there. Wordlessly, he let her in. He saw her wander aimlessly around the room until her eyes fell on the letter that he had been writing. She saw her name inscribed on it.

"May I?" she asked.

"Go ahead," Terence said, with a sweep of his hands. "It was meant for you anyway." While Colleen picked up the letter and read, Terence busied himself by cleaning up a bit. He couldn't imagine why she was here. Then he noticed that she had the crumpled annulment papers in her hand. Terence felt dejected.

He walked over to Colleen who was still busy reading and took the papers out of her hands. He made his way over to the little desk, took a deep breath, and reluctantly signed the papers.

Colleen looked up and saw him scrawl his name on the line. "What're you doing?"

"Signing them," he said, stating the obvious. "I would think that's why you brought them here."

She didn't answer, but she seemed to be stalling. Then she asked, "So, you meant what you said in this letter? You're ready to let me go?"

"Yes, I did." Terence handed her the signed documents. She took them and looked at them.

Colleen took the pen from his hand. She rested the papers on the coffee table and poised the pen to sign. Then she stopped. "I don't want to do this."

Terence reeled from her revelation. He leaned closer to make sure he'd heard her right. "What did you say?"

"I said that I don't want to sign these papers." She tossed the papers in the waste bucket. Walking over to him, she gripped his shirt and looked him directly in the eyes.

"You said something at Gina's wedding that really got to me. You said that I was different, and I was. I was hard and calculating, and I didn't like that person. I liked the person that I was with you, Terence."

Terence sounded like a dumb mule, but he asked anyway, "What did you say?"

"What I said was I like the person that I was with you," Colleen repeated. "I came over here to ask for another chance, but your letter tells me that you're ready to move on."

"I only said that because I thought that was what you wanted." Terence beseeched her. He cupped her face with his hands. "Bump the letter. I love you, Colleen."

"I know that—by the way, was that true what you said?"

Knowing exactly what she was talking about, Terence blushed with embarrassment. "Yes, it was. I never slept with Dana, but I did come close."

Colleen thought about what he said for a moment, and then said, "I can appreciate an honest answer. Were there others?"

Lord, what do I do? Terence hedged, but decided to give Colleen a straight answer. "Yes."

Colleen dropped her head and shoulders with a new grief. She shook her head with obvious disbelief. She twisted her body toward the door. "I must have been mistaken thinking this could work."

Terence rushed ahead of her and guarded the door. "It was before we got married, though. We were dating for such a short period of time, and even though I knew early on I wanted to marry you, I still . . . I was messing around with a couple of other women." He felt his second chance slip through his fingers. He grabbed Colleen's shoulders and shook her. *Look at me.* His will prevailed, and she faced him. Water crystals were forming in her eyes. "Colleen, I did fool around. But not once after we got married. I meant those vows, and besides that one act of stupidity, I kept them. You've got to believe me. Our marriage has changed me. I'm not the same man I was a few months ago. And it's because of you."

He waited while she debated. Finally, she spoke. "Thanks for telling me the truth, Terence. Even though it really hurts. I love you too much to not forgive you."

When her words registered, Terence dared to reach out to hug her in an intimate embrace. *Thank you, Lord.* "I'm really sorry, Colleen. If you'll give me another chance, I promise you that you'll never have cause to regret it. Ever."

Colleen looked Terence in the eyes. "I see your earnestness, and I'm going with my instincts here. I'm miserable without you, and I'm choosing to believe in your sincerity. I'm taking a chance. Just.don't.hurt.me."

Terence gathered his courage to ask his wife a question. "Colleen, if you wanted to give me another chance, how come you brought the annulment papers?"

Colleen wiped her eyes and smiled. She went over to get them. "To do this." After that last comment, she took the papers and ripped them up.

Terence smiled.

Colleen smiled.

Then he took a step toward her.

Colleen stepped toward him.

The two hugged, and then kissed. It was minutes that felt like an hour before they separated.

Colleen broke contact first. "I love you, Terence. I can't believe that you were writing me a good-bye letter. I think hellos are much nicer."

Terence felt humbled by the renewed love reflected in her eyes. "Me, too," he agreed. Then he shouted, "Thank you, Lord! Hallelujah!" Looking at Colleen, he confessed, "You don't know how much I prayed for this."

Colleen went to the door and opened it. "Come on," she said, with an outstretched hand, "let's go home."

Terence grabbed her hand and held it. Desire sprang to life, and she drew him closer to her. Those were the last coherent words, she uttered for a long time.

Keith walked around his home feeling lonely. Eve had called with the news that Bass was her son's biological father. He admitted that he felt relieved, but it was accompanied by a momentary pang. He knew that a child with Eve only would've complicated things.

Michael and Gina were on a mini-honeymoon in the Poconos. Gina wanted to wait until summer for a full honeymoon, when they could explore Europe at their leisure.

His mother had also flown back to Cobb County, anxious to get back to her life and friends. Keith told her about his intentions to move, and she perked up at the idea. She felt the move would be good for him.

Keith looked at a snapshot of Gina and Michael he had on his mantle. He picked it up and studied it. He took his finger and ran it alongside Gina's face in a sweet caress.

"Good-bye, Gina," he whispered, sentimentally, before placing the picture down.

Gina waited in the car. It was time to say good-bye to her and Michael's wonderful love cottage. Their time in the Poconos had been well spent. They had bonded as a couple.

Up here in the mountains, away from Keith, Gina could be happy with Michael. She realized that Keith was probably right. He had to move. Distance was the best solution in order for her and Michael's marriage to work.

Michael pulled the door closed with finality. He entered the car. Impulsively, she reached over and kissed her husband. "I love you," Gina announced.

"I love you too, babe."

Before he put the car in gear, Gina yelled for him to stop. There was something that she had to do. Michael looked perplexed but handed over the keys to the cottage. Grabbing her pocketbook, Gina ran back inside. She raced toward the bathroom and securely locked the door.

Slowly, Gina unzipped her pocketbook and retrieved a picture from one of its compartments. She looked at a picture of Keith she had taken at her house during winter break. She looked at it for several seconds before bringing it to her lips. Gina placed a lingering kiss on Keith's lips.

"I love you, Keith," Gina whispered.

Then she slowly ripped the picture into tiny little pieces. She felt as if her heart would burst, but she knew that this was what she had to do. She was married, and she couldn't carry around any reminders of what could have been. She couldn't look back. She had to look ahead to her new life with Michael.

Gina rolled a wad of tissue paper in her hands and put the bits and pieces inside it. Then she threw the contents in the toilet before flushing the entire thing down the drain.

"Good-bye, Keith," she said, and held onto her heart. She heard Michael toot the horn and knew it was time to go.

When she returned to the car, Michael helped with her seat belt. "Thanks," Gina said and looked at him.

"You're welcome."

He smiled. And, just like that, Gina knew everything was going to be all right. She closed her eyes, accepting her prince, and awaiting her happy ever after.

Coming soon . . .

The saga continues in the next installment of the On the Right Path *series.*

My Steps Are Ordered

Team Keith? Or Team Michael?
God's side? Or, is there really any other choice?

Gina Ward has it all. A husband, a child, and all the finer things life has to offer. She doesn't see herself as one of the less fortunate who needs God. But what happens when her only child, Trey, falls ill? Will she turn to the only one who holds the whole world in His hands?

Keith Ward is a respected minister, but he cannot shake his inappropriate feelings for his brother's wife. When his nephew falls ill, Keith knows he has to drop everything to be by her side. Will he finally find healing for his broken heart?

Michael Ward is living the dream life. But life as he knows it changes drastically when his son falls ill. Everything he thought to be truth will be brought into question. What will he do when he realizes he is living one big lie?

Readers' Guide Questions

1. Colleen and Gina have been friends for years. Then Colleen got saved and married Terence. Should a newly converted child of God remain "best" friends with someone who is not saved?

2. Colleen and Gina's friendship went through significant changes and transitions. Most friendships are transitory. What do you think contributes to building lifetime friendships?

3. Colleen didn't see herself how others saw her. How can a person's self-worth and self-esteem influence the mate he/she seeks?

4. One of the main reasons that Colleen invested so much in her marriage was that she didn't want to end up alone like her mother. Do you believe that is a valid reason to stay in or seek a relationship? Have there been times when we have made decisions in our love lives strictly because we didn't want to be alone?

5. Gina felt that Colleen was always preaching to her since she became saved. Do others perceive you like this? How can we effectively share Christ with others without coming across as "holier-than-thou"?

6. Gina was not ready to hear about salvation or to go to church. Should Colleen have done more to encourage her friend in the Lord? Was Colleen being a true example to her friend to lead her to Christ?

7. Terence urged Colleen to get baptized again. How do you feel about the idea of getting rebaptized? Should it be encouraged, especially since we know that God looks at the heart?

8. Colleen changed her appearance and even quit her job to please Terence. Do you think that a woman

should give up her independence and do all she can to please her husband? Why or why not?

9. Colleen fought back in an abusive relationship, which is not common. Do you think that was a wise move on her part? What measures does your church organization provide to help battered/abused women?

10. As a married woman, Colleen realized that there were some issues that she couldn't share with her best friend, Gina. Do you agree with this? Are there certain topics that should remain between a husband and wife? How do we draw the line between what we share and don't share about our personal relationships?

11. When a man marries, he leaves his family and cleaves to his wife. With Terence, we see his struggle with pleasing his mother versus his wife. Have you ever been in a situation where you made your significant other choose between you and his mother?

12. Should Colleen have given Terence a second chance after he abused her and admitted to cheating on her?

13. Gina was in love with two men. Is that possible? If so, why or why not?

14. Keith and Gina decided to keep their one-night stand between them. Do you agree with their decision? Do you think they should have told Michael about their betrayal?

15. Francine felt she would lose Terence once he married Colleen. There are many parents who face this empty-nest syndrome. What are some activities or pastimes in which parents of adult children can get involved? Does your church have a ministry for seniors?

16. Do you think that parents should have a life separate from their children, or is that selfishness? Why should/shouldn't parents make their children the center of their lives?

About the Author

Originally from Jamaica, West Indies, Michelle Lindo-Rice calls herself a lifelong learner. She has earned degrees from New York University, SUNY at Stony Brook, and Teachers College, Columbia University. When she moved to Florida, she enrolled in Argosy University, where she completed her Education Specialist degree in Education Leadership.

A pastor's kid, Michelle upholds the faith, preaching, teaching, and ministering through praise and worship. From a young teen, Michelle discovered a passion for reading and writing and feels blessed to use her talents to bring God glory. Michelle currently works as a Reading Specialist for exceptional student learners, and is the proud mother of two teenage sons.

Her first Christian fiction novel, *Sing a New Song,* was released in January 2013 to favorable reviews. *Walk a Straight Line* is her second work of fiction, and its sequel, *My Steps Are Ordered,* will be out soon. For more information or to leave an encouraging word, you can reach Michelle online at Facebook, LinkedIn, Twitter @mlindorice, or join her mailing list at www.michel-lelindorice.com.

UC His Glory Book Club!

www.uchisglorybookclub.net

UC His Glory Book Club is the spirit-inspired brainchild of Joylynn Ross, Author and Acquisitions Editor of Urban Christian, and Kendra Norman-Bellamy, Author for Urban Christian. This is an online book club that hosts authors of Urban Christian. We welcome as members all men and women who have a passion for reading Christian-based fiction.

UC His Glory Book Club pledges our commitment to provide support, positive feedback, encouragement, and a forum whereby members can openly discuss and review the literary works of Urban Christian authors.

There is no membership fee associated with UC His Glory Book Club; however, we do ask that you support the authors through purchasing, encouraging, providing book reviews, and of course, your prayers. We also ask that you respect our beliefs and follow the guidelines of the book club. We hope to receive your valuable input, opinions, and reviews that build up, rather than tear down our authors.

What We Believe:

—We believe that Jesus is the Christ, Son of the Living God.

—We believe the Bible is the true, living Word of God.

—We believe all Urban Christian authors should use their God-given writing abilities to honor God and share the message of the written word God has given to each of them uniquely.

—We believe in supporting Urban Christian authors in their literary endeavors by reading, purchasing and sharing their titles with our online community.

—We believe that in everything we do in our literary arena should be done in a manner that will lead to God being glorified and honored.

We look forward to the online fellowship with you. Please visit us often at www.uchisglorybookclub.net.

Many Blessing to You!

Shelia E. Lipsey,

President, UC His Glory Book Club